WHAT
WE
BURIED

WHAT
WE
BURIED

KATE A. BOORMAN

HENRY HOLT AND COMPANY • NEW YORK

Henry Holt and Company, *Publishers since 1866*
Henry Holt® is a registered trademark of Macmillan Publishing Group, LLC
175 Fifth Avenue, New York, New York 10010 • fiercereads.com

Library of Congress Cataloging-in-Publication Data
Names: Boorman, Kate A., author.
Title: What we buried / Kate A. Boorman.
Description: New York : Henry Holt and Company, [2019] | Summary: Told in separate voices,
Jory, whose face is partly paralyzed, and his sister Liv, a former reality television performer and
child beauty pageant contestant, join forces to search for their missing parents.
Identifiers: LCCN 2018006861 | ISBN 9781250191670 (hardcover)
Subjects: | CYAC: Missing persons—Fiction. | Brothers and sisters—Fiction. | Disfigured
persons—Fiction. | Beauty contests—Fiction. | Reality television programs—Fiction. | Family
problems—Fiction. | Mystery and detective stories.
Classification: LCC PZ7.B64618 Wh 2019 | DDC [Fic]—dc23
LC record available at https://lccn.loc.gov/2018006861

Our books may be purchased in bulk for promotional, educational, or business use.
Please contact your local bookseller or the Macmillan Corporate and
Premium Sales Department at (800) 221-7945 ext. 5442 or by email at
MacmillanSpecialMarkets@macmillan.com.

First edition, 2019 / Designed by Rebecca Syracuse
Printed in the United States of America

1 3 5 7 9 10 8 6 4 2

Reality is merely an illusion, albeit

a rather persistent one.

—Albert Einstein, maybe

SLIPPERY
AND
CONDITIONAL

Radio News FM:

"Reno PD have been called in to help with a case of arson in Mineral County, as a recent discovery has turned it into a potential criminal investigation. Bones were uncovered in the wreckage of a burnt lakefront property, discovered by a local man during his walk. Police did not confirm whether or not the remains are human; the investigation is ongoing.

In local news, LVPD are asking for the public's help in locating two people who disappeared from the Clark County area Friday—"

JORY

MY DAD SNAPPED the radio off as we pulled into the parking lot of Princess Liv's Spectacle of Justice, otherwise known as the Clark County courthouse. It wasn't to spare us some sort of upsetting news story on an "already upsetting" day; my dad generally wasn't aware of those kinds of things—you know, other people's realities or emotions? No, he was trying to read the parking instructions to see if he could pay by credit card, and the radio was irritating him.

Not that my reality was affected either way. Some random news story held as much relevance for me as this court date; the only one emotional about today was my mom. And as I stared at the courthouse through the tinted window of my backseat prison, I couldn't remember why I'd agreed to waste my time.

My dad cursed and began rummaging for change in the console, and I peered at the building, which shimmered and danced in my vision like it was threatening to wink out of existence. It was a trick of the light, a common sight in

Nevada—land of infernal sun and dry, cracked earth—but something about the way it wavered made me want to look harder, make sure it was real.

It made me want to do the same to myself.

My chest tightened. Sinking into the leather of my dad's SUV, I squeezed my fist tight and watched two tendons appear on my forearm as the muscles strained. I closed my left hand around my wrist and squeezed harder, feeling my pulse thud, picturing the blood rushing through the vein toward my fingers and back toward my heart.

You know the saying "seeing is believing"? It's a problem, when you think about it. I mean, it's reasonable for people to want proof before they accept something they've been told. I do. I'm a fan of logic and demonstrable facts. But the idea inherent: that you can believe what you see? That's majorly flawed, because people usually have no clue what they're looking at. It's why people think my sister is a lovely, tragic victim. It's why they so often assume I can't tie my own shoes.

"We're here, Jory-boy," my mom announced belatedly, glancing back from the front seat. "It's time." My mom was a classic stater-of-the-obvious. I relaxed my hand without meeting her gaze and said nothing, even though I knew she was hoping for some reassuring response. This was her new thing. The moment my sister had filed her lawsuit, I'd materialized before my mom's eyes.

Now I existed.

My dad's cell went off—his ringtone was the first four bars of "Janie's Got a Gun," which gives you an idea of how irritating he is—and he answered it as he parked, turning away from my mom dismissively.

She was used to that. We all knew that plastic forks and printed paper napkins and whatever other party supplies were distributed by my dad's company, Par-T-Own, didn't sell and ship themselves.

But lately, my dad's phone calls had become louder, more excruciating to witness. His volatility hadn't ever been completely contained to the home front—it bled into customer relations from time to time—but this seemed next level. He was less cocksure, a bit desperate even, and I wasn't going to hang around and listen to him swear or, worse, *wheedle*.

I opened the back door to freedom, and a breath-stealing blast of heat, and stared at the blurry courthouse, forcing it to come into focus.

There. Solid as the asphalt trying to melt the bottom of my Nikes: a nondescript building with no imposing columns or archways. It blended into the surrounding box stores dotting this strip of road like it was trying to appear as if it was for common people. Ironically, it was also situated on the outskirts of Vegas—where the common people's transit didn't run.

Not that I'd take transit. People on the bus are the worst for staring.

I slammed the door of my chrome-rimmed holding cell and headed for the shade without waiting for my mom. As I climbed the front steps, a shadow passed over the entryway—dark fingers trickling along the stucco overhead like cool water.

My pace slowed. It was a cloud passing over the sun—I knew that—but I had the sudden urge to put a hand on the railing and grip the metal tight. Maybe lie down on the steps, feel the concrete.

Stop it.

The air felt heavy, like the very rare time rain was imminent.

"Hotter than a snake's butt in a wagon rut," my mom observed, catching up to me. She was breathing hard and clutching her oversize purse. The tassels and bits of bling swung, hitting her elbow and her side alternately.

The saying was "snake's ass," but my mom never swore. She said it didn't reflect well on a person's character. I guess for my mom, words spoke louder than actions.

The entry led into the open-air atrium of the courthouse. In the center, concrete planters surrounded a fountain in the shape of a decidedly nonaquatic lizard, which spouted water from its mouth. Fitting, for Vegas—where nothing was too incongruent or illogical.

"Let's wait here for your dad. He'll just be a second."

I looked at my watch. It was twenty to ten; our court appearance was at ten o'clock. The fact that my dad had taken that call spoke volumes about his opinion of the court date. The fact that my mom didn't protest when he took it spoke volumes about . . . everything else.

She plunked herself down on the edge of the concrete, like she needed a rest after a hard-won battle, and glanced around. A weird mix of disdain and concern crept over her face. "She sure doesn't draw the crowds like she used to." The look morphed into alarm. "I hope to heck she doesn't wear her hair up."

The hell?

"She knows her ears stick out too much for that."

As I digested the complete inanity of that comment, my mom's first observation registered. She was right: there hadn't been any media outside the courthouse, and the atrium wasn't empty, but it certainly wasn't packed. It didn't seem like throngs of rabid fans had shown up to see this all go down.

Huh. Maybe the case wasn't as big a deal as Liv had hoped. Maybe, after three identical lawsuits pitting ex–beauty pageant kids against their parents, public appetite for this kind of spectacle had waned.

Awkward.

Liv had been texting all week, trying to confirm I'd be here. Her last message was full-blown desperation: *Need to talk. Can I come over?*

I hadn't answered. I had no idea why my presence mattered that much. Maybe she was thinking of the family photo op: the triumphant queen and her big brother, united in justice. There wouldn't be a shred of truth in the image, but who cared? The illusion was what mattered. Liv's entire existence proved that.

"I need caffeine." My mom fished around in her purse and extracted a twenty-dollar bill. She waved it at me, gesturing with her other hand at the coffee bar in the corner of the atrium. "It's gonna be a long morning, Jory-Jore." The layer of makeup she'd caked onto her eye-bags was shiny in the heat. "And it sure would help my nerves."

Because caffeine is a proven relaxant.

"Not sure I can get in that courtroom without a little help." She punctuated this with a dramatic sigh. "Not sure I can get in there at all, actually."

I studied her. She did look unsteady, like that moment last week when she'd had a panic attack at the grocery store. I took the bill from her outstretched hand. "What do you want?"

She dug in her purse again, found a fan, snapped it open, and started to flap. Her free hand fluttered up to fiddle with her necklace. "A Frappuccino—Grande."

Of course. I crumpled the twenty in my fist. Of course it had to be a Frappuccino.

"Get yourself something, too!" she called as I turned away.

The atrium was shaded by a variety of umbrellas and awnings that did nothing to combat the heat; I could feel my collared tee sticking to my back and hoped the checked pattern actually was sweat camouflage like the label promised. Maybe a cold drink wasn't a bad idea. It wasn't in my Sixty-Day Shred regime, but: one, I hated buying bottled water, and two, I had worked out twice yesterday, so didn't it all balance out? I worked out because I didn't want to feel weak on top of everything else, and I used the regime because it was good to have a schedule, but I didn't portion out my meals or worry how my clothes were "accentuating my progress."

I wasn't screwed up like my sister.

Before me, a table and umbrella wavered in and out of focus.

I paused and stared, willing it to stop. An unpleasant splintering feeling was working its way through me, bringing an equally unpleasant thought: I was looking at an imitation of the actual table with umbrella. The wavering I saw was the veil between this copy and the real thing, and the veil was drawing back . . .

Dry eyes: that's what it was.

I pulled a small bottle of artificial tears from the front pocket of my jeans. The relief was instant but, as always, the blurriness took a while to subside. It was hard to decide what was worse for clinically dry eyes: the heat or the air-con. In summer, I was screwed either way.

That's probably what had happened as we parked; my eyes had been drier than I thought, and the heat did its mirage thing. No need to get all metaphysical. I mean, I was into that kind of thing: my film club was always discussing illusion, the line between real and the hyperreal, and, honestly, I considered myself a bit of an expert on it all, considering everything. But today was going to be surreal enough without me questioning my grasp on reality.

I put the artificial tears back in my pocket and joined the line at the coffee bar.

The girl at the register looked a couple of years older than me. She was cute: dark auburn dreadlocks, huge eyes, and a cheek piercing. I turned slightly to the right so she was looking at my best side.

As I waited for the line to move, a shadow passed over the courtyard again. The air was denser still, and the smell in the air . . . it was definitely going to storm. Bizarre. I glanced up to look for the clouds, but like some hapless moth to a light bulb, my gaze was drawn instead to three girls cutting across this corner of the atrium.

My sister, Liv, and her entourage.

They walked with textbook posture, confidence radiating off them like nuclear waves, and they were all done up in faux defiance of perfection: designer tops, teased hair that was supposed to look careless. But the most obvious crack in their rebellious facade was how their flat dress shoes slapped the tile together; they were pacing one another in perfect unison.

You can take the girl out of the pageant—hey, you can convince her those pageants caused her "irreparable and lasting harm" worthy of a million-dollar lawsuit—but you'll never fully take the pageant out of the girl.

I glanced back toward the fountain. My dad had arrived; he stood with one dress shoe on the edge of the fountain, leaning forward, hand to his ear. He was still on his call. My mom was facing away from us.

They hadn't seen her, and Liv had probably deliberately avoided them. She'd been staying with her friend Asia, the blond—or was the red-haired one Asia?—ever since the hearing date was set more than nine months ago, so she hadn't had to endure my mom's histrionics. I mean, sure, she had endured them for years—so did everyone who tuned in to the reality TV show *Darling Divas*—but Mom's more recent antics? The spontaneous crying and binge eating and impulse buying? My sister hadn't had to deal with any of that, even though her court case was ground zero for Mom's psychosis.

Liv saw me and raised her hand in greeting. She didn't smile—she knew better than that—but I saw her confident expression falter when I didn't return the gesture. She wasn't going to come over here, was she? To "talk"?

"What can I get you?"

I turned back to the counter, caught off guard and forgetting my sideways trick, which gave the hot barista a clear look at my face. There was the usual moment of *pause* followed by an obviously forced *this is totally normal* smile.

To her credit, she didn't look around to see if I had an aide, if I should've been standing in a coffee line on my own. And that smile dimpled in the side of her cheek where the silver stud was, pretty much killing me. I forgot all about Liv.

"One Venti iced tea," I said slowly, "and one Grande Frappuccino."

There was a silence. Her eyes flicked to her screen. Back to me. "An iced tea? Venti?" she asked.

I nodded.

"And . . ." She cocked her head forward, gesturing to her ear with a raised finger like the reason she didn't know what I wanted was because she hadn't heard me. "Was that a mochaccino?"

I thought about changing the order, picking something easier to say—I mean, "Frappuccino" has got to be the stupidest goddamn word for a drink in the first place—but a spike of irritation killed that idea. Lately, going out of my way to make sure other people didn't feel uncomfortable was getting old.

"A Frappuccino." I was trying not to care about her reaction, but she was concentrating really hard on my mouth, and I could feel my face getting hot.

Her eyes lit up. "A Frappuccino!" She said it like she'd figured out the cure for cancer, which should've grated on me, except that dimple . . . Okay, she was so hot her glee was kind of adorable.

I nodded. "Grande."

She paused for one more second, then tapped the screen. The cash register drawer popped open.

"I like your ink." She looked at my outstretched arm as she took my twenty.

A tattoo of a two-toned, oblong *ouroboros*—a snake eating its own tail—stretched along the inside of my forearm. It symbolizes infinity, life from death, creation from destruction. The universe in balance.

Sort of.

I wanted to ask her if she knew what the symbol was, if she knew what book it was from, and there was a crazy moment where I imagined she answered yes to both, and then she asked why it was oblong and not a perfect circle, and I told her the reason, and she thought that was cool. And then she asked me out, which wasn't weird because she assumed I was eighteen on account of the tattoo.

"Where'd you get it done?" She gave me my change, grabbed a cup from below the counter, and started scribbling on it.

"Revolt."

She cocked her ear forward again and grabbed a second cup.

"Revolt Tattoo."

She marked the cup and set both aside, sucking in her bottom lip like she was thinking hard. "Oh! *Revolt!*" she said. I take cute back; she was gorgeous. Her eyes were a light brown and her skin was lightly freckled, like she'd been dusted in whatever they put on the top of the whipped cream—

"Sorry," she said. "I'm sorry." For not understanding me, she meant.

Spell: broken.

I stuffed the change into my pocket and moved along the counter toward a different barista—a guy with dyed blond tips who had picked up the cups with my order on them. The hot girl greeted the next person in line.

"Your name?" the guy with the terrible frosted hair asked, cup in hand, Sharpie at the ready. "She forgot to ask."

Forgot, or didn't want the hassle.

"Jory." I didn't look back at the barista. I hoped she stayed distracted.

He squinted. "George?"

"Jory."

He pursed his lips, like he was deciding whether or not this was even worth his time. A hot feeling crept into my throat. He scribbled on the cups in turn and set them aside.

I moved along to wait at the far end, forcing myself to count down from ten, like our family doctor insisted. My parents hadn't taken her advice to find me a shrink, so she'd tried to help me herself.

"Outwardly expressing anger is new for you," Dr. Levy had said. *"It's important we find techniques to help you do that it in an acceptable way."*

Technique number one: count down from ten.

I wasn't exactly sure if she knew what she was talking about, but I'd figured it was worth a try. I didn't want to end up flying off the handle and doing something I regretted.

Technique number two: while counting down from ten, unpack the situation that made you feel angry.

Okay, the interaction with the girl at the register hadn't gone the way I'd wanted. That wasn't anything new. I was also used to people apologizing for not understanding me. So . . .

My train of thought paused as I scanned the atrium.

Liv had disappeared.

"Rory!"

I counted again before stepping up to the counter and taking the drinks: a Venti iced tea and a Grande Frappuccino. For Rory.

I guess my parents couldn't have known when I was born that I'd always have trouble pronouncing my own name—that a *J*, for someone with paralyzed sixth and seventh craniofacial nerves, was a bitch of a consonant to negotiate, second only to plosives—consonants like *P* and *B* and *T*. The one surgery helped my left side a bit but came nowhere close to fixing my pronunciation. If I'd done the series of surgeries, like the doctors had suggested, my own damn name wouldn't have been such a challenge. There was even a chance I could've smiled—or something close. But then, my parents would've needed to see it as an investment. You know, like a Child Glitz Pageant?

Like that.

I walked back toward the wrinkled silk pantsuit that was my mother. My dad was still on his call.

"I understand that!" he snapped into the phone. "And I said I'd sort it out. I need time. You need to give me that—" He pushed off the fountain with a dress shoe that needed a serious shining—the round buckle was dusty, another sign that he was unraveling by the minute—and strode out of earshot.

I looked at my watch again; it was now ten to ten.

"We'd better get in there," my mom said, dropping her necklace back against her throat and reaching for the drink. She made no move to get my dad's attention. "Judas Priest, but I'm all aflutter."

Aflutter was a hilarious understatement; she knew what was coming. Liv's lawyer had won three straight cases in a row the past three years: all beauty pageant kids who'd participated in the *Darling Divas* reality TV show. And none of those girls had the footage Liv had.

Even my parents' lawyer had advised us all to prepare for Liv winning. He meant emotionally, I think. As in: prepare yourselves for Liv's legal emancipation and the estrangement that would follow, because after this circus was over and all that was left were crumpled popcorn boxes, we were going to be sad little clowns indeed, without our main event—our Liv.

Well, at the end of summer I was moving away from all this and restarting my life at Boston University, so, yeah, I'd prepared. I looked down at the hand that gripped my iced tea. Blood pumped oxygen through my veins, along my wrist, into my palm, my fingers, and back. A continual loop. Never-ending. I was a walking *ouroboros*.

It was the courthouse, with its ironically cheap stucco, that was temporary; it was what it stood for that was ephemeral.

About a year ago, Liv told me that she had learned from her new friends ("pageant survivors," she called them) that it isn't selfish to want retribution; that if you've been wronged, bringing light to the issue by punishing the perpetrators helps those who've been similarly wronged.

I didn't tell her we would first need to agree on a definition of "wronged" before I'd concede that she was enacting a public service. There was no point in having that conversation; Liv would never understand that justice was slippery and conditional, that it only existed for certain people in certain circumstances.

She didn't realize that she was, still, firmly center stage in an inane and self-absorbed fiasco. All that was missing was the mile-high tiara.

LIV

THE HALLWAY OUTSIDE the courtroom was long and airy; it echoed with the clip of business heels and a low murmur of voices. All that space made me nervous—I am way more comfortable in crowds.

"Where is everyone?" I scanned the pencil skirts and tailored suits, chewing my upper lip. We'd breezed into the courthouse no problem, but I'd told myself that was because the media was probably inside. Now we were right outside the courtroom and I still hadn't seen a single reporter. I hoped Asia hadn't noticed.

"They're coming," Cherish replied, looking at her phone. Asia peered over her shoulder. "But Brooke texted she'll be a little late." Cherish glanced up at me. "Or did you mean *everyone* everyone?"

A hot flush washed over me. I waved a hand like I didn't care. "I meant *us*."

Cherish flipped her long auburn hair. It had natural shine,

the kind I had to use a special product to create. "Kaylie will be here any minute."

"How soon?" I said it more to keep Cherish off the topic of all the people who hadn't showed.

"Soon. Like five minutes."

With effort, I clamped my teeth together, tasting Brindled Glass, the matte lipstick I'd reapplied. My mom had tried to break me of my lip-chewing habit for years—she even had my pageant coach coat my upper lip in some kind of gloss that tasted like garbage. It would work for an hour or so, but the gloss would eventually sweat off during routine practice, and by the afternoon I'd be back to chewing my lip raw.

"Thank heck for lip liner and airbrush gloss," my mom used to say, *"or you'd be a horror show."* She said it often enough that the cameras caught it, then they played it on about seven different episodes. It was a "frankenbite": a clip taken out of context and spliced together with other footage to create a particular scene. A typical clip went like this:

Hairdresser, doing my hair: *"Wow, Livy. Your hair is holding curl so well today."*

My mom's voice: *"Thank heck . . ."*

Close-up of eight-year-old me, looking in the mirror.

My mom's voice: *"Or you'd be a horror show."*

I guess when they used it like that, they were trying to show how unkind my mom could be. Later, they used the frankenbite in combination with my tantrums. Like at the Little Vixens Pageant in Tallahassee when I was nine and I'd thrown my Rich Wear Queen crown in the garbage because I hadn't won Ultimate Grand Supreme. For that, they'd dub the whole quote over footage of me acting poorly. It was supposed to be so ironic it was funny, right? Clearly no amount of lip gloss could help me.

I watched those episodes the most of any of the footage, because it was like watching a stranger who looked like me. I didn't have memory of the really bad tantrums, where I'd flail and scream and rip at my cupcake dress. My therapist told me it is possible for a person to be so emotionally distressed that they basically black out and that this happened most often to children.

I guess that's what happened to me. Once, I raked a cameraman's face and drew blood. That episode had the most hits on YouTube—along with comments that advocated instating capital punishment for spoiled children.

I scanned the hallways for Kaylie. Media or no, I wanted all my girls here to share in my victory—*our* victory. We'd worked so hard on this, I couldn't imagine winning without them. That was kind of funny, considering I used to think I hated them. Considering I had said as much on national TV.

I'd said a lot of things on national TV.

But that didn't matter now. I was finally in control of the things I said, of my image, and I could write a new story for myself. I just hoped people were paying attention . . .

"Hey, don't be nervous." Cherish was frowning at me.

"Sorry."

"Don't apologize," Asia said. "Cherish threw up before she went into her final hearing."

"Seriously?"

Cherish made a face. "That wasn't nerves!"

"No? Residual bulimia?" Asia smiled wickedly at Cherish, who laughed. But when Asia's eyes met mine, I saw the unspoken question, the concern.

Part of me loved that she cared, but it bothered me that she obviously wasn't sure if I was over all that. I shook my head.

I hadn't thrown anything up in more than a year; I was strong, like her.

Strong. Brave. Fierce.

"I saw your brother on the way in," Cherish said.

"Yeah."

"Is he still not talking to you?"

"Jory doesn't talk much," I said lightly. "So how would I know?"

"What's that called again?" Cherish asked. "I know you told me a few times, but I can never remember."

"Moebius syndrome."

"And it's . . . like paralysis, right? God. I can't imagine. Because he's all there, right? Like, he understands?"

I nodded, picking at the pinkie nail on my left hand before I realized what I was doing. I tucked it into my fist. "Scholarship to BU in the fall. Majoring in . . . rocks? Something science-y."

"Wow. Are they all like that?"

They. "People who have Moebius? No. Like, some have . . . what's that called—autism? But he doesn't." A fluttery feeling was starting in my stomach.

"He's not very friendly. Though I guess why would you be? It must be so hard."

I made an *uh-huh* sound, hoping she'd drop it. I didn't like to talk about Jory much, and Cherish had a way of asking things that could be irritating. I didn't black out anymore, but my therapist had identified some "problematic thoughts" I'd have when I was upset. We'd worked on ways to redirect my thinking when I felt that darkness creeping in.

And there it was, hovering at the edge of my mind like a black cloud.

"It's hard on everyone," Asia said firmly. Her statement didn't bother me, because she knew the whole story. She knew Jory and I had never been close, even though he was only eighteen months older than me, and that since I'd filed against my parents it had gotten so much worse. He hadn't spoken to me in months, and I was pretty sure it wasn't out of loyalty to my parents; it wasn't like they were besties.

Probably he thought I had nothing to complain about. And yes, the lawsuit had put us back in the public eye, and he is a private person, so he could've been annoyed about that. I'd tried hard to keep him out of it, though; I'd done interviews and appearances on the condition that he was left alone.

But Jory had always been a prickly pear. Even as a kid he was hard to get along with.

I was going to change that. He didn't know it yet, but we *both* needed this. And when the judge read out her ruling, he'd see.

"Does he work out?"

"Cherish!" Asia chastised.

"What? I'm just asking!"

I took a sip of air and mentally pushed at the dark shadow. "I guess?"

"You can tell," Cherish continued, raising her eyebrows in appreciation. She wrinkled her nose. "Like, it's kind of tragic that—"

"Where's Sandra?" I looked around. "She said she'd meet me at a quarter to."

"She's here." Asia waved to someone behind me.

I turned. Sandra, my lawyer and Asia's former lawyer, was striding toward us, dressed to kill in a seersucker skirt and jacket and patent maroon heels. I suddenly wished I'd chosen my maxi dress and heeled sandals. They were the first things

I'd picked out, but then Asia had said she thought we should look teenager-y.

I risked a look back at Cherish, inwardly cringing that I had cut her off. But it had been that or letting myself slap her insensitive—

Stop it.

I took another small sip of air and shoved down the person I used to be—the person my parents had made me. I needed to show people, the judge, that it had been the pageant world that caused my blackouts. Sandra had found me a therapist to make sure I could deal with my anger and not do anything that might compromise our win.

Redirect. Focus on something good.

Okay: Cherish didn't look annoyed with me.

"Good morning, Lavinia. Hi, girls." Sandra always used my full name. I didn't mind so much; she had a way of saying it that made it sound kind of fancy. The way my mom said it, it always sounded trashy. A spicy perfume settled in the air. The courtroom was a "scent-free zone"—it even said so on the door—but Sandra wasn't the type to let anyone tell her how to present herself. She was so fierce.

She touched my arm. "How's my warrior?" She didn't look the least bit upset that there wasn't a crowd of media and onlookers.

If you can't make it, fake it. I pulled my stomach toward my backbone and squared my shoulders like I'd learned in Pro-Am modeling. It had been good for something, at least. "Ready," I answered.

"Great. Now, remember that you won't have to say anything. You'll just need to sit there while the judge delivers her decision."

I nodded.

"I can send it out when it comes in, right? The verdict?" Cherish gestured to her bright-blue phone.

"If that's all right with Lavinia." Sandra looked at me.

"Totally," I said quickly. "People will want to know. Won't they?"

"Everyone is so proud of you already," Asia cut in. "But this moment of your absolute self-actualization will be the icing on the cake."

I smiled, hoping I didn't look unsure. Asia sometimes spoke in a way I didn't understand, but she never made me feel stupid for it. Still, I was pretty sure she hadn't really answered my question.

"And afterward we're going to do something symbolic of your new freedom," she continued.

"Like putting all of Liv's pageant crowns in a pile in the parking lot and driving over them?" Cherish suggested.

Asia snorted. "Nothing that juvenile," she said. "I mean like taking our picture in front of the Eiffel Tower—a placeholder until we visit the real thing."

A flush rose up my neck into my cheeks. Driving over my pageant crowns was pretty much exactly what I'd planned to do. I hadn't told Asia; I was going to pretend it was a spontaneous thought. She liked spontaneous people.

But she was right: the idea was childish.

"Horror show."

"All right." Sandra moved past us and opened the door to the courtroom. "You girls can sit in the first row behind our table. Lavinia, after you."

Asia squeezed my arm and gave me a reassuring smile. "You'll be great."

A thrill rushed through me at her touch. "Thanks," I said, and then, feeling bold: "And thanks for the other day."

She tilted her head. "For what?"

"Worrying about me."

Asia frowned. "What do you mean?"

I paused, my cheeks growing warm. "Oh! I thought . . ." She'd texted me a bunch, wondering where I was, how I was. I'd just assumed . . . a dizzying sweep of humiliation hit me.

"Thank heck for lip liner and airbrush gloss."

"Sorry," I said. "Forget it." I was dying inside, but I drew myself up to my fiercest and entered the courtroom.

"Where are they?" Asia's whisper was unreasonably loud in the silence.

I glanced over my shoulder at my friend's anxious face. She was wedged between Kaylie and Brooke. Cherish sat on the bench at the far end. They were all taking turns glancing back at the doors.

I scanned the room. There were a handful of people: a few women who must've been from my mom's homemade jewelry group, my mom's sister, whom I'd only met twice when I was little, some men I didn't recognize, and a few people with notepads who looked like press. Definitely not a high-profile-case kind of crowd.

Beside me, Sandra shook her head slightly. I turned back around.

The judge, a large woman with bright-red lipstick, checked her watch. The clock on the wall behind her read twenty past ten. My parents were way late. And it was flipping freezing in the courtroom.

I shivered, pulled my arms close to my sides, and glanced over at my parents' lawyer, a skinny middle-aged man with thinning hair. He looked confused, like he also hadn't expected them to be late.

Where the flip were they? Were they doing this on purpose? I'd seen Jory in the atrium. There was no way he'd take the bus, so he would've had to catch a ride with them. No. They were here. My mom was taking her sweet time climbing those steps.

It was a little power play. Fine. She could enjoy it while it lasted. Because once the verdict came down, her ability to manipulate me, or anything related to my life, ever again, was over.

Behind me, Cherish sighed loudly.

Sandra checked her phone. The clock hand ticked over another minute.

Silence.

And then the door was flung open with a thud so sudden, my heart stuttered. Everyone turned.

A security guard strode in. He ignored us all and made his way past Sandra and me to the judge's bench.

No one was following him.

The judge bent to listen to the man's low murmurings. She asked him something I couldn't hear, and as he answered, she took off her glasses and rubbed at her eyes. She held her glasses in both hands, scanning the courtroom. Her gaze stopped on me.

"Lavinia Brewer?" she said.

I leapt to stand, but Sandra put a hand on my arm, keeping me in place.

"Yes?"

"I'm sorry to inform you that we'll have to delay."

Now Sandra was out of her chair. "On what grounds?"

The judge swung her gaze to Sandra, unhurried. "On the grounds that we currently don't know where Mrs. and Mr. Brewer are."

"I'm sorry?" Sandra didn't sound sorry.

"Mrs. and Mr. Brewer are nowhere to be found. I'd like them present for my ruling. So we'll delay until we locate them."

"Nowhere to be found," Sandra repeated.

My parents' lawyer was also standing, looking bewildered. "That's correct."

"They're in the atrium!" I blurted out.

The judge shook her head. "Not anymore. Security has scoured this building inside and out. Their vehicle is in the parking lot, but there's no sign of them."

"I just saw my brother." My voice was doing that whiny thing I hated. "Where could they have gone?"

"Your brother didn't go anywhere; he's still on the premises." The judge repositioned her glasses. "He's the one who reported their disappearance."

JORY

I DON'T KNOW from previous experience, but I'm going to go out on a limb and guess that being questioned by overzealous authority figures on an ordinary day is like dealing with wet sand in your underwear. Being questioned by said figures when you have my syndrome, on the most messed-up day ever? Gritty nether regions would be a welcome reprieve.

I'd been speaking with two of the courthouse security guards for ten minutes, and I'd counted down from ten a dozen times. They were asking me questions really slowly, like I was from another planet, and they kept looking at each other when they didn't understand my answers.

At least focusing on that was helping me keep it together.

"So you went and got your mom a . . ." The dark-haired guard paused, like he was waiting for me to fill in the blank, and squinted, his already too-small eyes shrinking further. He had a strange quirk to the side of his mouth. Most people tend to tune out extraneous information when they're under duress. Not me: I've always focused in on details when I'm uncomfortable.

"Coffee."

He exchanged a look with his companion. "And then you and your parents started across this atrium toward those steps."

I nodded. "Yeah."

"You didn't leave to go anywhere? Even for a minute?"

"No."

"You were directly in front of them—leading the way?"

I'd told them this three times already.

"Yeah."

"And then?"

"Then," I said, mimicking his greeting-a-being-from-outer-space tone, "when I got to the stairs and turned around, they were gone." I held the guard's gaze. He hadn't caught on to the fact that I was mocking him. He was too busy playing detective, trying to figure out if I was telling the truth by looking at me. This was an upshot to having Moebius: there was no way he could tell that I was lying.

He looked like he was going to make me go over it a fourth time, but we were interrupted by a flurry of movement swooping down the stairs.

Liv and her entourage arrived like a troop of shellacked Barbie dolls. They'd doubled in numbers, and Liv's lawyer was with them.

Great.

"Where are they, Jory?" Liv demanded, striding over to me.

The security guard held up his arms. "Slow down, little miss."

"Do *not* 'little miss' her," the lawyer barked, matching pace with Liv. "I am her representative, and my client would like to speak with her brother."

The guard stepped aside, and Liv pulled to a stop, her lawyer at her elbow. Her entourage filed in behind. The blond one looked super pissed, and the other three were too busy staring at me to remember to look like they were backing Liv up.

"Well?" Liv crossed her arms. "What happened?"

I looked at Liv's lawyer. Even in those ridiculous heels, she only came up to my chest. She also had these really tight curls and beady eyes, and she was wearing a diamond necklace that was close to choker length . . . Yeah, the whole thing gave the distinct impression of some sort of lapdog.

"*Jory.*"

I looked back at Liv. She uncrossed her arms and waved her hands impatiently.

"I turned around and they were gone," I said.

I'm sure there are things I do when I'm lying. I must have some kind of tell—a gesture, a head bob, something. But only a person who's spent a lot of time with me would recognize it for what it is, and that person was definitely not Liv.

"You know, this is really uncool," the blond one spat out. "After all that Liv's been through? What are you trying to do, break her?"

Liv drew back like she'd been slapped. Her eyes darted away from mine and toward her friend.

"Don't worry, Asia. It would take more than that," Liv's lawyer said.

Liv blinked. Then she straightened her shoulders, like she was resetting—a small gesture, but I saw it. She locked eyes with me again. "Were they even here?" she asked.

"What?"

"Were they here?"

My ability to see far still isn't great, which is part of why I got fixated on things in my immediate proximity, but Liv wasn't similarly nearsighted, was she? She had to have seen my parents in the atrium when she saw me.

"Yeah." My answer sounded tentative, even to me.

"Are you sure?" She stepped toward me, so close I had to put a hand up to warn her to back off. "Are you sure they didn't just send you to make it look like they were coming?"

"Lavinia." The lawyer gently touched her arm. "I don't think this is helping. At this point, we're going to have to file a report and let the police do their job."

The woman's tone was so condescending, I expected Liv's fury to be redirected at her. Instead, she paused. And then it was like a switch had been thrown.

"Okay," she said, stepping back. "Fine. We'll file a report." She turned to the lawyer. "But . . . doesn't some time need to pass—forty-eight hours or something?"

"That's a myth. A person is missing as soon as their family says they are."

"Okay." Liv nodded. "Good." Then, like she remembered something: "What about . . ." She gestured toward me. "You know."

"Right." The lawyer stepped forward. "Jory, the judge asked that you stay with your sister until we locate your parents."

"What? Why?"

"Because your parents have miraculously disappeared the day of the verdict, and she didn't feel it wise to leave you alone."

Alone. I looked at the lawyer and Liv. "She thinks I'll disappear, too?"

The lawyer paused, deciphering my words. "Oh. No, that's not the issue. But there will be police action—a search—and in that time, everyone related to the case should be accounted for. It's for your own protection."

Stay with my sister until they could locate my parents. So . . . stay with Liv until the end of time? Because—

Don't think about it.

The lawyer looked at Liv's blond friend—the one who hadn't stopped scowling at me. "Asia, Lavinia's been staying with you. Would it be all right if—"

"No." The word was out of my mouth before she could ask Asia the question. There was no way I was staying at Asia's apartment. The sunglasses in her hair looked like she'd hair-sprayed them in; anyone stupid enough to render their sunglasses useless in this weather would probably need help brushing their teeth. "No, thanks."

"Whatever," Asia muttered.

The lawyer sighed. "If you'd rather, Jory, we can arrange to have someone stay at the house with you."

I shook my head. A stranger, babysitting me? This was bullshit.

"Hey." The lawyer's attention was pulled to one of the Barbies. "I hope you're not talking about this on social media?"

The redhead paused, blue phone in hand. "I was just texting my boyfriend."

"Well, make sure he doesn't either. The last thing Lavinia needs right now is a bunch of online speculation." The lawyer's tone was one of admonishment, like she was talking to a six-year-old. "I'll send out a statement."

Red rolled her eyes. "Like anyone is paying attention to this online," she muttered, pocketing her phone.

Liv's cheeks went pink. She cleared her throat. "I'll go home with Jory."

Asia's mouth dropped open. "What?"

"Just until this is over."

I studied my sister. The look on her face was unusual: guilt or embarrassment, or both?

"Maybe there's something there that'll help find my parents."

"The police will handle it," her lawyer said.

"But maybe I can help."

Need to talk. Can I come over?

Her text messages. What had she wanted?

"Are you sure?" Asia asked. "I mean, you don't have to."

"I know." She shrugged, like she was trying to look nonchalant. "But I think it's best."

Her lawyer looked back and forth between us. "If you're both sure?"

"I'm sure." Liv fixed me with a stare. There was a spark of desperation there. "Jory?"

My pulse skipped, and there was a palpable throb in my throat. Shutting her down in front of her groupies would be so damn satisfying. After all, she'd wanted a circus, and here she was, center of the ring like a trained lion: on display and clinging desperately to some semblance of dignity.

I pulled my gaze wide. Behind Liv was her little entourage, a couple of security guards milling nearby, and the atrium gaping. She'd wanted a circus, had tried her best to create one, but no one had shown up to see her jump through the hoops.

Damn it. "Fine." I tried to ignore the flash of gratitude in her eyes.

"Do you need to pick up your things from Asia's?" her lawyer asked.

Liv shook her head. "I still have stuff at my parents' house."

"All right. I'll drive you both." Her lawyer looked at her watch. "We'll stop at the station and make the report first."

"What about their car?" Liv asked.

Right. My parents' Armada was still in the lot, which was part of the reason the security guards had questioned me for so long.

"Not our concern."

Liv turned and huddled her groupies together. Asia unfolded her arms to give Liv a hug, and she shot me another look of disdain. The rest made soothing noises and took turns touching Liv like she was some rare object that could break.

But Liv wasn't either of those things; she wasn't unique or fragile. So maybe her suggestion of returning to the house wasn't a way to save face. Maybe it was some kind of calculated move I couldn't figure out yet. Or . . .

Or maybe she was right.

Maybe there was something at the house that would set it all straight. Maybe my parents were back there right that second.

Maybe I hadn't seen what I thought I saw.

LIV

THE GLASS CASE in my parents' living room had been cleaned recently. It was huge, at least twelve feet tall, and full of my pageant crowns.

Not the early ones, obviously. Mom didn't display any of my prelim crowns—the small, local pageants that fed into state. And none of the Queen crowns from early state pageants were displayed either, since those were a "waste of money" according to my mom. Winning Queen of your event meant you had no shot at the good titles and no chance at winning Ultimate Grand Supreme. And since we always entered the required number of categories to qualify for Grand Supreme, pulling—winning— the Queen crown of any event was sort of like the loser crown. Definitely not showcase worthy.

There were more than sixty. Some of the Grand Supreme crowns were eighteen inches tall, and they literally glittered; my mom had set the track lights in the room so that they hit the case just so. In the middle of the second shelf there was a framed photograph of me as a kid, maybe ten years old. Red swimsuit, hair in pigtails, sand stretching out behind me. The sun had caught a glint of gold at my throat and the sparkle in my eyes as I posed.

So aware of the camera. So aware of my smile.

I'd been doing pageants for a few years by then; I knew how to turn it on.

I kicked off my ballet flats and sank down on the white couch.

When we had arrived twenty minutes ago, Sandra had helped me do a quick look around to make sure my parents weren't there. Of course they weren't; I'd never thought they would be, which was something I told her straightaway, pretending the reason I'd volunteered to come was to help out Jory. She thought, like, maybe he'd be worried or scared or something? And that my being there would make things more comfortable, in the circumstances.

She didn't know Jory—his needing me around had never been a thing.

No. I was here for answers. There was something about all this that felt off, like Jory knew more than he was saying. Plus, the idea of going back to Asia's after everything: the pathetic crowd turnout, the epic fail at getting a verdict . . .

"Thanks for the other day." My skin crawled with the memory of Asia's confused frown. How pathetic was it that I'd thought she was *"worrying about me"*?

My therapist would tell me to let it go, to redirect. So how was this for redirection: I'd question Jory myself and figure out where the H my parents were.

I'd asked Sandra to check my room for me. I was sure my mom had made a flipping shrine, readorned it with the pageant sashes and photos I'd torn down and thrown at her during one of our arguments, and I was afraid that if I'd guessed right, I'd trash the place. That wouldn't look very good to the judge.

Plus, the police had told us to disturb as few things as possible at the house, in case they decided to apply for a search warrant and look for clues or whatever. Sandra told them that, considering my parents had missed their court date, these were "exigent circumstances," which I guess meant the police shouldn't need a warrant. The cops said they needed some time to look into it all and took down Sandra's name as our liaison while they conducted their missing persons search.

So, who knew how long it would be before they were actually looking for my parents? And Jory . . . well, he'd told the police exactly what he'd told Sandra in the car on the way to the station. And he was shaken, for sure. I could tell because ever since we were kids he'd get really fixated on small details when he was upset. Like, he'd zero in on people's faces, kind of zone out, and he was doing that the whole time we were at the police station.

But was he upset because my parents had disappeared or because he'd played a part?

Judas Priest.

He was so frustrating and unhelpful with his one-word answers. I wanted to scream at him, but giving in to that impulse was the old me—I didn't do that anymore. I pulled myself off the couch, resisting the urge to check my phone. I'd turned it to mute at the police station after Sandra told me I could post that my court date had been postponed, and it had blown up with tweets and messages. Like, part of me was relieved—people were obviously watching the case—but I couldn't deal right now. I didn't even have it in me to Snapchat something snarky about that stupid showcase of crowns.

I tracked down Jory in the kitchen. He was standing in the far corner, making toast—a smell that reminded me I hadn't eaten all day. Wrapping up at the courthouse had taken some time, then at the station, there were all these questions—some I couldn't even begin to answer ("What were they wearing?" "What was the last thing they did?"), so Jory had to, which took forever—and then there'd been the drive home.

I opened the fridge, knowing before I looked that it was packed with everything I didn't eat. Sure enough, a full-fat, high-sugar spread greeted me: cans and cans of soda, bricks of cheese, some kind of layered cake, three loaves of bread, two enormous jars of peanut butter, take-out containers . . . I grabbed a yogurt cup. It was that awful, brightly colored stuff, but it was as close as I was going to get to dinner.

I wandered to the island and leaned against it. "Jory?"

He didn't turn around.

I tried my smile-voice trick, forcing a smile before I spoke. Whether or not I felt like smiling, it always made my voice sound happier. "Look. I know you don't want me here, and I know . . . you've been upset about the court case. I . . . I just hope that wouldn't cause you to do something you might regret later."

No answer.

Smile. "Because what Mom and Dad are doing? It's not right. It's . . ." I racked my brain for the phrase. "An *obstruction* of justice." *Whew.*

Jory made a sound—a laugh?—and popped his toast.

Smile. Barely. "And I don't want you involved in anything

like that. Because they're going to be charged, you know. When they're found. And you need to go to college in the fall. And you can't do that if you're being charged . . ."

He plunked the toast on a plate and began buttering it.

I gritted my teeth. "Jory, *please*. If you know something, I need to know. I need to know if you were involved."

A pause. "I wasn't."

"Do you swear?"

Jory put the knife down and turned. "Yes."

I peered at him. It was so hard to tell with Jory. Best to keep him talking. "But had Mom been acting strange lately?"

"Um, yeah."

"Really?"

He tilted his head, holding my gaze. It took me a second to realize he was mocking me.

"Jory! You know what I mean!"

He went back to buttering his toast. How much flipping butter did he need?

"I mean was she, like . . . nervous or . . . different?" The knife scraped against the toast. "I just want to know if she—"

He wheeled. "That?" He pointed with the knife to the fridge behind me. "That food? She buys that amount *every other day*." He picked up his plate. "The bar for strange behavior is pretty low."

As I worked out his last sentence, he turned and bit into his toast, keeping the hand holding the plate up near his face. I turned and fished in the island drawer for a spoon. Jory was messy when he ate, and he was self-conscious about it. I didn't have his chewing issues, but I could sympathize. I hated eating in front of people, too.

Still, did he think I didn't know strange behavior? The months before I filed and moved out, my mom had upped her control game to epic levels: combing through my room, stalking my social media. Overbuying at the grocery store was nothing.

I pulled the tab of my yogurt back and wandered over to the kitchen patio doors, peering out at the pool. It was already dark, and the outdoor lights caused shadows to flicker and dance on the surface of the water.

The pool was maintained like it was used all the time. But we didn't use it and we never had guests; my parents didn't have any friends they'd invite over. They'd always been too busy for that sort of thing, my dad with his business, my mom with my pageants. Being friends with other pageant moms wasn't really her thing.

"We're here to win, not make friends, Livy." My mom had said that when you're putting a bunch of money into something, you have to give it one hundred and ten percent—you're cheating yourself if you don't. And . . .

"No one likes a cheater." Once, she'd said that exact thing to a nine-year-old contestant, accusing her of deliberately taking too long in hair and makeup and making my own appointment rushed. I hadn't had time to get scales painted on my arms for my Deep-Sea Wear costume, and my mom was furious. On YouTube, that episode was unofficially titled "Sea Monster: Brenda Brewer loses it."

Yeah. She was big on no cheating. Until it came to what she was willing to do to me, I guess. That wave of powerless fury surged up. I was so close to being done with my parents' nonsense forever. And now . . .

"What are you trying to do, break her?"

Asia's words from the courthouse echoed through my

head. Did she really see me that way—as someone who could break? Did she think I was that fragile?

"Horror show."

That black shadow swelled in a corner of my mind.

Tomorrow was Saturday: if the police decided they needed a warrant to search the house, they couldn't get one on the weekend, could they? And by Monday, who knew where my parents would be?

I had to do something. If there was evidence in this house, maybe I could find it. After all, I had so much invested in getting my parents into that courtroom—wasn't I cheating myself if I didn't give *a hundred and ten percent*?

I stared out at the pool. It shimmered in the yard lights, shadows writhing along the aquamarine like black snakes. The surface wavered and then flashed, suddenly so shiny it could've been reflecting the sun on a cloudless day.

The skin over my collarbone pinged, like something hot had touched me, and I heard a familiar click: a camera shutter.

But my eyes were drawn to the body.

Facedown. Drifting like a clump of garbage. Suit jacket splayed out on the surface of the water, dark hair . . .

The yogurt cup dropped from my hand and hit the kitchen floor with a splatter.

"What the hell, Liv?"

My mouth opened, but no sound came out. I raised my hand, clutching the spoon and feeling like I was moving in slow motion, and pointed, pressing my finger to the glass.

Jory crossed over to me and peered out. "What?"

Seriously? I looked at him. He was squinting. Right. He was nearsighted.

"It's Dad." My voice was barely a whisper.

"*What's* Dad?"

I looked back at the pool. The bright, shiny surface was gone, though the shadow snakes were still there, weaving along the bottom.

The far end of the pool was empty.

"But . . ." I unlocked the door and pushed it open, my toes squishing through yogurt as I stepped out. The night air was sticky and the stone tiles were warm under my bare feet. I ventured to the edge of the pool, gesturing with the spoon. "He was here." I turned. Jory was stepping over a gob of pink dairy fat to follow me outside. "He was floating."

"In the pool?"

"Yes." I swallowed. "He was facedown . . . He looked . . . dead."

Jory stopped. He crossed his arms.

"I swear I saw him."

Jory was silent.

"I . . . swear." I looked back at the empty pool. Except . . .

Except there was no way. Dead bodies don't get themselves out of pools and then over an eight-foot-tall concrete wall enclosing the backyard. I shivered despite the heat. Jory was still staring at me. He probably thought I was cracking. Like Asia said I would.

"I'm tired." I shrugged. "My eyes are playing tricks on me." I met Jory's gaze reluctantly, expecting him to say something cutting.

Instead, he tilted his head. "You really didn't see them today?"

It took me a moment to figure out what he meant. "No," I said. He was sticking with his story, obviously.

He was quiet again. He looked over my shoulder at the pool.

I fiddled with the spoon. I was tired. A little spooked. Like, it's not every day your parents disappear. Especially when you're finally about to make them pay for ruining your childhood.

Okay. Maybe I was more upset than I thought. Maybe I'd done the adult version of blacking out.

Jory muttered.

"Pardon?" I looked up at him.

"Wish. Fulfillment." He said it slowly, deliberately.

"What do you mean?"

He gestured at the pool. "What you saw."

I frowned, trying to understand. *Was he saying*—"I don't wish Dad drowned!"

He crossed his arms again.

I didn't—did I?

I stared at the flickering shadows on the pool. No. I was upset, and it had triggered a memory. A scary image I'd seen once or something.

"What did you need to talk about?"

I looked back at Jory. "Pardon?"

He sighed. "Why are you here, Liv?"

I frowned at him. "To help." He stared at me, clearly expecting me to offer a better explanation. Well, he could wait. What I'd wanted to talk about, which was what I was planning to do with my lawsuit winnings, and the reason I was here now were two different things. And before I told him anything, I needed to find my parents.

I stepped around him and headed back to the kitchen. I'd have to clean that yogurt. The housekeeper never came on the weekend. I was sure they still had one; I couldn't imagine Mom cleaning. I couldn't imagine her doing anything, much less drowning my dad—

Wait. Where had that thought come from? Something my mom had said once—not caught on camera. We were near water somewhere. The surface was so shiny . . .

"Sometimes, I wish to heck he'd drowned."

I stopped dead and spun around. Jory had his hands shoved in his pockets and his head bowed like he was thinking. "Jory." He looked sideways at me. I took a deep breath and spoke as I exhaled to steady my voice, the way Sandra taught me. "I think I know where they are."

IT'S ALWAYS THIS
DARK IN THE
DESERT

JORY

THE HIGH BEAMS of my parents' Audi illuminated small shrubs clinging to the shoulders of the road and glinted off the tar winding across the highway before us. I had to imagine the dry desert stretching toward low mountains in the distance because there was no moon and the occasional oncoming car was the only other source of light. Our sight was basically confined to the tunnel cast by the headlights of the car.

I could tell it wasn't my shitty eyesight; Liv was sitting up over the wheel, peering ahead intently. She noticed me watching her. "It's so dark out here."

Wow. The apple didn't fall far from the stating-the-obvious tree. Why had I agreed to get in the car with mini-Mom?

That's right: because I didn't have a better option. Was I really going to let my sister drive off into the wilds alone on the most screwed-up day in history? Plus, the alternative was staying home and . . . what? Play Cloud Dynasty or some other online RPG like it was an ordinary Friday? *Not* wonder about my grasp on reality?

That moment at the courthouse stairs hovered in a corner of my mind.

"We'll be late."

I stabbed a finger at the radio station scan button, interrupting the acid jazz that had been upping my irritation for the past ten minutes.

"Seriously, I can hardly see a thing. Is it always this dark in the desert?"

It was going to be a long drive. Walker Lake was more than three hundred miles from Vegas but, according to Liv, it was where she'd find our parents. She'd bought herself the weekend by telling her friends and lawyer she needed time alone—and that she'd check in periodically. But I knew she thought she'd find our parents, alert the Mineral County authorities, have our parents arrested for failing to appear in court, and breeze back into Vegas all by the next morning.

What I couldn't figure out was why she was so sure about Walker Lake. That was something she either couldn't explain or didn't want to.

"I'm glad you're coming with me," Liv had said as we backed out of the driveway. She'd found the ever-misplaced keys to my parents' Audi no problem and asked me to hop in like we were going for ice cream. Stranger still, she'd sounded so sincere. Was that even possible?

I pretended to adjust my seat belt and glanced at her again.

She was humming along to some vapid pop song on the radio and gripping the steering wheel tight, a weird combination of nerves and confidence.

But that was Liv. Even as a kid, she'd had this bizarre energy about her, like she was completely on edge but somehow fully in control of the situation. Except for when she wasn't. Except for when she "blacked out" and screamed for forty-five seconds straight. She hadn't done that in a long time, not since the TV cameras went away. But I knew that she was less out of control in those moments than everyone thought. The timing wasn't coincidence—her fits and the cameras were related—but it wasn't cause and effect the way her lawyer had alleged.

No. She was still playing a role, and her sincerity and gratitude were part of the act. She wanted me along because if I stayed in her sight, I couldn't do anything to sabotage her plan—like alerting our parents to her stroke of genius. I knew she thought I had something to do with it all.

But whatever. At least if I was with her when she realized she was wrong, she'd know I wasn't involved. Then maybe she'd move back to Asia's while the police continued to search.

And search, and search, and search . . .

I stabbed at the radio again, changing the station.

"Hey!" Liv protested. "I was listening to that."

"It sucked."

"Nice, Jory."

The sad whine of a steel guitar drifted through the speakers.

"Like this is any better?" Liv huffed.

We drove in silence for several minutes. I heard Liv take a breath and looked over at her. Now she was smiling. Why was she smiling? God, she was so weird.

"I wonder if the road to the cabin is still passable." Her voice was a notch lighter. "We might have to hike in if it hasn't been used recently."

Hike in. Like she backpacked regularly.

"I'm pretty sure I remember how to get there. It's the turn after that corner store outside the town, if that still exists. Like, I can probably remember the corner, at least. And then from there, it's a gravel road to the lake. I think . . ." She trailed off. "I think I'll recognize it."

"Well, we could ask." I looked at the clock on the dash. It was 9:32 P.M. "If we weren't going to arrive in the middle of the night."

"It couldn't wait until morning, okay?" Liv said. "I couldn't waste another minute." She stared out the windshield, chewing her upper lip.

Jesus. That hope in her eyes: she was so sure she was on the right track. I mean, it would be good if she was; it would actually be the best-case scenario. My shitty eyesight plus my parents pulling a fast one on both of us would explain the unexplainable. The impossible. The thing I couldn't let myself think about, let alone tell Liv:

That my parents had vanished—literally—in front of me.

Stop.

The tightness in my chest was back. I fished a package of Rolaids out of my pocket and took two.

"What are those?" Liv asked.

I shoved them out of sight. "Antacid."

"You eat an awful lot of them."

"Heartburn."

"That often? You eat them, like, every other hour."

I shrugged.

"Have you ever considered finding what's causing the heartburn? Maybe you should eliminate the cause instead of treating it with drugs." Her voice had that Pro-Am thing going on suddenly, like she was being interviewed for the Miss Teen Universe contest.

"The cause is stomach acid."

"But what's causing *that*? Like, we're so quick to pop a pill for things that bother us that we never really take time to understand the root of the problem."

I was silent, which I guess she took as disagreement, because she continued. "I'm serious. Do you know how many people are addicted to prescription drugs in the US? Addiction kills sixteen million people a year."

Wait. Was she comparing my reliance on Rolaids to an OxyContin overdose?

"It's because everything's so easy to get now. Doctors prescribe you anything without a second thought."

"I see." *I see* as in: *please stop talking.*

"Like, I'm not saying I'm smarter than doctors, but people should take responsibility for their own happiness. Instead of masking their pain by using something that makes them feel good for a minute, people should address why they're unhappy. And then deal with that."

By suing their parents? I didn't say it because my parents were actually beside the point. On point: it takes a special kind of righteousness to believe the trauma of being told you're beautiful since age four deserves national attention.

"Part of my recovery and transformation is holding people accountable," Liv continued. "I need to help others in my situation know that they can say no, that they can stand up for themselves."

I had to shut this down or I'd say something I'd regret. "You don't mask your 'pain' with drugs?"

She laughed. "What drug would I be on?"

I thought of her posing in front of the Audi for a lightning-quick selfie before we got in. "Snapchat?"

She opened her mouth, closed it. Squinted at the road.

I settled back in my seat as the steel guitar wailed softly. The occasional road sign glinted past, its top stripe reflecting the car's headlights. Maybe I could pretend to sleep the rest of the drive. We'd been on the road only an hour or so; there was no way I could take four more hours of Dr. Liv. I'd fling myself from the moving car first. It had been years since I'd been confined to such a small space with my sister, and I couldn't even remember the last time we'd driven up to the cabin. I remembered being there, but not the drive.

I was standing on the shore—water shoes on because I hated the feeling of sand between my toes, especially the gooey wet sand on the bottom of the lake.

My dad was at the end of the pier with a glass in his hand, which is why I'd chosen to stand on the stupid beach. Behind me, Liv was posing in a strawberry-red two-piece swimsuit, and my mom circled around her with a camera, snapping shots. I wasn't allowed to stay in the cabin because we were having "family time."

When the kids at my school had "family time," did it feel like this? Like a car crash waiting to happen?

"Hey, Jory!" my father called. His speech was slurred. "You want to see a monster?"

I blinked out at the dark highway. It occurred to me that we hadn't seen another car in a while. A long while, for being on the 95 an hour or so from Vegas. I cleared my throat. "Is this even the right road?"

"We follow the 95 all the way. Check my phone."

I reached into the console and pulled out her obscenely glittery Android. On the screen was a message notification. "You have a text from Asia—"

Liv reached over and snatched the phone from my hand.

"If you care," I finished.

She set the phone in her lap and tucked a lock of hair behind her ear. Her gaze darted toward me, then away.

"Um, I wasn't going to read it," I said.

Liv gripped the steering wheel, suddenly looking vulnerable.

"Seriously. I don't care what you two are sexting." I was trying to make a joke, but Liv's eyes went wide, then wider, until she was blinking back tears.

What the hell?

"Kidding," I said. "Liv?" I felt a twinge of unease. It wasn't like her, and this whole damn thing was already so screwed up. I scrambled for a distraction and, in my slight panic, blurted out something I'd vowed to myself I wouldn't bring up again: "What did you want to talk about? This week, I mean."

She frowned at me. "What?"

"Your texts?"

For a second it looked like she was going to pretend she didn't know what I was talking about—again—but then she sat up straighter. "Oh, that." She shrugged. "I wanted you there for the verdict."

"Why?"

She hesitated. "It's—well, it's hard to explain right n—" Her eyes locked on the rearview mirror. "Geez Murphy," she said. "Someone's in a hurry." Her sentence was punctuated by the sudden glare of headlights streaming in at us from behind.

The roar of an engine grew as the lights swept up blindingly and then moved to the side. The car sped past us on the left, a blur of black and chrome, with tinted windows. It swerved back into our lane and braked suddenly, red taillights screaming crimson.

"Holy!" Liv jammed the brakes in turn, but the other car was already speeding up again, gaining distance. A circular logo above the license plate glinted in our headlights before the car sped away into the dark.

"Weird," I said. "That was a black Armada."

"I saw it." Liv stared out the window. "Did you catch the license plate?"

"No."

"Me neither. But . . ." Liv chewed on her upper lip, like she was nervously considering something. Then a look of determination settled on her face. She gripped the steering wheel and stomped on the accelerator.

"What are you doing?"

"It's too much of a coincidence."

Coincidence? Oh. Oh no . . . she thought—

"That's Mom and Dad." The speedometer climbed over seventy. "And I'm going to catch them."

LIV

"IT'S NOT THEM," Jory said.

"It has to be them."

"But why would they—"

"Mess with us? I don't know! Why would they disappear in the first place?" I leaned forward, my eyes glued to the road. "Maybe they didn't know it was us until they passed us. Then they thought about stopping, then thought better of it. Whatever it is, I'm not losing them. There!" The glow of taillights came back into view. Then the Armada's headlight beams flashed in a giant arc and disappeared from our view as the SUV turned left. "They're turning off!" I said. "Hold on."

"How about slowing down?"

We swung onto the intersecting road with a slight squeal of the tires.

"What road is this?" Jory asked, putting a hand on the dashboard.

"Who cares?" I accelerated. Eighty miles an hour was doable.

It was a straight desert road after all, and Asia and I had done faster than that on the straightaways outside Vegas in her 8 Series. Tarred cracks flew under the car as we gained on the SUV.

"Liv, slow down."

"I can't lose them."

"You don't know it's them."

"Why else would they be driving so fast? They're trying to lose *us*. It's them. I know it is."

The taillights ahead moved to the left as the road took a sweeping curve. Dark shapes loomed on either side of the road—low mountains. The taillights moved right. The SUV was taking the middle of the road on the turns so it wouldn't need to slow down.

But the curves were getting sharper as we headed west. The Armada had to throw on its brakes now and again, and I had to slow a bit too.

As the low hills became rocky cliffs, the turns became even sharper and closer together, so that we'd lose sight of the Armada around one corner, then see it again on the straightaway before the next.

I was losing them. "Sugar." I accelerated. Fast. Too fast.

The next curve screamed toward us, and I had to brake hard. The tires locked, and the back end of the car fishtailed as we skidded into the oncoming lane. I jerked the wheel to the right, which made the back end swing harder. We arced around in a half circle, screeching to a halt on the opposite side of the road, facing the way we'd come.

"Jesus Christ!" Jory yelled.

I clutched the wheel, staring out at the deserted highway. It had happened so fast there wasn't time to be scared. Now adrenaline was flooding me, and my heart was beating triple time.

Breathe. Focus.

Sitting up tall, I craned my neck to look out the back window. The Armada was gone. I slammed both hands on the wheel. "We lost them!"

"Are you serious?" Jory sounded pissed.

"What?"

"You could've killed us!"

"I didn't."

"You could have." His chest was rising and falling rapidly.

"Well, I *didn't*. And I had to follow them." What did he expect me to do?

"It wasn't them."

"It was totally them."

"No, it wasn't!"

"You said you don't know where they are!"

"I don't!"

"So what makes you so sure?"

He stared at the radio display. The tinny sound of a steel guitar whined out at us from the speakers. I reached forward and punched the radio off. *"Jory."*

"What?"

"I said, what makes you so sure?"

"Because—" he started. Then he rubbed his hands over his face. "This is stupid. This whole thing is so stupid."

"It's stupid to want justice? Mom and Dad ruined my childhood. It's stupid to let them get away with it."

Jory clenched his fists in his lap like he didn't know what to do with his hands. I checked over my shoulder again. The highway was dark. Empty.

I breathed deep and picked up my phone to use the maps app. If this road led in the direction of Walker Lake, I may as well keep following it. The text from Asia sat, unread and un-responded to, on the screen.

How's it going with Talky Tom?

Let me know if you need backup. Ha, ha.

I noticed then that I had no service. The maps app couldn't even find us on the grid. *Frick.* I sank into the seat and looked at Jory. "I'll go back to the highway. Happy?" My hands were shaking, so I tightened my fingers on the steering wheel and pulled ahead.

Jory was quiet as I guided the car through the twisty roads, retracing our route. He was right; I had been driving these curves pretty fast. But I had been following my parents, I knew that much. Except . . .

Except hadn't their car been left in the courthouse parking lot? Maybe that's why Jory was so sure. Still, it was possible they'd returned to retrieve it after nightfall.

I reached for my lip balm in the console and caught sight of my phone screen.

Talky Tom. Asia and I had created nicknames for my family members based on opposites. We called Dad Type B, Mom was the Giver—which Asia said was doubly ironic because it was also the name of one of her favorite books, and she couldn't stand my mom—and Jory was Talky Tom, for obvious reasons.

I glanced at him. He was fixated on the tattoo on his arm, tracing it over and over with the fingers of his left hand. It was some weird looping symbol, and I still couldn't believe my dad had signed the consent form. But then, neither of my parents really ever said no to Jory. I think because it was easier than dealing with his moods.

If Jory wanted a cookie or a new book or, more recently, to lock himself in his room for hours, he was allowed. Wouldn't want him to stop talking completely so that you had no idea what to make him for dinner. Wouldn't want him to pretend to be sick and ruin a rare family outing. It wasn't fair: all my worst moments were still online—I'd need to sue the *Darling Divas* producers to get them taken down—but there wasn't a single shred of video evidence of how difficult Jory could be. Like that time . . .

I checked my phone: 2:37 P.M.

If we didn't leave right away I was going to be late, and if I was late, I may as well not show up at all. The kids from my class had said three P.M. at the Atmosphere north gate, but since I didn't have anyone's number yet, I couldn't text to let them know if I was running behind. Finding them in that amusement park would be impossible.

I paused at the hallway mirror and reapplied some lip balm to calm myself. Mom didn't like me wearing too much makeup when I wasn't auditioning, but I felt funny with none on—kind of like I didn't have a face.

"Found them," my mom announced from the top of the stairs, dangling car keys from her hand.

"Okay, good," I said. "Come on, Jory!"

Silence from the upstairs hallway.

"I'll go see what's taking him." Mom disappeared.

Geez. She was insisting on coming, even though most of the other kids were going to be dropped off. And since Jory had had his staying-home-alone privileges taken away for "accidentally" smashing a bottle of Dad's expensive whiskey the last time he was left alone, he was coming too.

Mom had told me they'd keep a distance—hang out at the food tents or whatever. It sucked, but I wasn't about to pass up this chance.

Now that I wasn't on the circuit anymore, I had time to have friends. To make friends.

I fiddled with my phone. They were taking forever.

I was about to call up again when my mom reappeared. "Sorry, Livy, but I don't think it's going to work out. Your brother's sick."

Sick. Except that he'd been absolutely fine ten minutes ago.

"What's wrong with him?" I glanced at the time again: 2:41 P.M.

"Headache." My mom smiled like she was apologizing, even though she didn't look particularly sorry. "You know he gets those."

Oh, I knew. They somehow happened anytime he didn't want to do something. "Can't he take an aspirin?"

"It's real bad. He's going to lie down."

"Well, can't you just drop me—"

"It's not going to work this time," my mom said. She didn't have the car keys in her hand anymore. "Next time."

Jory was turned toward the passenger window even though there was nothing to look at in the dark. He was probably giving me the silent treatment because he couldn't fake a headache to get out of this. Irritation spiked through me as I remembered that day: how I'd snuck upstairs and spied into his room, where he was playing his stupid video games with the sound off. I didn't try to convince my mom he'd been lying, I just spent the next week pretending I couldn't understand a thing he said. He didn't seem to care, but then he'd "accidentally" spilled water on my phone, which took a week to replace—

"Did you miss a turn?" Jory's voice broke into my thoughts.

"What? No." I squinted. "Why?"

"Been ten minutes." Jory pointed to the digital clock on the dashboard.

"So?"

"Too long."

I considered this, replaying the SUV chase in my mind. He had a point. We couldn't have been following that Armada for more than a few minutes before we stopped.

"But the only turn we took coming out here was off the main highway. And we haven't reached it yet."

Jory shook his head and muttered.

"What?"

"This isn't the road."

I peered around at the dark, tall shapes that rose up on either side of the car. We should've been out of the mountains by now, but the road *was* straightening out. Maybe I hadn't noticed the mountains right away during the chase?

Strong. Fierce. "The highway has to be up here." I applied some lip balm and tossed it back in the console, scanning ahead for a break in the hills, for the glow of headlights that would signal the approaching 95.

Several minutes later I slowed the car to a crawl. The road had been narrowing for the past several miles, and my heart jumped a bit when we clunked off asphalt onto gravel. The road we followed the SUV on had been paved, I was sure of it.

"Okay, this isn't the road," I said. "Should I turn around?"

"GPS?"

I glanced down at my lap again. "No."

Jory slumped against the window. "Yeah, I guess."

I pulled the car over to the shoulder, then swung around so we were headed the opposite direction.

"I don't understand. I only turned once. This should be the road."

Jory was silent.

I scanned the sides of the road desperately for some side road or turn I might've missed. Maybe I wasn't remembering the chase properly. Maybe the road had forked and I didn't remember, and we'd passed it in the dark on the way back to the highway. But several miles later, we were still on the same highway, and no intersecting roads had shown up. When we arrived at the curvy section of road again, a sinking feeling started in my stomach.

"What now?" I asked. "Turn around again?"

Jory was no longer slouched in the passenger seat. He was sitting up, peering out ahead and bouncing one knee like he was agitated.

"Jory?" The high beams of the car illuminated a curve up ahead.

"Your show," he said. "Your call." His voice was off. Like he wanted to say something else but thought better of it.

I ground my back teeth together and swung the car around a second time. I drove slowly, scanning harder for a hidden intersection, a side road, anything . . .

Fifteen minutes later we arrived on the gravel again. This time, I pressed on. I'd been on a kind of high during the chase; maybe the road actually hadn't been paved when we turned off.

But this road became narrower and narrower, the terrain more bumpy. The headlights swept ahead of us, showing dark potholes.

Jory said something.

"What?"

"I said, something's wrong."

My stomach churned. I pulled it to my backbone to sit up straighter as I navigated the dusty tracks. I would've remembered this. The road was getting too rough to drive on.

Ahead, the gravel came to a dead end. I pulled the car to a stop, put it in park, and stared out at the tunnel of light ahead of us. Beyond the last two feet of road was nothing but cracked, dry desert and scrubby brush.

Outside the glare of the headlights, shadowed figures dotted the landscape.

They're just cactuses. Or cacti, or whatever.

I fumbled for my phone. Still no service.

"We missed the turn again." I tried to make my voice steady. Jory was fixated on the dead end in front of us. "Jory?"

Silence.

Judas Priest.

I thought about Asia's texts, wondering how it was going with Jory. I should've brought her instead; I should've told her everything. When I'd grabbed my stuff to leave though, I was thinking about how amazing it would be to do this on my own. And then . . . well, it was hard to explain, but I had this overwhelming feeling like Jory *had* to come with me. Big mistake. Having him along was like bringing a pumpkin—no, a jack-o'-lantern. Scowling, unhelpful . . .

My panic turned to anger. That SUV had been my parents'. And they'd led me out here to get us lost, or scared, or something, because they knew I was on the right trail. And Jory with his little "it wasn't them" routine. When I'd grilled him on that, he'd zoned out. And he'd been fixating on his arm when we drove . . . He was hiding something, I could tell.

And we were wasting time.

I threw the car into drive and pulled it around.

"What are you doing?"

"I'm going to the cabin." I gripped the steering wheel and accelerated. To heck with looking for intersecting roads. "We'll follow this road out of these mountains and then get back on the 95."

"If we find the 95, we're going home."

"Why? Because you know where Mom and Dad are after all?"

"No, because this is useless and—"

"Shut it!" I snapped. "This isn't a flippin' trip to Atmosphere you can sabotage!"

"What?"

"This is serious! So unless you're going to help or tell me the truth, just shut your mouth!"

I turned the radio on to fill the silence and was greeted by a blast of static. I changed the channel. More static. I changed it again.

Nothing but static.

IT WASN'T
SPARKLY
CAKE

JORY

DRIVING AROUND IN the middle of nowhere with an unhinged, narcissistic Barbie was obviously exactly how I wanted to spend my Friday night. Add in the fact that we were completely disconnected from the outside world and, oh, the little detail that we were trying to find two people who'd vanished right in front of me, and all that was missing was the party mix—the one with the Cheetos.

Don't think about it.

Except I couldn't stop. I'd been telling myself that there was an explanation for all this, but now that the road had mysteriously morphed into something neither of us remembered, everything felt like it was going to splinter again. My chest was tight.

I'd almost told her. That moment when the road ran out, I'd almost told her about what I saw in the courthouse. How Mom touched my shoulder as we approached the stairs. How Dad was right beside her. I have no peripheral vision, sure, but his cat-ass cologne was always impossible to miss. I was half a step in front of them when I started up the stairs, and Mom was hurrying us along.

"We'll be late," she'd said, but there was something different about her voice. Something . . . distorted. I turned back to see—I could swear her hand was still on my shoulder and . . .

They weren't there.

They weren't anywhere.

It was like they'd . . . evaporated. And the sensation I'd had when we'd pulled up to the courthouse, that everything else—the lizard fountain and the tables with their patio umbrellas and the too-warm air—was about to disappear too, just shatter into a million indiscernible pieces, layer over layer until one thing was indistinguishable from the next: that feeling rolled over me in waves. I sat down on the stairs, gripping the steps with both hands and staring at the spot where my parents should've been. To quell my panic, I'd collapsed my focus inward, listening to the blood rush through my ears, picturing it looping through my body. I was trying to keep myself there, trying to keep it together.

I sat like that for a good five minutes.

And then I wandered off to find security.

It was impossible. Any way you looked at it. I mean, vanishing was obviously impossible, and my mom moving fast enough to give the *impression* they had vanished was equally impossible. And then . . . how far could they have gotten when their car was left in the parking lot? Without any surveillance cameras catching anything?

Wish fulfillment.

I couldn't get the idea out of my mind. Not the genie-in-a-bottle kind of wish fulfillment; more like . . . seeing what we wanted to. A kind of lapse in our consciousness, maybe.

Once, I got in a discussion with Mark "Everything Is Black and White" Mietzka from the film club about consciousness and time. We were discussing that classic film *The Matrix* and the idea that reality is an illusion. I just had to look at my sister's little stint on *Darling Divas* to know that, even if we weren't living in an actual computer program, it was stupid to assume everything you saw was real. Everything about that show was calculated: reality could easily be nothing more than a set of carefully constructed images.

But I was making the case that time is part of that illusion: that our experience of reality is only our perception of time. Mark had agreed but launched into a completely unrelated rant about time-travel movies.

Now, what I'd been trying to articulate—the idea that time and reality are the same thing—was stuck in my mind. Maybe I'd lost moments in time, and it had only seemed like my parents had vanished. And maybe I'd lost that time because I'd wanted to. Wish fulfillment could be more like . . .

"Refocusing our consciousness."

Liv frowned. "What?"

I didn't mean to speak out loud. I shook my head. "Nothing." Liv would never understand. Ironic, because wasn't it trauma victims—something she purported to be—who often reported losing chunks of time?

My thoughts churned. Could I have somehow skipped over the moment my parents left?

"Whatever," Liv huffed.

God. Forget wish fulfillment: this little road trip was purgatory.

Seriously. If I believed in such a thing, I'd be convinced I'd died en route to Liv's court date and was now awaiting judgment for that time I put a piece of dissected cow's eyeball in Gary Lapinga's Diet Coke during science. Not that he hadn't deserved it. Lapinga insisted on calling me Rocky, from that damned grief-porn movie from the Eighties starring Cher and her non-Moebian-but-similar-enough-for-grief-porn-lovers son who exists to show everyone a slice of humanity before he dies without realizing any of his dreams (I read the Wiki page). If there were any kind of divine presence ruling the universe, Lapinga would have been flattened by an errant steamroller long ago.

No. I was alive, and God didn't exist, and my sister was driving us further into lost with every minute, convinced we'd find my parents at some dead lake—at a cabin that could well be a heap of rubble after all these years. I must've been ten or so the last time I was there, and I doubted my parents were keeping it livable. Liv's hunch had to be wrong.

So why was there a familiar feeling about all this—sitting next to Liv, driving in the Audi? That wasn't possible, either: we hadn't gone anywhere together in years. Maybe I was remembering a time we'd driven up to the cabin and I was conflating the two: a memory of the past and our current situation.

"You want to see a monster?"

I popped another Rolaid. We drove for several minutes more in silence. At least Liv wasn't doing that creepy smiling thing anymore.

A chime broke the silence. Another. And another. Then two more in succession. "I have service!" She grabbed her phone and shook it at me triumphantly. "See? I knew it would be okay if I kept driving."

The constriction in my chest eased. I barely used my phone—I hadn't even thought to bring it along—but knowing we still had a connection to civilization, to reality, dissolved the panic I was trying to keep at bay. "Who needs you so badly?" I didn't want Liv to know I was relieved, so I feigned irritation. "Your fans twittering over the scandal? Hashtag princess court case oh em gee?"

"I took all my social media off my phone," Liv said absently, holding her phone up to unlock it as she drove.

"Why?"

"Just . . ." Liv squinted at the screen. "Weird. Asia's wondering if I want her to come get me. I told her I'd call her. Oh— and now . . ." She frowned.

"What?"

"'Maybe you should've waited until after'?" Liv read. "What's that about? And—" She frowned again. Then she looked up, let out a surprised "Oh!" and swerved violently back into our lane.

"The hell!" I hadn't even noticed we were drifting. God. I'd never wanted to be able to drive so badly in my life.

"Oops." She didn't sound particularly remorseful. "Okay, see where we are." She unlocked the screen and tossed the sparkly device into my lap, smiling at me like she hadn't nearly ripped my hand off for touching her phone earlier.

Right: I was allowed to help Liv when it was on her terms. It had always been that way.

I raced to the kitchen to get Oreos and make a glass of chocolate milk for a Dragon Empire *marathon. I needed the sugar rush: if I made the next level, my warrior would reincarnate with twice the Qi and I'd gain a new pressure-point move.*

The front door opened and my mom's voice filled the house. "You ruined your chance! You didn't even try." She sounded super pissed.

I stirred the chocolate syrup into my milk more quietly.

"I did try*! I just forgot my lines!" Liv, sounding equally pissed.*

Ever since Liv had stopped doing pageants, she was home a lot more, but she still went to auditions for dumb commercials and photo shoots.

"In an audition for Tween Talk Las Vegas, *Lavinia? That was a major stepping-stone, and you threw it away. It could've been your way onto Bravo or Lifetime!"*

"I'm sorry, okay?"

"I'm sorry too. We should've never stopped doing the circuit."

My mom's phone rang and she answered it. A split second later, Liv stormed into the kitchen. She pulled up short when she saw me, her eyes red and a little swollen. I hadn't seen Liv cry in a really long time. She had a face full of makeup, complete with those false eyelash things, but somehow she looked way younger than thirteen, not older.

"It's over." My mom was in the foyer, but she was talking so loud we could hear her plain as day. "No, she blew it."

I didn't know what to say. It was obvious I'd overheard them.

"What?" Liv demanded. There was a tremor in her voice.

"I honestly don't know," my mom said. "Like, you should've seen—no. They were all there: the producers, the crew, and she . . . Geez Murphy, I can't even describe it." She was probably complaining about the audition to her sister, who'd called from Virginia. My mom used to do that exact thing when Liv first started pageants. Liv and I would sit in her room, listening, while Mom went over everything Liv did right. And wrong. The times there were more wrongs than rights and Liv's eyes got teary, I'd pantomime my mom talking on the phone to make her smile.

Standing in the kitchen with me, she looked like that much younger Liv.

I offered her my chocolate milk. "I can make another one."

Her face hardened. "You know I can't have that!" she snapped. "Geez, Jory. Get a clue." She brushed past me and banged out the patio doors.

I picked up her phone from where it rested on my knees, anger spiking in me. My sister had always been a master manipulator. The same day she'd cut me down after her botched audition, she'd asked for my help, begged me to "back her up" on a request to go to some girl's pool party.

"Tell them it's a good idea. Jory—please. I have to go. Marcy sent out handwritten *invitations."*

Always her terms, always her show. So now I could touch her phone as long as I didn't mention . . . "Asia's pretty needy."

She didn't take the bait. "She's just being a good friend." It looked like she was trying not to smile. In fact, it looked like what I said had pleased her immensely. Damn. She waved her hand at the phone. "So where are we?"

My desperation to be sure we weren't lost outweighed my desire to find a new way to annoy her. I peered at the screen, found the maps application, and tapped it. "On some dinky road east of the 95." I pushed at the screen with my thumb and forefinger. "I think it says 661."

"What does it meet up with?"

"The 11? You'll have to backtrack to the 95."

"Fine," she said. "That's fine." Her words were punctuated with a blast of sound from the radio. The song she'd been humming along to before I'd changed it blared out from the speakers. Jesus. Did every station play this garbage?

Liv glanced at me and changed the channel, clearly trying to keep her costume in place for the Conciliatory event. She was a formidable competitor.

"—public's help in locating two people who disappeared from the Clark—"

Liv punched the console absently, skipping by the announcer's voice.

"Hey, go back!"

She frowned.

"That was about Mom and Dad." I batted her hand away and pressed at the buttons, getting static, then acid jazz, then a pop station in succession. "Shit."

"You really think they'd put out an alert already?" she asked.

She had a point. We'd only filed the report eight hours ago, and the cops hadn't seemed to be taking us too seriously at the time, despite her lapdog lawyer's yapping. And it's not like they would've received other complaints: Who else would even notice my parents were gone? Besides someone trying to ship plastic forks, I mean. "Maybe not," I said. Anyway, what did it matter? What information would the radio announcer have that we didn't?

That *I* didn't?

Don't think about it.

Liv took her phone from me and placed it in the console, then took a water bottle from the cup holder. As she took a long drink, I realized I was super thirsty. I waited a few seconds, then started rummaging in the backpack I'd grabbed before we left the house. It contained my hoodie, a package of gum, more Rolaids, a bottle of artificial tears, and my wallet. No water bottle.

Well, wasn't this fucking perfect? I slumped back in the passenger seat and tried to think about anything else but the cool liquid she held in her hand.

Liv held out her water bottle like she'd read my mind. "Want some?"

I stared at the clear blue plastic.

"Want some?" Liv offered me a thin green straw. We were standing in the hallway outside the hair-and-makeup room. The carpet

was patterned with diamonds and it was a little dirty. The hotel wasn't very nice, but Liv didn't seem to care.

She was excited. She'd only been doing pageants a year, but she was already winning a bunch and she was totally ready to win the Halloween Scream Theme event. She was dressed like a mad scientist, with black-rimmed glasses, black gloves, and a white wig that looked like cotton candy fluff. Under her white lab coat was a black bodysuit with painted-on scars like little neon railroad tracks.

She waved the straw at me. "Pixy Stix. It really gets your energy up. Everybody uses it. I heard one girl's mom call it pageant crack."

I didn't know what that meant, but it sounded kind of cool. "Okay."

"You have to rip off the end and then pour it into your mouth."

I did as she said, but it rushed out so fast that I could only get some of it into my mouth. Most of the sugar ran down the side of my face and into the collar of my costume—a white lab coat, like Liv's.

A blond girl Liv's age was passing by in a really short black witch dress. "Oh my god!" She started to laugh into her hand.

Liv snatched the straw back from me, staring at the girl, her face white. She glanced around quickly . . .

Oh. She was wondering if anyone else had seen.

My stomach dropped. I'd embarrassed her. "I didn't mean to." I quickly brushed at the sugar, which stuck to my fingers. "Liv?"

My mom was suddenly back from talking with hair and makeup. "Come on," she said. "We need to practice the tear-away lab coat bit. It needs to be fast and right on cue."

"I could help." I wanted Liv to forget about what had happened with the sugar, but the stupid stuff was still stuck to my hands.

"No," Mom said, fussing with Liv's wig. "As soon as Livy turns into the monster, you leave the stage."

"Jory?" Liv was still holding out her water bottle.

"No."

She closed the lid and put it back in the cup holder. The memory of the pageant lingered, and a hot flush ran through me as I thought about how naive I'd been, how pathetic, following Liv around like she wanted me there. Jesus. That little girl who'd walked by . . . she'd won the big crown, the one Liv wanted. And Liv had lost her mind . . .

"You want to see a monster?"

Liv was chewing her upper lip again, staring out at our underwater tunnel of light. That weird feeling of déjà vu was back.

"Why Walker Lake?" I asked. She'd ghosted me when I'd asked her this back at the house, and I'd let it slide since I didn't have a better plan. "Why there?"

"It's . . . it's a hunch. Something at the house reminded me of it."

"What something?"

She glanced at me. "I remembered an argument they had there."

Which was like saying "I remembered brushing my teeth there" or something else so routine it becomes mundane. My parents' constant arguing had only stopped when Liv got the TV deal, I think because my mom had something to focus her efforts on.

"It was about selling the cabin."

Again, my parents had argued about selling the cabin all the time. My mom had inherited it from her dad—some dude from Reno who'd had a variety of investment properties and a deadly heart murmur—and she clung to the place for "sentimental reasons." My dad wasn't the sentimental type, and he wasn't the sort who took no for an answer. He won eventually, but all the fighting was for nothing: it turned out that the property couldn't legally be sold.

A conservation group had petitioned the state of Nevada to declare that area of the lake an "ecologically sensitive area," which effectively put an end to any further development for twenty years. Property couldn't change ownership unless you were surrendering it to the state of Nevada for reclamation purposes, and my dad was far more interested in waiting out the reclamation period for potential profit than in being a friend to the earth. I waited for more from Liv, but she was quiet. "*That's* why? Because you remembered an argument?"

"No."

"Well?"

"Why do you want to know?"

I stared at her. "Seriously?"

"It seems a bit weird, is all. First you're trying to convince me they're not there. Now you need to know exactly how I know they *are* there."

I sighed. She was still suspicious of me. Hilarious. Not hilarious: telling her about what had happened at the courthouse was obviously not an option. It would only confirm her "hunch" that I was somehow involved. Like I'd go this far out of my way to mess with her. "Tell me we're out here for a better reason than 'they fought.'"

She looked at me for a frustratingly long time, and I realized she was deciphering my sentence; I'd spoken too fast. That never used to be a problem. When we were kids, Liv would've had to pretend she didn't understand me. And when she was being a real bitch, she'd do exactly that.

"I. Don't. Know. Where. They. Are," I said.

"Fine," she said, though I could tell she was still unconvinced.

"It was . . . it was more than that. Do you remember the last time we went up there? There was a break in filming for *Divas*, and Mom said we needed to get away. And . . ." She hesitated. "And Dad fell off the pier and hit his head on the pilings?"

I shook my head.

"They'd been arguing all day, and Dad drank too much and went out on the pier and ended up in the water. I saw him; Mom pulled him out."

I didn't remember any of this. "So?"

"Well, a couple of days later Mom said something to me about wishing he'd drowned. And then when I thought I saw him in our pool . . . It's hard to explain, but the two felt connected."

"'Felt connected.'"

"Yes. It was like the memory was trying to tell me something."

I wanted to shred her for this, but something made me pause. That moment at the courthouse—wasn't that feeling significant at the time? Hadn't I known, somehow, that things were about to come apart?

Liv took my silence for disbelief. "Look, even if you think that's stupid, them being up at Walker Lake makes sense. Where else would they go where no one would know them? Like, that was the whole point of the cabin, wasn't it?"

"What do you mean?"

Liv looked at me like she'd spoken out of turn. "Oh."

"Oh what?"

"Well, Mom liked it there because it was . . . private. There was no one around, you know?"

I shook my head. "Sentimental reasons." It couldn't have been the wilderness; Mom was so far from being one with nature, she would've breathed bottled air if it had come in convenient-sized packs.

"That's what she *said*."

"But?"

"But the real reason"—Liv cleared her throat—"was that there was no one to . . . bother us."

And I finally picked up what she was putting down. *Bother us* was code for no one around to stare at Jory, no one to speak slowly and loudly to Jory. No one to ask if I was *born like that?*

It was no secret my mom was obsessed with aesthetic perfection. I'd long suspected that having a kid with Moebius was what prompted her to put Liv in pageants in the first place. She was proving to the world that she could make a beautiful kid too. So why was this revelation grating on me? It was par for the course. It was annoying that I hadn't pieced it together, sure, but it shouldn't have bothered me like this.

I looked down and traced the tattoo on the inside of my arm.

"It's never-ending deadweight," my dad said into his phone, drink in one hand. I stood in the doorway, unnoticed. "But I still want to double it to at least a half mil. Who knows? We might get lucky and lightning will strike it. Or it'll be washed away in a flash flood." He laughed. "Okay, yep. Thanks, Jim." He set down his phone, took a sip of his drink, and placed it on the kitchen island, like he could care less about it—like it wasn't going to be attached to his hand all night. He'd only just poured it, so now was my chance: I had to ask him while the night was young and his handwriting was legible. His phone pinged and he frowned down at it, scrolling with one hand.

"I need your signature," I said.

He barely looked up. "For what?"

"A consent form." I pulled it from my back pocket and unfolded it. I walked over and smoothed it out against the granite counter.

He tore his gaze away from his phone to skim it over. "What's Revolt Tattoo?"

"A tattoo parlor. You need to be eighteen, or have signed consent."

He laughed. "Right." And looked back at his phone.

"In two months I won't need the form." I set a pen beside the paper and waited.

He glanced at it. At me. He sighed and put down his phone. "Just tell me it won't be something wussy." He picked up the pen.

"Nope. Really manly." I watched him sign and quickly gathered the form back. "It's going to be a bottle of Jack." I tucked the form safely in my pocket.

A muscle worked in his jaw. "You have a smart mouth, you know that?" He tilted back the rest of his drink, clinking the ice against his teeth. He put the glass down and stared at me. "But I guess you had to have something."

"Jory?" Liv had this saccharine, sympathetic look on her face. I knew that look: I'd seen it before.

Like when I was fourteen and I'd been invited to go paintballing by a kid in my homeroom. I was actually a little stoked to do something on the weekend beyond my usual RPG. I mean, junior high is the holding pen for assholes who hide their latent insecurities behind spitballs and Axe body spray; the pickings for friends were a little slim.

But Liv heard from the kid's younger brother that their mom had made him invite me because "Jesus had to hang out with lepers, too." She'd told me that over the breakfast table, wide-eyed, face full of faux concern. *I don't think you should go, Jory.* As if worry for me was her motivation.

She was looking at me that way now. Like I was that kid with the pity invitation and she cared so much she was going to save me from it all. "I'm sor—"

"Save it," I cut her off, clenching my hand into a fist. "I don't give a shit."

She pressed her lips together and went quiet. The road we were on T-intersected with a new one. Liv stopped the car, put it in park, and looked at her phone.

"This must be the 11 you were talking about," she said. "So I should turn east, right?"

I was silent. She could figure it out.

"I think I should turn east," she said brightly, like she hadn't noticed I was being a dick to her. And okay, yes, I *was* being a dick to her, but I didn't feel capable of much else, suddenly.

She put the car in gear and turned right.

A dark shape darted out in front of us.

"Holy crap!" Liv slammed on the brakes, screeching to a halt to avoid hitting it. Inexplicably, it had frozen in our beams but was looking the opposite way down the road. Pointy ears and a lithe, small body crouched low to the ground.

"Cat," I realized.

"Where did it come from?" Liv wondered aloud. "We haven't seen a house or anything since we turned off the 95." The cat swung its head toward us.

"Jesus."

The bottom half of the cat's face was missing. Its eyes were wide and yellow, its nose and top teeth intact but . . . the jaw was gone. Just gone. A bloody, mangled mess of tissue and bone comprised the space between its nose and its throat.

Liv made a strangled sound and grabbed at my arm, her nails digging into my skin. The pain registered only slightly over the full-body rush of adrenaline that coursed through me. I swallowed hard, not wanting to look but unable to turn my head.

The cat stared back, like something out of *Pet* freaking

Sematary. It cowered in the glare of the beams for several seconds. Then it extended up on its legs, turned its head parallel to us—the profile was more horrifying: a cat with half a face—and sauntered off the road. Like it had all the time in the world and no particular place to be.

We sat in shock for several seconds.

"Geez Murphy," Liv whispered. She cleared her throat. "What do you think happened to it?"

Hit by a car, probably, but what was the thing doing in the middle of the desert? Not exactly its natural habitat. There had to be houses in the hills, places we couldn't see from the road.

The thought didn't comfort me. Who builds their house in the middle of nowhere, hidden away? Survivalists, that's who. People with a cellar full of canned goods and guns and an assload of paranoid thoughts. People who rip their cats' faces off? The last point was unlikely, but whatever the case: it wasn't anyone I wanted to chance upon in the dark.

"Go," I said.

Liv accelerated down the road, leaving the mangled cat to recede into the shadows.

LIV

THE HILLS ON either side of the road felt like they were clos-ing in on us, but that was because I was still freaked out about that cat. The little thrill I'd felt seeing Asia's texts was long gone. The headlights lit up small stretch after small stretch of high-way. Not another car in sight.

Sugar. My hands were shaking again. Worse, Jory was back to his frustrating one-word answers. I pushed away any thoughts of what else was walking around out there in the dark, focus-ing on Jory to keep the panic at bay.

He wasn't truly upset about what I'd said about the cabin, was he? I mean, he knew how our parents made decisions, and it wasn't like he loved strangers or crowds either.

But I could see him *pretending* to be upset to make a point.

He thought my lawsuit was dramatic and over-the-top, so he was pointing out how easy I'd had it compared to him. But I had something that could change his mind about my court case in a hurry. I just needed to win. Unless . . .

Unless he was involved in my parents' plan. He was weird—weird*er*—than I remembered. He kept fixating on his stupid tattoo, and what had he mumbled about "refocusing" something? More and more, it felt like he was hiding something.

And really, was it such a stretch to suspect him? He used to sabotage me all the time. But did he hate me so much that he'd actually help my parents?

I glanced around at the endless nothing, a hollowness settling in my stomach. We had to reach a sign or a town or something soon. The longer it took to get to the cabin, the more chance my parents had to get away and the more likely it was that Sandra would notice I was gone. She'd be angry with me. And Asia—would she be hurt that I hadn't let her in on my plan?

I wondered if she could tell something was up. Her texts were strange. Like, I was pretty happy she was checking on me, but . . . still. It was sort of unlike her?

Ping me and I'll pick you up.

9:41 P.M.

Maybe you should've waited till after.

?

Aren't your parents home by now? You should get out of there.

10:05 P.M.

Hello?

What's going on?

It was weird that she thought my parents would show up back at the house—what did she mean about "after"?—and pinging me that often was weirder. Asia never looked needy. But I thought back to before we'd entered the courtroom; she'd acted like she didn't know what I was talking about when I mentioned her texts from yesterday. So maybe she worried about me more than she wanted to admit. It made my stomach do little cartwheels, thinking about her feeling overprotective of me. I hoped it wasn't on account of the drama of my verdict fail. She did like drama—all the girls did.

Sometimes I worried that was the most interesting thing about me. Cherish was always fixating on the worst details of my case: my blackouts and tantrums and stuff. She always wanted to know what I'd been thinking in those moments, and it didn't matter how many times I told her I didn't know, that I couldn't remember. Still, when we were all together, watching a movie or ordering takeout or something else that was normal, I was happy, because I was finally creating moments that were *worth* remembering.

And the best of those were moments with Asia.

"How about special friends?" the woman behind the camera asked. "Do you have a boyfriend?"

Mom and I sat in front of Mr. Anton's rows and rows of hairpieces. The crew had positioned us so that his big mirror with the glittery frame was in the shot. My mom looked at me.

I put my hands under my legs and rocked a bit. "No."

"No? No boyfriends?"

My mom smiled. "She's a very busy nine-year-old. She can worry about boyfriends later."

"I never want a boyfriend." I looked away, which wasn't okay. I wasn't supposed to "close down," but I was bored and I wanted the cameras to go away. We'd been at Mr. Anton's all day, filming me trying on hairpieces and extensions. They even filmed Mr. Anton and his little dog, Chico. "Boyfriends are weird."

My mom laughed like this was the funniest thing ever. "Pretty sure you won't have a choice."

The actual truth was that my mom was terrified of me having a boyfriend. When I was fourteen, I caught her tracking my periods on a calendar—she was convinced I was going to "get into trouble" and "ruin my life." I hadn't even kissed a boy at that point. When I told Asia about that, she said it was beyond creepy.

It was, but I'd been so used to my mom knowing everything about me, being in my business, scheduling my life, that at the time it had almost seemed . . . normal.

The radio let out a burst of static, making me jump.

"—*public's help in locating two people who disappeared from the Clark—*"

The radio crackled again. More static. Jory's hand shot forward to turn up the volume. The static hissed and whined loudly.

"Yikes!" I protested. "Jory—"

"Shh!"

The announcer's voice returned: "—*a gold necklace with a letter* P *pendant, and blond hair. Anyone with information about the Brewers' whereabouts is asked to contact local authorities. And now for a look at our short-range forecast, we go to meteorologist—*"

Jory turned the volume back down.

So they *were* doing alerts about our parents. That made me nervous. If other people were looking for them, then the chances of me getting to them first weren't as good. Especially with the details of what they'd been wearing—

"They got the necklace wrong," I realized.

Jory looked over at me. "What?"

"She was wearing her Busy Bee, right? I thought that's what you told the cops: a necklace with a bee?"

He considered this. "Plosives," he said, emphasizing the *P*. Then the *B* when he added: "They're a bitch."

I didn't know that word, but I guessed it had something to do with certain sounds Jory couldn't easily make. I wasn't about to ask and risk his sarcasm again. I also wasn't going to ask him what I was wondering: if that wrong detail would make it more difficult for people to locate our parents.

A part of me hoped it would, so that I could still get to them first.

For a long time I hadn't believed I had the right to sue my parents. Deep down, there was a part of me that loved the pageants. I loved knowing I'd nailed a routine. I loved the rush of winning the big crowns. I loved it when my mom made a big deal and told me I'd done everything right.

I'd confessed all that to my lawyer while we were reviewing evidence for the case. But Sandra said that children can't be held responsible for doing things they are groomed to do; that's why minors are tried and sentenced differently. Besides, she said, I'd committed no crime.

She was right: the charges hadn't stuck.

I looked over at Jory.

He was standing at his mark on the stage.

"What's wrong with me?" The music started.

I made my way to the front of the stage and posed, making a show of glowering at the judges. I felt a little nervous; judges like you to smile. I moved back and forth across the stage, posing, showing off my lab coat, which was Velcro'd for an easy tear-away.

"You can smile later," my mom had told me. "When you become the monster."

The music boomed, a voice sang about something creeping up inside you.

I danced back toward Jory and the cart, grabbing at my fluff of white hair, pretending I was hearing voices in my head. On the cart was a dummy dressed exactly the way I was under my lab coat—black bodysuit with little glow-in-the-dark scars. I posed near the covered head of the dummy, in front of the giant cardboard prop—an electrical switch that could move up and down.

I grabbed the handle.

And then I saw the witch, standing offstage. She was hunched over and she was looking at me like . . .

I froze. I heard the bass drop: my cue. I knew I had to move, I had to hit my mark, but I couldn't tear my eyes away from her.

". . . you might just go under."

I was behind the music now. I forced my hand to pull the switch down.

A flash of light exploded in the room.

"Watch the road!"

My attention snapped back to the highway. We were drifting over the center line again. "Oops!" I corrected quickly. We'd driven into a series of curves—kind of like the ones where we'd lost the SUV.

Jory muttered something about "Barbie's Deathmobile."

"I didn't mean to! Geez. I'm tired, okay?" I glanced at Jory, keeping one eye on the road this time. He was tracing that dang tattoo on his arm again.

"What is that anyway?" I ventured.

He didn't look up. "The future."

I waited for him to explain further, but he didn't. "Hey, do you remember the pageant you helped me with?"

Jory's attention snapped away from his arm. "What?"

"It was in Pasadena. The Halloween Scream Theme one? I was a mad scientist."

"So?"

"I was thinking about that."

Jory shrugged and looked out the window. He had to remember. He'd only helped me with one pageant, and that one was a doozy. For sure he remembered the fallout with the pageant authorities afterward. And the cops. "That . . ." I hesitated. "That shouldn't have happened."

"What?"

"Well . . . you shouldn't have been there."

"Why? Didn't want me to see you go postal?"

My cheeks flushed. "It's not that. The entire world has seen me . . . do that. It's . . ."

"That was ground zero, you know."

"What do you mean?"

"Your first tantrum."

"Oh. Yeah. I know."

"First Blackout Rage Performance."

I paused, frowning. "It wasn't a performance."

"Oh?"

"It wasn't! Sandra says that kids who have been through trauma sometimes get so upset that they lose control."

Jory looked at me.

"So yeah, like, I did 'black out,' but that's what happens to kids who are put in bad situations."

He nodded. "Right. And what about kids who make money when they do it?"

"What?"

"What about the kids who get more viewers when they 'black out'?"

Was he serious? "Are you saying that you think I *pretended* to be upset for the TV show?"

He was quiet.

"Seriously. Is that what you're saying? That I was acting?"

"You were that upset you weren't the prettiest?"

Anger surged in me. I tried to breathe deep and redirect the way my therapist had taught me. Jory had trauma, too—I had to remember that. "You of all people should know how awful it is to get judged by how you look."

"Not the same thing."

"Well, being pretty isn't always easy."

"Right."

"It's not! Usually people hate you before they even know you. That's the joke, right? 'Oh, she's beautiful and she's nice, so I can't even hate her.' Because it's all right to hate someone for the way they look when they're pretty? It's not the same thing as hating someone for being ugly?" He stared at me. I winced. That had come out wrong. I tried to soften my voice. "You think you're alone. You're not. You're not the only one who feels scrutinized constantly."

"I don't give a shit what people think."

"Well, I don't believe that. Everyone wants friends." He looked away. "I know it's hard, but you should give something a chance. You could, like, Instagram your rocks—"

"My what?"

"Or get a Tumblr," I rushed on.

"Thought you went off social media."

"I just took it off my phone—the notifications and stuff. I still keep my profiles active."

"Why?"

Was he serious? "To control the story."

"What story?"

He was. "Mine. The story about me." He looked at me silently. Did he not understand the purpose of social media? "Anyway, what I'm saying is: you could, you know . . . meet people. Online. Like, what about those foundations for people with Moebius?"

"Because everyone who has Moebius is best friends!"

I gritted my teeth. I hated it when he used that sarcastic tone, and he was always using it with me. "I didn't say that. But at least they'd understand. What you go through, I mean. Meeting Asia—the other survivors—has really helped me."

He snorted a laugh.

"What?"

"Helped you."

"They have! All of that competitiveness Pro-Am teaches you, all of that trying to be perfect—it took meeting others who'd been through it to see how wrong I was to base my worth on people's opinions. They showed me how to get past it."

"Right. You're way past it."

I paused. I wasn't going to let him bait me into losing my temper. "You don't know anything about it."

"I know you think having four thousand Instagram followers—"

"Fourteen thousand—"

"Whatever! You think it proves your life is important." He shook his head. "You are *totally* past basing your worth on others' opinions."

Had I seriously been considering apologizing to him for that day? I mean, it wasn't like it was the day he started being a jerk. It was a little weird, maybe even a little intriguing, to hear him talk this much, but that didn't mean I was going to sit here and let him insult me. "You know what? Forget it."

"I'm trying." He slumped down in his seat.

We were back to driving in silence. Fine with me. Because maybe he *was* behind this somehow. Maybe he was so mean that he'd sabotage my entire lawsuit to show me what he thought.

"Don't worry about the haters; think about your supporters." Asia told me that all the time. She said that there would be people who thought my case was stupid. They were the same people who commented on YouTube that I should get a bullet in my head, right through the culturally insensitive bindi I wore for my Bollywood Theme event in Texas when I was nine.

I didn't want to believe my brother was one of those people.

But he *was* hiding something.

My thoughts drifted back to the radio announcement and the detail of the necklace. Of course Mom'd been wearing Busy Bee; it was the good-luck charm she wore to all my pageants. Even though I was expected to give it *one hundred and ten percent*, she wanted me to remember that luck played a role in my success too: I wasn't *that* talented.

"You're just lucky you're pretty, Livy."

When I was thirteen, I stole Busy Bee from her jewelry box. I'd wanted to go to the mall with some girls from my school that Saturday, but she'd booked me an audition for a local cable station instead. *"We buy you all the clothes you need,"* she'd said. When I told her it wasn't about shopping, she laughed like I couldn't be serious.

Jory caught me burying the necklace in the poolside potted cactus and told Mom. It was actually pretty humiliating, because, really: Burying a stupid necklace? What was I thinking? Still, something about handing it over all dusty and dull made me feel better. But I was grounded from my phone for a week.

My mom had probably worn that necklace to the courthouse to remind me I wasn't in control and never had been. She was probably trying to tell me I got all kinds of things I didn't actually earn. I felt darkness bloom in a corner of my mind, the way it had earlier at the courthouse.

"Hi, Lavinia, I'm Mr. Day." *The man was wearing a suit and holding a napkin with a piece of cake on it. My mom was across the room, talking to the pageant organizer.*

The counter holding the glasses of juice was too tall. I put both hands on it and leaned forward, deciding between lemonade and orangeade.

The man grabbed my chin and turned my face toward him. "Don't you look at the person who's talking to you?" *His eyes were pale. A lump in his throat bobbed up and down.*

My mom appeared over the man's shoulder. She smiled brightly. "You met Livy."

He let go of my chin and straightened up. "Yes."

"Didn't she look good up there?" *my mom asked, fiddling with her Busy Bee.* "Livy, that's your eighteenth Grand Supreme title now." *I knew this, of course. She wasn't really talking to me.*

"Well, I think that deserves cake." *The man handed me the napkin he was holding. I didn't want cake. I didn't even want juice anymore. I looked up at my mom.*

"Go on, Livy."

The white cake had pink icing and was covered in sugar sparkles. It felt heavy in my hand.

"Our agency is looking for under-tens," *he said to my mom, and gave her a little paper card.* "Let me know if you'd like me to take a look at her." *He waved to someone in the crowd.* "Excuse me." *He disappeared.*

"You hear that?" *my mom said.* "He wants to take a look at you."

"I don't feel good." *I set the cake on the counter.* "Mom?"

My mom was looking at the card like it was magic. She touched the bee. For luck.

"Mom? I don't feel good."

She looked down. "When did this start?"

"When that man said hi."

"That's just nerves." She looked back at the card in her hand. "I'm going to tell him we'll be at the Little Miss pageant in San Diego next month."

"But I don't want him to look at me."

My mom laughed. "Don't be silly." She looked over her shoulder at me as she left. "Just eat your cake. But not too much."

I stared out at the lonely highway. The moon was finally out, glimmering behind a low bank of clouds, and the radio was playing some kind of annoying country music again.

"Just eat your cake."

"Horror show."

I sped up. *Redirect.* I didn't care what Jory had to say about any of this. He could hate me if that made him feel better. He could sabotage his own happiness by pretending to be above what people thought. But he didn't get to take this away from me. I was getting to that cabin, and I was, finally, going to get what I truly deserved, and it wasn't sparkly cake.

I drew my shoulders back and sat up taller. The hills around us were definitely getting closer—it wasn't my imagination. The road was becoming narrower, and the curves had less distance between them. I slowed to make the next corner.

And then, to my left, movement in the dark. So quick I almost missed it. I snapped my head as we passed in time to see something on the face of the nearest rock wall. Climbing.

And it looked—

I braked. Hard.

JORY

I'D BEEN GETTING ready to pretend to sleep when Liv performed her kamikaze rapid-halt maneuver. Guilt over shutting her down so completely was needling at me, but it evaporated into fresh annoyance when my seat belt caught fast and held, pinching my collarbone through my T-shirt. "What the hell *now*?" I sat up.

Liv had pulled to the side of the road. She was staring into the rearview mirror. "I saw something." She craned her neck, peering out the driver's side window.

"If it was another damn cat—"

"It wasn't." Her voice was breathy. "It was . . ." She trailed off. Then she faced forward again and put the car in reverse.

I threw my hand over and grabbed the wheel. "What are you doing?"

"I want to go back and see."

"You can't reverse down these curves in the pitch dark."

"We're the only car for miles!"

Except it would be exactly our luck for a giant rig with a sleep-deprived trucker at the wheel to appear as we swung out around that last bend. "You can't," I said again.

"But I can't turn around." She was right: the road was too narrow. She chewed her upper lip, like she was considering her options.

"Walking back: also a bad idea," I said, anticipating her next brilliant move.

"I wasn't going to," she said, but her tone indicated she absolutely had been planning to do that.

I peered at her. "What was it?"

She took the car out of reverse, her face pale. "I don't know. It . . . was climbing up the rock." Her eyes darted toward me. "Maybe it *was* another cat." She cleared her throat and pulled back onto the road. "Yeah, I think it was. Or no, maybe a . . . lizard, or whatever lives out here."

I unbuckled my seat belt to release it from its pinchy, life-saving mode and rebuckled, staring at her.

"Yeah. It was a lizard," she said firmly.

A lizard. Wow, was I ever done with this little road trip. Once we got back on the 95, I was going to turn this train around or hitchhike home.

Liv accelerated around the next curve, and the road straightened out to flat desert. It occurred to me how strange those hills were. They'd come out of nowhere: we hadn't been in a valley and there were no mountains nearby. Weird.

I flopped back in my seat, rethinking my options. I mean, I only really had one, because hitchhiking the 95 in the dark? That wasn't the premise for a horror movie at all. And leaving my sister to drive to Walker Lake alone: Why not start writing the screenplay now?

Yeah, no. Once we hit the 95, I was going to have to somehow convince her to head back to Vegas. And maybe the radio announcement would be enough. That was proof the cops were on it, wasn't it? I mean, if they were sending out APBs . . .

They're sending out APBs for two people who no longer exist.

No. I had to stop thinking like that. There was an explanation, but driving around on the creepiest highway on earth was not helping us find it.

I had to admit, though, the creepiest highway had its merits: maybe by the time we found the 95, Liv'd be so freaked out by faceless cats and lizards she'd turn around voluntarily. Maybe she'd figure it would be too late anyway . . .

"We'll be late," my mom announced.

And disappeared.

I clenched my fist. Impossible. The only people who could cease to exist like that were the cyber kind, the ones whose existence was fake to begin with. So . . . someone like Liv, really. Someone whose entire self-worth and identity were based on strangers' "likes." Someone who thought my creating a vlog about my syndrome and having randos tell me I was "brave" would give my life meaning. Because I had nothing else going on?

I couldn't be bothered to set her straight. When she'd stopped doing pageants when she was eleven, a small part of me thought she might revert back to a real person. Someone I could talk to, maybe even someone I could share my new kung fu obsession with. But she just refocused her pageant smile on those stupid commercial auditions, striving for the metaphorical mile-high tiara.

I wasn't about to justify my existence to her now. I wasn't going to explain a Wuxia RPG group or what film club was about. She wouldn't have the first clue what it was like to hang out with people who thought critically about images, rather than spend their time trying to be some perfect version of something other people wanted. She thought I still liked rocks, for god's sake. She was pretending she was so changed, but all she'd done was replace garbage Pro-Am philosophy with her survivors' bullshit. Same righteousness; same narcissism.

No apology; no acknowledgment of shitty past behavior.

"Look crazy, Livy," Mom had told her. "You can smile later—when you become the monster."

The music started. "What's wrong with me?"

Liv paraded back and forth at the front of the stage, posing and wiggling. She moved to the far side of the stage and took the "crazy" position. My first cue. I went to the back of the cart, near the switch, and took a crinkly sheet and a lighter out of my pocket. Liv wheeled toward me, throwing evil smiles over her shoulder at the audience. She danced around the cart, tearing at her hair.

I got ready.

She moved in front of me, put her hand on the cardboard switch, and posed one last time as the scientist.

My last cue.

But she wasn't moving. She was . . . looking at something offstage.

We were behind the music: ". . . just go under." But I waited. I wasn't going to make a mistake and embarrass her again. She was still looking away, but finally I saw her pull the switch down, and I sprang into action, lighting the flash paper and flinging it into the air over her head.

Bang!

A flash of light exploded in the room. The audience gasped.

Liv reacted by jerking this way and that, pretending to be electrocuted, and tore away her coat, revealing the skintight monster suit beneath as I threw a white sheet over the dummy.

Whatever moment she'd been in before was gone: her smile was huge and bright. She threw away her glasses and wig, uncovering a neon scar across her forehead, and cartwheeled across the front of the stage. Someone in the crowd let out an ear-piercing whistle, and I forgot what I was doing for a second. Liv was so good—

My mom's voice rang out. "Go on, get it, Livy!"

I snapped out of it. I pushed the cart forward and disappeared off stage.

I relaxed my fist. *"Go on, get it, Livy."* Of course I remembered the pageant I'd helped her with. And I remembered the crowning afterward, when Liv had her First Blackout Rage Performance. After that pageant, the *Darling Divas* producers had really keyed in on Liv and her potential for freak-outs. And then there was no stopping Princess Liv and her Tour de Spoiled Brat Force.

Liv's meltdown must've illuminated things for me, because that Halloween thing was the first and last pageant I attended. Talk about dodging a bullet.

And now, one bad decision to get in the car with her—why had I done that?—had landed me in the crosshairs of her disastrous life.

"Intersection!" she announced, slowing the car. Our headlights lit up a crossroads and a dark building to the left of the road. Liv smiled, looking vindicated. I didn't point out that an intersecting road could just mean we were *directly* in the middle of nowhere.

"What does that say?" She pulled the car forward.

The headlights swept the space, and I made out two pumps

situated in front of the building as we got close. A gas station. Or used to be. Now it was an abandoned shell: peeling paint, boarded-up windows, and pieces of twisted metal hanging from the roof. Graffiti across the sign read PUSSY CATS in scrawling, black capital letters. Not exactly the place to stop for a road map.

The road crossed ours in a perfect X, but there was no signage to indicate which of the roads was the route we wanted.

"This can't be the 95," Liv mused aloud. "It's too small, and there's no traffic." She glanced at her phone. "Shiitake mushrooms! I don't have service again!"

She drummed one hand against the steering wheel. "I think I should go right," she said firmly, though it was clear she wanted me to offer an opinion.

I didn't respond.

She smiled that creepy smile, then swiped at the screen of her phone, raised it, tilted her chin, and pressed its side. That familiar shutter sound clicked.

I stared at her.

She put it back in the console and threw me a look. "It's for later, okay? I should have some record of this trip."

She turned up the intersecting road, humming to herself, clearly planning her latergram photo chronicle: *Road trip of Justice. Hashtag fierce.*

She was "controlling the story," getting on top of what the trolls and the fangirls and -boys had to talk about, *carpe*-ing the hashtag or whatever.

And she'd been doing it all her life: putting forth her carefully-posed-selfie/inspirational-quote best. Creating an illusion. She was an expert at it.

"You created your reality; live with it." Who had said that? And when?

I risked a quick look at her, not wanting to engage further but suddenly aware of my thoughts on a new level.

Liv created her reality.

And there it was—an uncanny sense of temporality. Like my reaction to what was happening—the focus of my attention—was a better measure of time than the minutes clicking over on the digital clock. Everything was beginning to feel malleable and unfixed, like if I looked hard enough at the road illuminated by our headlights, I'd see beyond it, or behind it, or something.

The highway wound north through the shadowed landscape—at least that's what the dashboard compass was reading. I gripped my hand into a fist, trying to ground myself in the here and now. But the more I tried to pay attention to my surroundings—the way the leather seat back felt, the smell of the AC, the stretch of highway—the less real it felt. We rounded a curve, and another darkened building loomed on our left side.

Liv slowed, peering out the windshield with a frown. "What the heck?" She crawled the car slowly forward and pulled opposite the building.

It was the same gas station we'd just left. It had to be. I mean, what were the chances of two abandoned stations sporting the charming phrase "Pussy Cats" across their facades? The pumps were identical, as was the barren parking lot.

I fought a niggling panic and resisted the urge to root through my bag for the Rolaids.

"We got turned around," she said.

"You only turned once." Acid rose in my throat.

"I know, but obviously the road curved back." She chewed her upper lip. "And we didn't notice."

"Go back," I said.

Liv narrowed her eyes. "Back where?"

"To where you had service. We'll call someone."

"No!" Liv grabbed her phone and clasped it to her like an addict would a crack pipe. "We're not calling anyone!"

"We're lost!" I snapped. That panicky feeling was going to erupt into something uncontainable if I couldn't sort out some kind of plan.

"We are not! It's . . . We missed a turn or something."

"Again?"

She chewed her lip. I closed my eyes and tried to think. "How much gas?" I asked.

"Huh?"

"Gas?" I pointed to her side of the dash.

"Oh." She looked down. "Half a tank?"

Not enough to be driving around in circles the rest of the night. "We need to get back in range."

"I'm not calling anyone."

Fine. "Then we need light."

"I have the high beams on."

"*Day*light."

Liv looked at me blankly.

"We need to wait for daylight," I said slowly. There was no way she was going to wait out the night.

Liv tapped the clock display. It read 11:59 P.M. Somehow we'd been driving for more than two hours since I last checked. "But the sun's not coming up for another six hours. That's too long—it gives Mom and Dad too much time . . ." She trailed off.

As I predicted. Somehow the fact of getting lost in the middle of nowhere was less worrisome to her than having to abandon a fantasy of riding into Vegas on a milk-white steed with the villains in tow. She really was that self-absorbed.

Maybe I should tell her what happened at the courthouse.

Maybe it would wake her up. Or maybe it would send her into hysterical-land.

Or, more likely, she'd think I was making it up, and it would only add fuel to her conspiracy-theory fire.

Maybe if we stayed out of touch long enough, Asia or Liv's lawyer would get suspicious and start looking for us. And then maybe they'd get to us before we starved to death in the goddamn desert.

"Look, I'll go back to where we had service, but I'm not calling. I'll look more closely at the maps app." Liv pulled the car into the parking lot of the decrepit station, swung a U-turn, and headed back down the highway.

For several minutes the road was mostly straight—like I remembered. The headlights stabbed out ahead of us, lighting up an unnervingly small portion of the road. How long had we been driving before we'd hit the station? I couldn't remember.

And that, truly, was why I wanted Liv to call.

It was as if time was evaporating out here. It felt slippery, hard to measure. It all felt . . . wrong. The road, the dark outside the windows, even the dashboard: the more I looked at them, the more they started to lose substance. They looked like they could dissolve at a touch, or vanish completely if I stared too hard. Everything was fragmenting, pulling apart, or . . . no: colliding. Everything was layering, one thing on top of another, each moment in time taking up the same space . . .

Our beams reflected off metal ahead. Another building to our left.

No.

The gas station sat like a dry husk of insect shell, long abandoned. *PUSSY CATS.*

Liv slowed the car to a creep and came to a stop opposite it.

We sat, silent, for several moments. My heart hammered so hard I thought it would crack my rib cage. I fumbled for my Rolaids and ate the last three in the roll.

Liv cleared her throat. "We're . . . we're obviously getting turned around somehow," she said. "It's just so dark . . ."

I swallowed thickly, glancing at Liv's water bottle. It was three-quarters full, and there was a thin scratch along its clear blue plastic surface. Maybe she'd dropped it somewhere. It was obviously new, because it had only the one scratch—

"Jory."

I focused on Liv's face and realized she was looking to me for reassurance. She wanted me to tell her that she was right, that everything was okay. *Now* she needed me—exactly like Mom had needed me after everything went sideways for her.

"If we die out here, it's your fault," I said.

"Nice."

"It is."

"I didn't . . . I didn't mean to get us lost. I . . ." She chewed her upper lip again. It was swollen now. She looked down at her phone. "Frick."

"What?"

"It's dead."

"Of course it is."

"You're so helpful." She grabbed a cord from the console and plugged the phone into the USB port on the dash. Then she shook her head and shoulders to reset. "You were right. We need daylight." She nodded to herself, a little too enthusiastically. "I'm tired, you're tired, and none of this is making sense, but it will. It will. We just need to wait until morning."

She had the tired part right, at least. My eyes ached from

squinting at the road in the dark. And I was pretty sure Liv was used to a minimum eight hours of beauty sleep; an *overtired* narcissistic Barbie might accidentally drive us straight off a desert cliff.

No. It was not going to end that way.

Whatever was going on, I wasn't about to let her make the situation worse. They say that the first few decisions you make in a survival situation are the most critical. We were lost, so conserving gas and finding water were priorities.

Yes. That's what I needed to focus on. Not how we had ended up like this in the first place. Not the idea that time—reality—was nothing more than what a person focused on in the moment. That would mean that I was basically manifesting all this, wouldn't it?

Not possible. That would suggest I actually did care about Liv's court case and was hoping she'd fail, and not because I was siding with my parents. Feeling bad for a man who drank until his vision blurred and a woman who barely acknowledged my existence? No. It would have to be related to Liv: what she deserved. And I definitely didn't care about that.

"So we're sleeping in the car?" She tried to say it like it was no big deal, like she'd slept on anything but a memory-foam mattress her entire life.

I pointed. "Parking lot."

She pulled in as far away from the pumps and building as she could. The headlights swept over the store with its boarded-up windows and peeling paint as she parked. I opened my door when she turned the car off.

She looked at me in alarm. "Where are you going?"

"The restroom, a.k.a. that cactus over there."

"Do you think it's safe?"

"It's the middle of the desert, not the slums of Rio." Except really, the dark emptiness around us was beyond creepy. Not so creepy that I'd rather pee my pants than risk it, but still.

I chose a corner of the parking lot and hurried to finish. The air was cool, almost uncomfortably so, and about a million brilliant stars were smattered across the huge expanse of sky. It should've been an amazing sight—they were so bright and it was so quiet—but the spectacle of it only made me more uneasy. I got in the car and shut the darkness out.

I balled up my hoodie to use as a pillow and reclined my seat as far as it would go. Liv reclined her seat too, but sat forward, looking as though she was debating a similar bathroom break. She'd put on the blazer she'd tossed in the backseat when we left the house. That wasn't going to keep her warm through the night, but whatever. Not my problem.

I turned my back to her and tried to get comfortable.

"Jory?"

"What?"

"I didn't mean what I said earlier. That I didn't care what you think. I—" She hesitated. "I do. Like, obviously."

Obviously. In that moment, I wished I'd positioned myself to face her to freak her out. When I slept, I drooled copious amounts—the stuff of a Barbie's nightmares.

Though . . . I guess she'd seen it before. The two of us used to camp in the TV room when we were young. A memory swarmed into my mind: Liv pulling out her flippers—her fake teeth—from her sleeping bag, pretending they were devouring Mom's decorative pillows. Me laughing and not caring that it sounded like a fit of hiccups.

I felt a pang, which was stupid. What did a moment from ten years ago matter? Especially in our current state of disaster?

"I . . ." she continued. "I just want this so bad, you know?" Her fingers drummed against the steering wheel in a rapid staccato. "I used to think I wanted those stupid pageant crowns, but that was what Mom wanted. I know now what I truly want. And maybe you don't understand why I want it . . ." She paused, like she was expecting me to jump in.

I didn't.

"Maybe you've never wanted anything so bad you'd do anything to get it. Is that it?"

Yeah, Liv. "I'd never had dreams of my own. Aspirations. Goals. How could I? How could I when I'd never "given anything a chance"? Her smugness from earlier, her declaration that she "knew it was hard" . . . like my life was something she'd weighed and found lacking.

"Jory?"

"Away."

"What?"

"Away. I'd do anything to get away."

"From Vegas?"

I turned around. "From all of you."

Pain registered on her face. She quickly collected herself. "Okay," she said, her voice soft. "I get it." She didn't, but that immediate reaction . . .

Shit.

I just couldn't seem to help myself. She was so infuriatingly obtuse.

She took a drink from her water bottle and offered it to me again. I shook my head, annoyed with myself, and her, and all of it.

"Here," she said, unscrewing the top. "You don't have to get my germs."

"I don't want it."

"Take it." She thrust it toward me. "You have to be thirsty."

Of course I was thirsty. "No, thanks." I jerked my hand away as she let go of it. The water bottle bounced off the console and fell to the floor mat at my feet, soaking one of my pant legs. She reached over and grabbed it, but it was too late; there was barely an inch of water left.

"Judas Priest!" She glared at me.

"I said I didn't want it!"

"Well, you didn't need to drop it like it was going to burn you! Geez, Jory!" She screwed the top back on to preserve the last swallow. "Accept help when you need it."

Again with the helping. "I *don't* need it." Jesus. Why had I felt guilty about shutting her down?

She scowled. "Right. Well, congratulations. Now we're lost without water."

"We're lost because of you."

"And you made it worse!" She threw the water bottle in the console and crossed her arms. "If you weren't so busy acting like you're better than me all the time, it wouldn't have happened!"

I flipped over violently to face the car door, clenching my hands into fists.

"You think you're so different from me," Liv said. "But you have no idea how similar we are."

"Stop talking," I said. "You lower the IQ of the entire desert. And all there is out there is cacti."

There was a long silence. Then Liv took a sharp breath in. Oh, Jesus. Was she crying? I listened. Movement, shifting. The automatic lock on the doors activated, sealing us in. Then I heard her flop back down in her seat. Okay, so no, not crying. Maybe trying to make me think she was?

Like that time I caught her burying Mom's necklace in a potted plant. She'd apologized and cried massive crocodile tears when her phone was taken away, but they'd dried the instant Mom left. She'd straightened up and smiled at me like some deranged doll, looking incredibly satisfied.

Playing a role. Controlling the story.

"You created your reality."

The thought snuffed out my anger. I rolled the words over in my mind, trying to remember who'd said them and when. Somehow, it felt like figuring that out might explain a few things.

Like why I could almost swear I wasn't staring at those stars for the first time when I was outside the car, even though I'd never spent the night in the middle of the desert before.

Like why all this felt more and more like an illusion, a set of carefully constructed images, the farther down the road we traveled.

STASIS
AND
NOSEBLEEDS

LIV

I SQUEEZED MY eyes shut. I was scared; I was seeing things.

No.

Yes. Eyes playing tricks.

Tell Jory.

Yeah, right! He already thinks you're a disaster . . .

I cracked an eye open and looked up at the driver's side window. Nothing.

Maybe I'd imagined it? It had seemed so real—first a shadowy shape moving outside the car. And then, closer . . . a person. Shuffling sort of, lilting along with a bit of a hitch in their step . . .

Sugar.

I was losing it. Miles back, in those hills, I'd also thought I'd seen someone on the rock face. A girl, spidering up the cliff. Out for a climb in the middle of nowhere in the dead of night. Totally normal. Totally likely.

I watched for something to appear at the window, but it

stayed dark. Jory already thought this road trip was the worst idea ever. If I told him about these things . . .

I shut my eyes tight again. The doors were locked. Jory was here. This was a sleepover, like we used to have.

I pulled the flippers out from under my sleeping bag and held them out. The Christmas tree in the den was still lit up, and the fake teeth shone all rainbow colored in the lights.

Jory sat up in his sleeping bag and poked at them with one finger. "What are they?"

"They're for my teeth!" I put them in and smiled. In normal light, they were bright white and made me look like I had all my grown-up teeth. One of my front teeth was missing—the tooth fairy had given me five dollars for it—and I had two bottom teeth missing on the left side. Mom said they were taking "forever to come in."

"Creepy," he said.

I spat them into my hand. "They're coming to get you!" I held them with two hands and made them chomp toward him. Jory grabbed a cushion and held it up to fight them off. "Om nom nom!" I grabbed the tassels on the pillow with the teeth and pretended they were eating them. He started to hiccup.

"Livy!" Mom called from the next room. "I said you could sleep in there if you went to sleep!"

I put a finger to my lips, shushing Jory, then called, "I am!"

"Well, I hear shenanigans. You've got a big day tomorrow. Go to sleep or I'll take you back to your room."

I rolled my eyes at Jory and snapped the fake teeth at him again. "Don't tell," I said, stuffing the flippers into my pillowcase. Mom would've been so mad if she knew I'd taken them from their tray.

"I won't," Jory said seriously. We snuggled down into our sleeping bags under the tree.

Jory turned on his pillow to look at me. "How come she doesn't care if I go to sleep?" His hair was messy; it fell in front of one eye.

I brushed his hair back. "Because you can't win a crown."

A sharp rapping sounded near my head, and my eyes flew open. I blinked, wincing at the bright light. I was curled into a ball with my hands tucked under my chin.

It was morning. The windows were fogged, and as I tried to sit up, I realized I was so stiff from the cold that it hurt to move. Jory's hoodie slid from my shoulders onto my lap. Weird. Had I stolen it off him in the night?

The sound came again. Beside me, Jory was sitting bolt upright in the passenger seat. There was movement outside the car to my left, and a face appeared at the window. I jumped back.

A man cupped one hand to the pane to see in. "You all right?" His voice was muffled. He was wearing a dirty ball cap and his face was unshaven.

I rubbed at my face and handed Jory's hoodie over to him, staring at the guy. Was this who I'd seen last night? Something in me said no, though he did look a little familiar.

The man knocked again. "You okay in there?"

I looked at Jory and put my hand on the door handle.

"Don't," he said.

"He's . . ." My voice was croaky. I cleared my throat but kept my voice down. "He's the first person we've seen in hours. Maybe he can help us."

"Where did he even come from?"

I glanced at my phone. It was still dead. Right: the car needed to be running to charge it. I turned the keys in the ignition to power up the car and rolled down the window a bit—not all the way, but enough so that it didn't look like I was afraid of him. Jory never trusted anyone. I didn't want to waste our one chance at getting unlost by pulling a Jory.

"Hey there." The man's voice was easy, smooth. He touched the brim of his ball cap in greeting, which was a weird thing to do in this situation. It seemed like a customer-service gesture, and it wasn't like he was going to pump our gas.

"Hi," I said.

"You look lost."

"Yeah." Behind him, the Pussy Cats station was less creepy in the morning sun. It looked kind of sad, actually. "We, um, we seem to keep finding this gas station." I laughed a bit, like I was kidding.

The man nodded. "You won't reach the 95 doing that."

"Where *is* the 95?" I asked eagerly. "My phone is dead."

He scratched the back of his neck. "Well," he said. "You can't miss the turn at the ramshackle place five miles up this road to the north."

So we had taken a wrong turn last night. "So turn there and it'll take us back?"

"Does it for everyone else." The man smiled, showing a few missing teeth. He looked at me closer. "Should do it for a beauty queen."

A shadow passed over the sun. A chill crept along my skin.

"Sorry, that was a little forward. You got that air about you, if you know what I mean. And not in a bad way." His gaze flicked toward Jory. It was the first time he'd looked at him, which was odd. Usually people noticed Jory right away and spent the next few moments being distracted by how they should react. He didn't seem perturbed.

"But here I am, all mannerless and whatnot. Name's Frank."

"Oh." I didn't want to make small talk, but it seemed rude not to. "Um, is there a town nearby? Or . . ."

He waved his hand. "Nothing for miles. Was just checking on the place." He pointed at the graffiti on the station pumps. "People like to vandalize." He turned back to us. "Didn't catch your name."

He was staring at me a bit too carefully. I went with the truth. "I'm Lavinia," I said. "This is my brother." Jory didn't speak.

Frank nodded, his gaze sliding over us slowly. Then he slapped the roof with one hand, making me jump again. "I'll let you get on your way."

My water bottle in the console dug into my back. Water. "Wait! Is . . . would you happen to have any water? We're all out."

"Liv—" Jory started.

I raised my voice to drown out Jory's protest. "We've been in the car all night, and if the 95 is as far away as you say . . ."

"You bet. There's a pump on the far side, there. The water's good—I promise. I know water."

"Oh." I wasn't sure what to say to that. "Okay, thanks." I waited for Frank to move away from the car—head back to wherever he'd appeared from in the first place. But he stood there, like he was waiting for us.

"You coming?" he asked.

"Uh, yeah," I said. "Let me grab my water bottle." I rolled up the window and took the keys from the ignition.

Jory shifted in his seat, muttering something.

"What?" I whispered.

"How did he know we wanted the 95?"

I risked a glance at the man. He was standing back a few steps from the door, waiting for me to open it. I kept my voice low and pretended to fish around in the console. "It's the only major route here. Probably lots of people get lost looking for it."

Jory shook his head like he wasn't convinced.

"We need water," I said, trying to keep my tone light. Spilling my bottle sucked, but we would've needed water eventually anyway. Jory hadn't had anything to drink since we left the house, so I knew he was thirsty. Probably hungry, too, but that could wait, at least for me. I was used to that feeling.

"I know."

"Okay, so." I went to open the car door.

Jory grabbed my arm. "Don't," he said. "We don't know that guy."

I shook off his hand, hoping the man couldn't hear him, and opened the car door. When I stood up, I realized I was nearly as tall as Frank. He was thin, too, and didn't look dangerous or whatever. I thought about carrying my keys in my fist, but I stuffed them in my pocket instead. I forced a grateful smile— I was good at those—and straightened my blazer. My hair was awful, but there wasn't much I could do about that without some dry shampoo.

I heard Jory's door open. His hoodie was clenched in his hand, and he kept his gaze on Frank as he made his way to my side of the car. Frank tipped his hat again, but Jory didn't speak. It took me a second to realize that he was coming with us.

I remembered to smile at Frank again.

"Okay, then."

We trailed behind as Frank set off for the station. The sun was up over the lowest mountain behind us and the rays were shining on the tin roof. I lost Frank in the glare here and again.

Jory's gaze was still fixated on him. I recognized his stressed-out-obsessing thing—he didn't like this.

Truthfully, I wasn't crazy about it either. The beauty queen comment had disturbed me. Had he recognized me? And if he had, what did that mean for us?

I noticed his shoes, shuffling ahead of us: leather with a familiar round buckle. They actually looked a lot like the designer loafers my dad liked, only about a thousand times dirtier and more worn. And there was something even more familiar about him from this perspective—the way he walked or . . .

"Here she is," Frank announced as he led us around the corner of the building. A peeling metal pump, painted red a million years ago, stood on a cracked concrete pad. "One of you'll have to work the pump handle while the other holds the bottle. 'Course, you probably knew that."

I nodded, like I did know that, but I'd never seen one of these things in real life before—only in movies about the olden times.

"Take what you need, Liv. I'm going to check inside the station. It's my usual loop." Frank tipped his head at us and strode away.

I quickly moved to the faucet end of the pump; Jory was the right person to work the handle. But he didn't move. He watched Frank cross the dirt and head for a side door. He kept his voice low. "Did you hear that?"

"What?"

"He called you Liv."

"That's my name."

"You told him it was Lavinia."

My skin prickled. "Maybe he guessed, shortened it himself . . ." No, that wasn't likely. But hadn't Jory called me Liv in front of Frank? He had, though Frank wouldn't have been able to hear that unless he had supersonic ears. In that case, he'd know we were sketched out about him . . . No. He *did* recognize me. "Do you think he's going to call the cops?"

"Why would he do that?" Jory kept watching the store.

"I don't know! Maybe . . . maybe he's been following my trial and he knows it was postponed and thinks it's weird or wrong that we're out here?"

"That's not what I'm worried about."

"What then?" A flash of movement at the window; Frank was inside the store.

"Water, first. Then we leave."

"But can we trust his directions? Maybe he's been sent by Mom and Dad to lead us astray?"

Jory looked at me.

"Okay, I know that sounds stupid. But I swear he's familiar. It's like I've seen him before or—"

"Water."

I unscrewed the cap on my bottle. Jory pumped the handle several times before it sputtered to life. The stream of cold liquid was a shock as I let the bottle fill. I handed it to Jory, who promptly downed it and held it back to me to fill again.

"I knew you were thirsty," I muttered, filling and capping it.

"Let's go."

We headed back to the car, watching the window Frank had appeared in moments ago. Would it be better to confront him? Come up with some story about why we were out here so that he didn't feel like he had to alert someone? Or would that only make him more suspicious?

"Oh, what the fuck." Jory's voice came from ahead of me as he rounded the corner of the building.

I jogged a step to join him.

The parking lot was empty.

My mouth opened and closed. I scanned the space, hoping there was some mistake—that we'd parked somewhere else and were remembering incorrectly, or . . .

Jory walked forward a few steps. He turned back to me.

"Frank?" I called out, turning toward the store. "Frank!"

"He took it," Jory said. "He fucking took our car."

"No," I said. "He—" But he had. He totally had. But how? I hadn't left the keys in the ignition, and when we used the pump I was pretty sure I felt them in my pocket.

I patted at my jeans, my pulse racing. Empty. No keys. And we were in the middle of nowhere. And my phone was in the car. And the car was . . .

"Oh my god." The words left me in a rush. "Oh my god." I scanned the road. Which way would he have gone? Why hadn't we heard him leave? "What do we do, Jory?"

Jory was quiet, but my breath was getting faster and faster. I was going to pass out. I bent forward and put my hands on my knees, trying to get air. "My phone was in there," I said. "Oh my god. Oh my god." The sun was barely over the hills, but suddenly it felt scorching hot. If it wasn't, it'd get there, and soon. And all we had for shade was this creepy gas station.

I looked at Jory, panic skittering through me. "You should've stayed in the car!"

My brother had his eyes closed and his thumbs pressed to his temples. His shoulders were quaking slightly, like he was barely keeping back emotion, like there was something violent about to bubble up and out. And when it did, would it come out at me? He was muttering to himself. I caught "bad idea" in the mix.

"We needed water," I protested. He couldn't blame this all on me—

"Not the water!" Jory's eyes flew open. He fixed me with his dead stare. "*This.* This trip."

"It's not my fault everything is so screwed up! How was I supposed to know?"

"*I* knew. I knew it from the start." He turned away.

Cold waves crept up my stomach and into my throat. "What? What do you mean you knew?"

"I knew we wouldn't find Mom and Dad."

The cold flared red-hot as I made out his words. I stomped over and positioned myself in front of him. "How did you know that?"

He was silent.

"Jory. *How?*"

He shook his head.

A rush of anger swept through me, and the black cloud crowded into my vision. I could feel things coming apart around me, disconnecting—the water bottle in my hand, the dusty parking lot.

"You helped them," I accused, my voice tight and low.

"No. I didn't. I—" Jory shook his head again. He tried to step around me. "—need space. Can't breathe."

I got back in his face. "You helped them!" The darkness was furling over everything now, narrowing my vision into a tunnel. I felt my hand reach forward and grab the front of his T-shirt in my fist. I wanted to shake him.

Jory broke free in one fluid move, twisting my wrist and shoving me backward so hard, I staggered and dropped the bottle. Then he spun away and bent at the waist like he was going to throw up.

It jogged a memory so clear my anger vanished. I saw Jory as a kid—young, thin, maybe eleven? Standing knee-deep in water.

Bent like that, hands on his knees, gasping for air. As I watched him, I heard a camera shutter click.

I blinked hard.

The parking lot dust reached my nose, and the sun's rays blinded me a moment. I reached out to put a hand on something to anchor me, but there was nothing. Only empty space and warm air.

"*No.*" Jory straightened. "But I saw them disappear."

I stared at him, trying to get my voice to work.

He spread his hands like he was trying to get ahold of something invisible. "At the courthouse. They . . ." He looked up at me. "Disappeared."

Something buzzed near my ear. I realized he was waiting for me to say something, so I forced my voice out. It was like speaking underwater. "What are you talking about?"

"They were there. Then they weren't." He ran his hands through his hair. "I knew we wouldn't find them at the cabin. We shouldn't even be out here."

"When you say you saw them disappear, you mean—"

"They *vanished*. Into thin fucking air."

The ground lurched up at me. A bottomless feeling was sweeping over me. "People don't vanish," I whispered.

"No shit!" Jory snapped. "They also don't drown in pools and appear in ghost SUVs and trap us in some endless loop of deserted highway."

"Stop yelling at me! I'm not the one who lied!" I could be angry. I could be that. It was better than being scared.

"I didn't lie!"

"You didn't tell me the truth!"

"You would've believed it?"

Of course I wouldn't have believed it, and until this moment,

I would've told him that. I would've been sure he was working with my parents on some elaborate hoax, meant to . . .

To what?

And how could he have done any of this? I was the one driving, I had insisted on going to get water.

For him.

I tried to focus, but my thoughts were going a million miles an hour. At this rate, my mind was going to shatter completely.

What are you trying to do, break her? Break her? Break her? Break her?

Focus on something. Anything. "Frank had on Dad's shoes." I was suddenly sure of that. They'd looked similar in the first place, and now that I thought about it . . .

Jory didn't seem to hear me. He stood there, his mouth moving silently, like he was counting. I'd seen him do this before. He was always doing strange things like this. Saying strange things . . .

"Wish fulfillment," I remembered.

Jory stopped muttering. "What?"

"You said 'wish fulfillment,' back at the house. Did . . . did you say that because you *wanted* Mom and Dad to disappear?"

"I've wanted that more times than I can count." Jory turned to look at me. "And you have, too."

JORY

LIV STARED AT me. "Oh my god, Jory. Do you think . . ." She rubbed at her eyes. Her eye makeup was already smeared from sleeping, and now she dragged the dark color across the sides of her face to her temples. The effect was something like Zorro's mask. I had the sudden urge to pencil a thin mustache on her. "—to them?" Oh. She was still speaking.

"What?"

"Did we do this?" She started to pace back and forth. "Is that even possible? Like, I know I said I wanted this so bad I'd do anything to get it, but—" She stopped short. "But you said that, too. That you wanted to get away from them."

She was right: I'd said that exact thing last night. Except if we were somehow manifesting all this, did that mean that I subconsciously *wanted* us to perish in the middle of the desert? Or was my parents' disappearance the granted-wish part, and being stuck here the price we had to pay—the universe's way of evening the score? I sort of wanted to pace, too, but Liv looked unhinged doing it. I was not unhinged. I was the most hinged. Except for this pain in my chest—

"Okay. It's okay. We can figure this out. Maybe I'm dreaming." She held her arm out and pinched it. Because that worked in the movies? She looked up at me. "What was the last thing they said to you?"

"Why?"

"I don't know! Maybe it will give us a clue or something about how all of this happened."

I shook my head. "Mom said, 'We'll be late.'"

"'We'll be late,'" Liv repeated. She started pacing again. Detective Oblivious, on the case.

I sat down on a broken piece of curb, trying to breathe through the tight feeling.

Don't panic. Don't. Panic.

It was possible we had gotten lost and run into some carjacking hillbilly, wasn't it? I mean, something about him looked off from the start, though of course Liv hadn't listened to me. "Why did you follow that guy?"

"Why did you?"

"Because you did! I wasn't going to let you go alone!"

Liv looked confused for a second. Then she frowned. "Well, he was showing us the water."

"You should've asked, then waited till he left!"

"He didn't look like a carjacker! Plus, he was waiting for me. It would've been kind of rude—"

"So?" I stared at my sister. She seemed genuinely perplexed at the idea of being unfriendly to a complete stranger. Which . . . how could it be that her desire to be polite trumped basic self-preservation instincts?

The air around us was dead calm, and the only sound was

the soft chirping of desert insects. The sun was up now in all its glaring, burny wonder. The air was getting warmer by the minute.

I tried to recap everything that had happened from the first moment when everything felt wrong. The first time I'd had that splintering feeling was at the courthouse.

"We'll be late."

And in the parking lot of the courthouse there was something weird about the radio announcement—like I'd heard it before. And Frank. I hadn't wanted to admit it to Liv, but something about him had seemed familiar to me, too.

And time out here—it felt so . . . intangible. It's not like time was concrete anyway, but ever since we'd gotten in the car, it had felt wrong. I started thinking about infinite loops—sequences of instructions in a computer program that repeated endlessly with no terminating condition—

"Jory," Liv said, like she'd realized something important. "I think this might be my fault."

"You think?"

"Seriously. I . . . I think it has to do with the court case."

"Get to the point." I'd felt like I was onto something there, for a moment. Something about time versus temporality. Our perception of time creating reality . . .

"Well, all of this happened the day that I was supposed to get my revenge—sort of—on Mom and Dad, right?" She moved closer. "And maybe that was wrong. And this is my punishment now. And you're . . . you're wrapped up in the mix accidentally."

"Your punishment."

"Yeah. Like maybe God is showing me what it's like to not have parents anymore. Maybe it's a metaphor, you know? Lost sheep in the desert and all of that?"

She'd interrupted my thoughts for *this*? "Jesus, Liv," I said. "God doesn't give a shit about your stupid court case."

Liv drew back in surprise. Her jaw tightened. "You don't know that."

"Even if a god did exist, would it spend its time taking privileged people to task on behalf of other privileged people? I'm guessing there are a few starving kids it might attend to?"

"That's not how He works, Jory."

"Because you know? Or because it makes you feel better believing your actions have no impact on others?"

"If I think I'm being punished, obviously I believe my actions have an impact on others!"

"*Globally.* An omnipotent power controlling everyone's fate is pretty convenient. You never have to think too hard about buying your sweatshop designer jeans and drinking that stupid bottled water—" From the look on her face, I'd lost her at "globally," and it wasn't because I was speaking too fast.

Liv crossed her arms.

"But you know what? It *is* your fault." I wanted her to fight back. I wanted her to tell me I did plenty of things that an omnipotent being could, in theory, be punishing me for. Our entire existence was probably harming someone, somewhere. I mean, did she pay absolutely no attention to the rest of the world? Par-T-Own's shitty supplies were sourced from some factory in Bangladesh where workers probably inhaled deadly fumes, and I was going to college with those profits. The fact that she didn't understand privilege enough to extend the example to something relevant to me was, frankly, enraging.

This is what happens when you've been told since childhood that you're the center of the universe. You end up having no idea how it all works, how temporary your existence is, how meaningless it all is at the end of the day.

And it didn't matter if she hadn't started out this shallow; what mattered was where she ended up.

"Jory." Liv was staring at me. "Your nose is bleeding."

I felt the trickle as she said it. I sniffed, putting two fingers under my nose and coming up with a smear of bright crimson. The trickle turned into a stream, and I dipped my head forward, catching the drops in the palm of my hand.

"Here." Liv pulled off her blazer and offered me the sleeve, even though I was holding my hoodie.

"I'm fine." I stood and flicked my hand, spattering the broken bit of curb I'd been sitting on with flecks of dark red. I tilted my head back and pinched the bridge of my nose with my other hand. A fluttery panic started. What if I couldn't stop the flow? What if I just bled out—

"At least wash off your hand," Liv said, distaste in her voice. She picked up her water bottle and held it out.

I ignored it, focusing on slowing my breath, getting the flow to stop.

"Oh, right," she huffed. "You don't need any help."

Anger crushed my panic. I felt a sweeping urge to break something. I could feel the blood tapering off, so I dropped my hand, turned, and stalked past her.

"Where are you going?" Liv scrambled after me.

I dropped my hoodie under the pump faucet and grabbed the handle, then began working it violently. The water had come quickly when we'd used it before, but now nothing was happening. I jerked the handle up and down. It didn't so much as sputter to life. Impossible. I pumped violently. Over and over.

"It's not working," Liv said, her voice dull.

I gripped the handle so hard the tendons in my arm stood out like cords. I wanted to tear it off and throw it as hard as I could across the stupid flat desert. I stared at the surrounding nothingness and waited for that feeling of temporality to come. It needed to come, needed to give me a clue that all this was temporary—that whatever was happening, we weren't stuck in it forever.

But everything around me felt solid. Static. Never-ending.

And all that space was closing in, making it hard to breathe. I dropped the handle and closed my eyes. Counted down from ten. The blood was drying on my nostril and upper lip; I could feel my skin tighten where it was smeared.

And anger was burning hot and bright inside. I could feel Liv staring at me, waiting for me to do something, to fix this. Her fierce-survivor routine didn't work when her survival was actually at stake. Funny, that.

Funny like a faceless cat.

Anger swept over me in a wave.

I started counting down from ten again.

LIV

I DIDN'T BOTHER offering Jory my water again.

Mother-of-pearl. How could he stand there counting? We were more screwed than before: we were back to only the water I had in my water bottle, and my phone was gone.

We couldn't just stand here. I yanked my blazer back on even though the temperature was climbing. "What's our plan?" I demanded. He opened his eyes. "Like, should we . . . walk a bit? There must be houses around. Remember that nasty cat all those miles back?"

"No, I'd forgotten."

That sarcasm again. I ground my back teeth. "Well, do you have a better idea?"

"Let's click our heels together three times."

"I'm serious, Jory!"

"What do you want from me?" he snapped. "*Now* I'm worth the air I breathe? *Now* I have answers?"

That stalled me out. "What are you talking about?"

"Nothing," he muttered.

"No," I said. "It isn't nothing. What do you mean, 'now you're worth the air you breathe'? When have I ever said you weren't?" I grabbed at his arm, but he pulled away. "Jory? You don't get to say that and then not explain!"

"I can't explain it to you!" he said. "You're too much like Mom."

I recoiled, feeling the sting of his words like a slap. He did not just say that. How could he possibly think . . . *Redirect.* What he said shouldn't hurt me, because it wasn't true. And if I reacted, it'd be like admitting he was right. *Strong. Fierce.* "Okay," I said, "maybe I was like Mom at one time, but I'm not anymore."

"Whatever."

My temper flared. "Not 'whatever.' If I was like Mom, I'd still be doing the dang pageant circuit, not suing her!"

"Right. Your 'transformational' lawsuit."

I paused, caught off guard. But not because I hadn't expected him to say that—because I had. He'd said it before—when? Months ago, probably. "Look, I know it's hard to understand"— he snorted—"but the lawsuit is about more than me." I could feel that blackness hovering near my thoughts and tried to push it away. I needed to tell him what I was planning to do with the money. Then he'd see how important it was for us to get out of this mess.

"Oh?"

"Yeah. I was texting you, making sure you'd be at the court date this week because . . ." I hesitated. "I want to help you." It was supposed to be my big news, a major reveal, except some- how it didn't feel that way. It felt like I'd already told him. How was that possible?

"You just got us lost in the middle of the goddamn desert," he said. "I'll pass."

The darkness bloomed, crowding out that strange sense of déjà vu. "You know what? At least I can admit when I need help. And at least I don't pretend I don't care about anything!" This wasn't the way to get Jory on my side, but I couldn't stop the words once they'd started. "You know, if you didn't believe what Mom and Dad told you—that you weren't good enough because of the way you looked—you wouldn't have hidden away all these years. You wouldn't hate me this much!"

Jory's jaw worked. "It's my fault you're a drama queen?"

"I'm saying you hate me because you actually do care what people think."

"That is *not* why I hate you."

I hate you. He had never said it aloud before. I stepped back, trying to collect myself, but the pain was too intense. I lashed back, hard. "You think you're so above me! You don't even know the ways Mom and Dad have messed you up."

"Let's get something straight." His speech was getting harder to understand. "*You* are screwed up. Until now, I have avoided being collateral damage."

"Oh, okay, so I *do* have trauma from my childhood? Because I was under the impression you thought it was no big deal. Like, *God* certainly wouldn't think it's important."

"It isn't!"

"What would you know about it? You never had to be near any of it! You didn't have a camera shoved in your face for five flipping years . . ." I faltered because that, too, I'd said before. We'd had this argument before.

"I'm so lucky I was an embarrassment."

Focus. "You were left alone."

"TV's no place for monsters."

"Isn't it? Isn't that exactly what they wanted me to be?"

"Wow. Deep."

My anger swelled. Who cared if we'd had this argument a thousand times? My hands were starting to shake. "Do you think I liked spending every stupid minute of my free time practicing routines? Do you think I enjoyed having my meals portioned out? Or going for spray tans when I was six?"

"Honestly? Yes."

"Well, you're wrong. No little girl should be doing that."

"You've spent a lot of time on your fan page for someone who hates it."

My fan page. At the start, I'd spent hours communicating with people who were fans of the show, beauty pageant hopefuls or their parents, singing Pro-Am's praises, like my mom told me to. But now I spent time there because I was trying to set them straight about glitz pageants. Even so, at first . . . "They were my only friends."

"They weren't your friends."

"It's as close as I got, wasn't it? They said nice things. Told me I was talented. Some of them even said they understood why I was having tantrums. And you know what? Those are the people who helped me see how wrong it all was. That Mom was training me to care too much what other people thought. That I shouldn't base my worth on other people's opinions."

"Oh?"

"Yeah. And that started my search for other survivors. So you could say that those online friends are the reason I overcame it."

"Are you kidding?"

"What?"

"Caring about others' opinions?"

"What about it?"

"You still do. Asia and her gang? Sandra? Your online fans? *They're* why you're out here."

Something cold settled in my stomach, dampening my rage. "No, they're not."

"Bullshit. You're trying to be the 'survivor' they say you are. You care so much what they think, you'll do anything to win their approval."

"That's not true." But my voice had lost its strength.

"You know it is."

Did I? Was I intent on finding my parents because I wanted the other survivors to think I was the *best* of them? The cold in my stomach turned to queasiness. No. No, I believed in justice—for me, for others. Jory had a way of twisting things because he could never see the good in people. "If I'm doing it for other people, it's for other survivors, other girls who need to know that they don't have to define themselves based on—"

"Your stupid court case is not helping anyone!"

"That's not true." Dang it. I was repeating myself. "My blog gets thousands of views a day; my hashtags have *trended*—"

"You are proving my point."

He was right: I was. But I was completely flustered now, and I wasn't thinking straight. I had better arguments than this, but Jory always made me feel so stupid, and that black cloud was crowding my thoughts, growing faster than I could control it. "At least by the end of the weekend people will be looking for me. Who would even notice you were gone?"

His fists clenched. "People would be *happy* if you disappeared."

"No, they wouldn't."

"No? Haven't you read the comments section?"

Heat flushed over me. Of course I'd read the comments section.

Kill yourself.

Someone put that bitch out of her sequined, lip-glossed misery.

Delete your account. And your life.

In the months leading up to the court date, the tweets and comments had started to drown out the messages of support—at least in my mind. It had felt like I was losing control of the message, my story. Two weeks ago I'd had a panic attack at the mall and locked myself in a dressing room. It was humiliating because Asia had to call my therapist, who eventually talked me out and insisted I take all social media off my phone. But Jory wouldn't care about any of that, because he thought I'd brought it on myself.

My breath was shallow. Screw this. Screw my offer. He didn't deserve anything good. "I can't believe I was going to use my settlement money to help you."

"Help me?"

"Yeah. That surgery Mom and Dad never wanted to pay for? I was going to do that for you." Jory's mouth popped open like he was surprised. "But you know what? Forget it. The ability to smile would be lost on you anyway."

"*That's* how you were going to help?" He didn't say it like it was a good thing. He shook his head. "You are so far up your own ass."

"Pardon?"

"You're fucking clueless."

"At least I'm not a freak!" I wanted to shut him up, to hurt him, but it didn't slow him down a bit.

"I was born this way; you chose to be a horror show."

"Horror show."

The cloud was inside my body now, simmering under my skin, creeping dark tendrils through every part of me. I could picture myself lunging forward, grabbing his face, and pressing my thumbs into his immobile eyes until they popped. Tearing at his slack mouth with my fingernails, shoving him backward into the water pump . . .

"Your court case—your entire existence—is one big joke."

My hand moved freely, pulling back, whipping forward. I slapped him. Hard. His head snapped to the side, and one hand came up to grab at his cheek as he gasped. "Fuck you, Jory," I said. "You are a monster."

I stared at him, rage coursing through me. He was bent at the waist and . . . and I suddenly saw him as a child, standing shin-deep in the shiny water. Trying to get air.

Click.

Shame washed over me.

I turned and ran.

JORY

I COULDN'T SAY what stunned me more: the slap or the "fuck you."

I doubled over and, as the split second of shock left, watched her shoes pivot and disappear.

My nose was bleeding again. I straightened up, pressing the back of my hand under it and sniffing hard, swallowing the metallic taste of blood. I expected Liv to go hide around the far side of the station, but she headed for the highway.

"I was going to do that for you."

Who did my sister think she was? I didn't want her pity, and I didn't want her "help." Her dumbass offer was so perfectly Liv. She thought the surgery would make everything better because smiling pretty for other people was all she knew.

But of course I wanted the damn surgery. That was the worst part.

I looked down at my tattoo, running two blood-spattered fingers across it.

"Do you want to talk about anything while you're here?" The guidance counselor leaned back in his chair, contemplating the apple in his hand. "I heard about the lawsuit."

I shifted my weight but didn't sit down. Talking about the lawsuit was the last thing I wanted to do. I hadn't needed to come to his office to grab the BU application—it was online—but I couldn't take another lunch hour of questions and stares. The entire school was talking about Princess Liv and her quest for justice, but I was hoping for conversation about something that actually mattered, which he was generally good for. Like the day he was getting ice for my nosebleed and I'd noticed The Neverending Story on his shelf. We had a long talk about the book versus the movie, and he ended up pressuring me to join the film club. His "this is temporary; high school is just a brief moment in time" mantras weren't so bad, especially since the club made my particular brief moment a little better.

"I'm just here to grab that application."

He opened a desk drawer. "Sure. Just know that I'm here to listen, too." He handed me a plastic-bound application pack. "This next year might feel like an eternity. But remember that this, all of this, is temporary."

As if I could've forgotten. The idea of restarting my life, reinventing myself at college and creating moments in time I actually cared about—that was foremost in my mind. I was going to get a degree, a job, and then, the smile surgery.

For a while, it had felt like a piece was missing when I thought about starting over. But I'd finally figured it out: I needed something concrete that reminded me I could. Something inked onto my skin.

I looked at the bookshelf. The Neverending Story was spine out, but I'd been staring at the cover of my own copy at home for weeks. Yeah, a tattoo of an ouroboros was going to be perfect. Something that signified reincarnation, that I was choosing a new existence.

One without my sister.

I sniffed again and wiped my hand on my jeans. Liv was now halfway down the stretch of road that ran ahead, then curved out of sight around a rising hill. The thought of her disappearing from view probably should've spiked alarm through me, but I felt no urge to call her back.

She was good at leaving.

"You are a monster."

I stared at her retreating form. The glare of the sun was blinding, reflecting off the highway like water.

"You want to see a monster?"

My dad stood at the end of the pier with a drink in his hand, beckoning with the other.

It wasn't like saying no was an option. I stepped onto the wooden pier, leaving the solid safety of the shore. The lake was still, like glass, and as I made my way toward my dad the pier rolled with my weight, making him bob up and down. He didn't seem to mind; he was staring at the water.

Maybe at some kind of weird fish.

"There."

I peered down. The ripples I'd made had dissipated and the surface was calm. I looked harder, searching for what my dad was pointing at.

A feeling of disaster-waiting-to-happen was suddenly intense.

"Can't you see it?" His breath was acidic and sweet. He leaned close, and I turned my head away. "No," he said, pushing my chin and pointing at the water again. He put his other hand on my shoulder and gripped it so hard I bit back a whimper. "There."

And I saw it. It was me, my reflection staring back, one side of my face drooping as if completely exhausted, my eyes different sizes, my mouth turned down and agape. I looked to my mom and sister on the beach.

"Kissy-face!" my mom commanded, and Liv struck a pose, pursing her lips at the camera. Click. Gold at Liv's neck flashed in the sun. I looked back at my reflection, feeling something disconnect inside. The water, the pier, the sun shining . . . it was all coming apart.

My father laughed. "Just kidding, Jory." He crouched down and put a hand in the water. "We're all monsters, inside, you know."

My chest was painfully tight. I pressed a hand against my T-shirt and massaged, staring as Liv disappeared from view.

Was that memory from the last time we were all at the cabin? Had Liv started doing pageants? Was it before *Divas*— before the *horror show*?

I knew calling her that would hit her where it hurt. I'd seen the clips. But I'd been guessing about the online comments. I could never bring myself to read any of it because I knew it would be bad. It was a damn comments section after all—the online depository of people's subconscious self-hate—and I couldn't stomach the idea of strangers saying shit about her. I mean, I was *allowed* to hate her; she'd left me.

Just like right now.

Fuck her. Fuck all of this.

I grabbed the nearest bit of broken concrete I could find and hurled it at the boarded-up window of the station. It made a satisfying thud, but it wasn't enough. I picked up another piece and put my entire body into the throw. The rock smashed against the aluminum siding, leaving a dent. Bits of our argument rang around my head, blending and weaving with snippets of a different time, different place . . .

"I want to help you."

"You're so pathetic."

"I'm telling the truth!"

"Tired of being embarrassed of me?"

I threw a third piece at the siding. *Smash!* Had we argued about this exact same thing before? When?

"*What would you know about it? You never had to be near any of it! You didn't have a camera shoved in your face for five flipping years . . .*"

"*I'm so lucky I was an embarrassment.*"

"*Why won't you let me do this?*"

"*You think you can buy me?*"

I bent to pick up a fourth rock and noticed something shiny in the dirt.

My fingers fumbled for it, dusting away the coating of hot soil. It was a chain. Gold. I peered at the pendant as I held it up. A dirt-encrusted bee . . .

The sun blinded me a moment as I turned it around.

Busy Bee.

My mom's necklace.

The air around me closed in, roaring in my ears like a gale-force wind.

It had to be coincidence; it was just some necklace. I looked closely. No, the bee was identical—it was her necklace. But that meant . . .

My parents had been here. They'd been here before we were. What had Liv said? That Frank'd been wearing Dad's shoes? I'd dismissed it as Liv blathering.

I jerked my head up to call for Liv, but she was nowhere in sight. I took a few steps toward the road, scanning the parking lot for other traces of my parents we may have missed. The gold necklace was impossibly heavy in my hand.

Jesus. Whatever had started Liv down this road, it seemed as though she'd been on the right trail. Maybe that SUV *had* been theirs. Maybe they'd gotten lost like us and showed up here. Maybe Frank was capable of much more than carjacking . . .

"Liv!" I hollered. I jogged onto the road and scanned the distance—she was nowhere. I cupped my hands to my mouth. "Liv!"

Frank'd had nothing on him—no backpack. Which meant he couldn't have walked far to get to this station. He could be anywhere; he could be waiting for her. Though why he'd leave us here just to wait around the corner . . . that would mean he'd have to have known we'd part ways. He'd have to have known we'd argue and Liv would leave. And that was impossible.

Except he'd known we wanted the 95 before we said anything.

And he knew Liv's name.

How? Had we done all this before?

Infinity. Endless looping sequences. Temporality.

"You created your reality; live with it."

I scrubbed my hands over my face. I was starting to come apart, and I couldn't. There was only one thing to focus on now: I needed to go after my sister.

LIV

I HEADED FOR the bend in the road, scrunching my toes painfully in my ballet flats to keep them on my feet. Running in this heat was like running through water.

But I couldn't look at Jory anymore, and I couldn't take him looking at me.

I ran until I rounded the corner and was sure I was hidden from him. Then I had to slow to a walk. Sweat was prickling me everywhere and my lungs felt tight, full of dry air. The road made its way through a series of cliffs here—sort of like the one I'd driven when I'd followed that SUV, and miles back, too, where I thought I'd seen . . .

That darkness was dissolving, and in its place a feeling of emptiness was growing. My hand stung where it had connected with Jory's face. I'd slapped people before—the video footage doesn't lie—but never Jory.

"Horror show."

I stumbled off the highway and retched.

There was nothing in my stomach to throw up. My eyes were stinging and I rubbed at them with my fists. I wasn't crying. I wouldn't.

Strong. Fierce.

Except now those words felt so silly. They felt like a joke. I dry-heaved again, feeling the sun beating on my back, my neck. I tried to cling to what I knew was true and right, but the idea that had given me purpose every waking minute for the past six months—that my court case would change things, make a difference—suddenly felt slippery, hard to keep in my mind. In fact, when I thought about all of it, the other survivors, my lawyer, the courthouse, I could only picture a giant black hole.

"You chose *to be a horror show."*

I hadn't *chosen.* My stomach churned.

Had I?

"Good choice," the girl handing out Jell-O shots said. "Red is my favorite."

I downed the sweet vodka and looked around the party, trying to appear a little bored. I never went to house parties because I didn't have anyone to hang out with, but I was doing an English project with two girls who'd insisted I come to the Year Opener. I'd arrived late so I wouldn't be here first, but apparently not late enough: they weren't here yet.

Worse, my brother was. I'd seen him in the living room talking to one of the losers from the film club when I came in, and I'd made a beeline for the kitchen. Jory probably wouldn't have tried to talk to me, but the dork he was with might've, and I did not need to be seen at my first house party with that. Ugh. Why was Jory even here?

I took another Jell-O shot—green this time—and wandered around a bit, trying to find the girls. Twenty minutes later, they still weren't anywhere. I decided to give it a few more minutes and headed back to the living room to sit down, but as I rounded the corner from the hall-way I froze. The living room was packed with people now, and Jory was being held in place by a guy I didn't recognize—I think he was from a different school.

"Wow, are you that drunk?" The guy stood with a hand on Jory's shoulder, holding him at arm's length. The other hand grasped a red Solo cup to his chest. The varsity letters on his jacket glowed bright in the black light. He swayed slightly.

Jory tried to move past him, mumbling something.

The guy pushed him back. "Seriously, man, I thought I was wrecked. How much did you have?"

One of the girls from glee club was standing beside Varsity Jacket Guy. "He's not drunk; he just looks like that."

Again, Jory tried to move past him, but the guy held him fast. "No shit?" He peered at Jory's face. Jory went stock-still. "That's serious, dude. Sorry about that." He let him go. "Sorry."

I melted into a dark corner of the living room, my stomach hollow-ing out.

The emptiness was spreading like it was going to swallow me. I raised my head, staring at the cracks and crannies climbing the rock face, trying to anchor myself to something. Anything. I focused on one crack that raced upward in a diagonal line. A glint at the top of the cliff caught my eye. Something was shining up there, out of place in the dry soil and dusty bits of shrub.

I wiped my eyes again and stepped forward, staring at the object. It was way too high up for me to reach—I'd have to some-how climb up.

Which was probably a bad idea.

I set down my water bottle and moved close to the cliff face, losing sight of it. My fingers grasped at jagged rock as I pulled myself up; my shoes slipped as I tried to find footholds in the rock.

When I finally got to the top, I realized I'd misjudged the object's location—it was at least twenty feet away, on the next bit of rock. From here, I could tell it was a little silver box. I was looking at a cell phone.

A cell phone!

I scrambled down the rock to get to its level. It was lying at the edge of a little cliff. How had I even seen it from below? I started forward quickly, then froze, glancing around. What if it was Frank's? What if he was nearby? I swiveled, scanning the hills, bracing myself for the creep to magically appear from behind a boulder.

No movement. No sound. I turned around and moved forward again. The phone looked so familiar—

It jumped to life, shattering the silence with a heart-stopping wail.

I froze before realizing it was a ringtone. It had service! I dropped to my knees and scrambled forward, reaching for it. The phone was playing some old song—some hair-band song from my parents' time, something about a girl with a gun—and it stopped abruptly when I picked it up. And then my breath caught as I realized why it was familiar.

It was my dad's cell phone. It was his case—a black-and-white Par-T-Own logo. He'd had that ringtone for more than a year.

I peered at the phone. Whoever had been calling had stopped, and the missed call wasn't registering on the screen. But it had service. I could call with it—we weren't stuck out here. And more important than that . . .

My parents had been here.

My heart pounded as I spun around on my knees, scanning the hills again. I didn't want to go back to that station, back to Jory, but I knew I needed to show him. I pushed to stand. A resounding crack froze me in place.

The sound had come from under my feet.

JORY

I HURRIED BACK to the pump for my hoodie and then headed to the highway. Liv couldn't have gotten far. I broke into a run. The sun beat down unrelentingly, and the heat clung to me like an extra layer of clothes. The hill in the distance seemed, for an alarming second, to stay the same distance away. No. I was getting closer to that damn curve—it was not part of this stupid infinite loop.

How far could I run without water? That was a good question. I was in better shape than lots of guys my age, but not Death Race in shape. If I didn't find Liv right away, I'd be seriously screwed.

But so would she.

And then all at once I was upon the hill and rounding the curve. The walls of rock were hugging the highway here, almost like they were trying to squeeze it out. There was a series of curves, though she would've had to have been moving fast to be beyond my sight already.

"People would be happy if you disappeared."

"Liv!" I increased my pace, heading for the far curve, but I rounded that and . . . no Liv. Maybe she was faster than I thought.

I sped up again, gaze fixed on the far turn, which shimmered in the heat. As I came around the corner, the hills dropped away completely and I found myself staring at the flat desert again. The road was a straightaway. Nothing for miles. No rocks, no mountains, not even a cactus of any sizable sort. No Liv. I clenched my mom's necklace in my hand.

Why had I let her go?

I stood in a corner of the living room, listening to Mark Mietzka ramble on about the importance of opening images and watching my sister sit on the couch and pretend to be engrossed in her phone.

I'd watched her drift around the party for the better part of an hour, trying to look as though she belonged here. Everywhere she went, girls eyed her up and down and talked under their breath. Guys made lewd gestures behind her as she walked by. She was like a designer-jeaned antelope wandering through a bunch of scornful lions: tiaras didn't matter here, and Princess Liv was definitely out of her element.

But I'd expected that.

Earlier in the week I'd overheard her on the phone with one of her pageant friends, talking about the party and trying to convince whoever it was to come. Two girls from her English class had invited her, which was what caught my attention and made me linger in the kitchen, listening in.

Unsurprisingly, Liv hadn't noticed. Even people who don't assume I can't understand often still assume I'm not paying attention. It's a strange misconception of people who don't talk very much, as if constantly giving your two cents affirms your existence.

Liv and my mom had been arguing a lot. Liv had been spending more and more time online and on her phone, outright refusing the auditions my mom was booking for her with advertising and modeling agencies. But she hadn't acquired any real-life friends.

I suspected she'd been invited because she'd be unwelcome. The girls who'd invited her probably weren't even planning to go. It surprised me she hadn't figured that out, but I thought maybe she'd finally realized how vapid her life was and was trying to fill the void with something, even if that something was a party full of kids who didn't like her. I never went to those things either, but Mark's cousin was throwing it, so he'd had a pass—as did anyone he invited, as long as they didn't try to talk to the cool kids.

I didn't give a shit about the party. I'd learned a long time ago—like second or third grade at some kid's birthday party—that the questions and snide comments weren't worth the free admission. Liv had been invited under a similar, albeit opposite, premise: so people could ignore her and make her feel like an idiot for showing up.

I'd told myself it would be funny to watch Princess Liv try to keep her royal composure while the peasants mounted their passive-aggressive revolt.

But truly, I'd decided to come in case something worse had been planned.

I had nothing to lose. It's not like I'd fall a rung on the high school social ladder or piss off my sports team if I interrupted an ambush. I couldn't picture the girls in her class doing something truly heinous, but I'd had enough experience with assholes to know they could surprise you.

So I watched Liv wander around and take Jell-O shots, generally ignoring the looks and trying to keep her Pro-Am posture intact. Her new perch on the couch with her phone was an indication that she wasn't giving up on the idea she belonged here.

Jesus, it was sad.

I shifted my stance as that idiot who'd been in my face earlier *descended upon her. I'd seen her when he was talking to me—she'd retreated into a corner of the room and listened. I watched now to see how she'd react. He collapsed onto the couch beside her, obviously drunk, and said something I couldn't hear.*

Liv set down her phone and flashed him a pageant smile. He leaned closer, touching her arm and gesturing at her dress like he was complimenting it.

And I could see it on her face: she was totally buying whatever this guy was selling.

I decided Princess Liv could handle herself.

I left.

I stared out at the straightaway and scanned the horizon for movement. Nothing.

Liv was nowhere.

And maybe it was better that way.

Why was I looking out for her when she only ever thought of herself? I wasn't that naive asshole anymore. The entire reason we were stuck out here was her unwillingness to get over herself, her "trauma."

I looked down at my tattoo. I'd had the *ouroboros* drawn oblong, not in a perfect circle, because life is imbalanced and messy, but the snake eating its own tail, signifying life from death, is the antidote to the chaos: reinvention.

Liv hinging her future on "fixing the past"? That was stasis. *That* was a dead end. And me chasing after her like this was the opposite of moving forward.

I turned around and made my way back through the series of hills. They were completely out of place, sitting as though they'd been dropped here from the sky, no dried-up riverbed or series of canyons nearby to explain them.

Like the ones we'd passed through miles back. Identical, almost.

I pressed forward, annoyed I'd expended so much of what little energy I had running after her. I should've been conserving my strength, thinking about where to find water and food. And that's when I noticed her water bottle on the side of the road. Placed there, not dropped.

And definitely not there on my way past.

I stopped, searching the sides of the road, the hills. Everything was quiet, dead calm.

"I want to disappear," Liv said.

I put down the tinfoil and looked over at her. She was drawing a huge button on the cardboard switch. The dummy sat nearby, clothed in its black leotard. It needed scars, and for that we needed neon paint, but Mom hadn't been to the dollar store all week. It's like she didn't want me to be part of Liv's event and was trying to make it difficult.

"To become the monster," she said, finishing the circle and looking up at me. "Poof."

"It doesn't work like that." I gestured to the pieces of flash paper sitting near the cardboard box I was wrapping. "It doesn't create a big cloud of smoke or something that you can hide behind."

"I thought you said it was like what magicians did."

"It is. It makes a big bang and a bright flash."

"But no smoke?" She frowned.

"Not enough to disappear." I was a little embarrassed now. Had I let her down? "But it makes a huge flash. People will be surprised, trust me."

"Yeah," she said. "Okay. But . . ."

"But what?"

"What about when I become the monster? How can I change without them seeing?"

I thought for a minute. "Maybe you don't need to do it without them seeing. You can transform before their eyes."

Liv chewed her lip. "Will they like that?"

"It would be more of a performance."

"Yeah, okay." Liv smiled. "You have really good ideas, Jory."

I shrugged, but secretly I was happy she'd said that.

"So can I see it? The flash?"

I fanned out the pieces of paper. We had about six—Mom had bought them before she knew it was my idea, before she knew Liv needed my help.

I went and got a lighter out of the junk drawer in the kitchen and came back into the living room. "Watch." I lit the paper and threw it in the air.

A flash of light exploded with a BANG! Liv screamed.

I blinked. The sun was reflecting off the metal band of Liv's water bottle.

The scream came again. Not from my memory this time, though—no, this was from right here and now. It had come from somewhere above me.

LIV

THE EARTH SHIFTED under my feet. I screamed again. There was a split second of nothing: no sound, no movement. Then the cliff gave way and I was slipping backward, scrabbling at the rock in front of me that was breaking apart into a cloud of dust and shale. I flailed, feeling everything move, slide, come apart . . .

I threw myself forward, banging my chin on something hard, then stopping all at once. The chunk of rock under my feet had gotten stuck against the side of the hill, bringing me to a halt and a bunch of dust down around me. I held my breath, trying not to cough.

When the slide didn't start up again, I risked a slow look over my shoulder. About two feet below my shoes, the cliff dropped away really sharply—at least thirty feet—to the bottom of a ravine. A dizzying flush of terror struck me. I hugged the incline, pressing myself into the dirt and forcing myself not to try to scramble upward. The chunk of rock I was resting on felt unstable; shifting on it might start the landslide again.

Shiitake mushrooms.

My heart was beating so loud in my ears. Jory was too far away to hear me if I called out. Someone else was obviously out here somewhere, but if that someone was Frank, would he help me or send me to the bottom of this gorge? I wasn't sure I could risk that.

I tried to slow my breathing and stay calm. I always had to stand perfectly still during crowning; I could stay still now if I concentrated. And maybe Jory would come looking for me. Maybe he'd notice my tracks or something.

No. He'd never notice my tracks—his eyesight wasn't that good. So how long could I stay here? Not long. The sun was brutally hot, beating against the side of the cliff, and I had no sunscreen or hat or water. I was going to fry to death on the side of a cliff.

Geez Louise. Why had I climbed away from the highway?

Stay calm. Don't move.

I pressed my forehead to the hot earth and pretended I was onstage for judging.

Relax your shoulders, focus on a point in the distance . . .

Gradually, I stopped trembling. Taking a slow sip of air, I raised my head. A glint drew my gaze up the cliff face.

That stupid little phone had come to a rest on a bit of protruding rock and was lying above me to my right. It lay there like it was taunting me.

It rang again, shrieking to life with that awful chorus.

Frick! Who could be calling?

Not important.

Trying not to shift my weight too much, I slowly stretched

out my hand above my head. My fingers grazed the edge of the phone, pushing it farther away.

Stop.

Whoever it was, did I think they'd arrive here before this landslide restarted? They definitely wouldn't, and moving wasn't a good idea. Even so, as if I couldn't help it, I reached for the phone again. It wasn't so much the idea of answering; it was the idea of having something that proved my parents had been here. I looked down as I stretched up, feeling for it. A trickle of sweat left my hairline and rivered down my cheek. I almost had the phone—it was almost in my hand . . .

The earth shifted under my feet. My stomach jammed up into my throat as I lost my footing and—

And then a hand was around my wrist.

My head snapped up. Jory was leaning over the cliff above. He had me by the arm. And now, somehow, he was lifting me. I scrabbled at the soil with my free hand and my feet, trying to climb as he brought me up to the edge. He was inching backward, rising to his knees as he pulled.

I grasped for the top, pulled myself over, and rolled away from the edge. I scrambled up to sitting and scooted backward. "Come away!"

Jory was too close to the edge, sitting with his arms on his bent knees, head hanging. "It's okay," he said in between labored breaths. "It's solid."

I wrapped my arms around myself. I was shaking uncontrollably.

He looked over at me. "You're fine. You're okay."

I was fine. I was okay. I was on solid ground.

So why did I feel like I was going to cry? I hugged myself, taking several deep breaths and trying to get it together. When

I was sure I'd swallowed any tears that were threatening, I spoke. "You saved me—"

"You left me."

"I know, that was stupid. I shouldn't have run away."

"No." Jory shook his head. *"Before."*

I studied his face, trying to get some clue. He looked away, holding his wrist with the opposite hand and moving it in a slow circle.

"Are you hurt?"

"No." He dropped his wrist. Then it was like he noticed his hands. He held them out, stared at them a moment, and started looking around on the ground. He stood, frantically patting his pockets, digging in them. Then he took another step to the side of the cliff and bent over, hands on his knees, peering down. And I saw him as that little boy again. Doubled over. Trying to get breath.

"You are *a monster."*

The wind gusted around us, hot and dry.

Jory peered into the ravine.

"He's not drunk; he just looks like that."

Again, Jory tried to move past, but the guy held him fast. "No shit?" *He peered at Jory's face. Jory went stock-still.* "That's serious, dude. Sorry about that." *He let him go.* "Sorry."

I melted into a dark corner of the living room.

A half hour had passed when the guy found me on the couch, pretending to text with someone. He didn't know I was Jory's sister, but he said he'd heard that I was that "stuck-up little beauty queen."

He told me I was easily the hottest girl at the party. I let him stick his tongue in my ear and put his hand up my shirt.

Then I excused myself, threw up in the bathroom, and went home.

The nausea was back. The memory churned inside me.

There was a time I never would've done something like that to Jory, but when?

I stared at him, crouched dangerously close to the edge.

I spent so much time controlling the story. But where was my ability to write my story in real life? Where was my fierceness when it actually mattered?

"It's buried," Jory said. "It's buried way deep."

JORY

"WHAT'S BURIED?"

Liv's question barely registered. I was transfixed by the floor of the crevice, a monochromatic canvas of crumbled shale and broken sandstone. There was no way to climb down to search, and besides, the necklace could be under a ton of rubble. My eyes were so dry they were burning, and the wind snaking through the hills wasn't helping.

"What's wrong with me?" That damn song was playing over and over again in my head.

I looked at Liv. She was hugging her arms around herself, chewing her upper lip. *Jesus.* She was going to have to stop doing that.

I stared back down the sheer drop, searching for a glimpse of proof that our parents had been here.

"Can't you see it?" My dad's breath was acidic and sweet. He leaned close, and I turned my head away. "No," he said, pushing my

chin and pointing at the water again. He put his other hand on my shoulder and gripped it so hard I bit back a whimper. "There."

It was me, my reflection staring back, one side of my face drooping as if completely exhausted, my eyes different sizes, my mouth turned down and agape. I turned my head to look at my mom and sister on the beach.

"Kissy-face!"

My father laughed. "Just kidding, Jory." He crouched down and put a hand in the water. "We're all monsters, inside, you know." He leaned closer, as if he was trying to reach something on the side of the pier.

And I put two hands on his back and pushed him in.

"Come away from the edge," Liv said. "Please?"

I pulled myself to standing and backed up, staring at the ravine. Dad hadn't fallen in the lake that day. Liv remembered Mom hauling him out, but she didn't remember me running away, stumbling off the pier into the shallows before I doubled over, trying to get a breath.

"I shouldn't have hit you."

I looked at her. She was a mess: her hair was tangled and sweaty, that eye-makeup Zorro mask was streaked down her cheeks—she'd been crying, obviously—and her blazer and jeans were coated in a fine layer of dust.

"I shouldn't have." Her face was white. "You didn't deserve that."

Didn't I?

I'd been home an hour when I heard Liv get back from the party. Our parents were already in bed, even though it was only midnight. Mom and Liv'd had an argument before Liv left, so Mom not stay- ing up to wait for Liv was her way of winning it. And Dad, well, he

*was likely in a Jack Daniel's–induced coma. It was the weekend,
after all.*

*I opened my bedroom door a crack as Liv came up the stairs. I saw
her as she passed to get to her room—she was disheveled, her makeup
smudged in dark streaks under her eyes.*

She'd been crying.

She glanced over at me, looking as though she was going to stop.

I closed my door.

The wind gusted, hot and dry around us. Liv's raccoon eyes
were wide and serious. She was waiting for my reply, but my
thoughts were all jumbled together now. She'd apologized for
something, but I couldn't remember what. And the sight of her,
all clown faced and pathetic, sparked a strange desperation in
me. "What were you thinking?" I demanded.

"I said it was stupid, okay?"

"No. Not now . . ." I could feel my knees sticking to my
jeans—they were obviously seeping blood. When I'd heard Liv
scream, I scrambled up that rock face so fast I'd skinned both
knees.

Liv still had her arms wrapped around herself. "I thought
I saw something," she said. She shook her head. "No. I did see
something. I had it right in my hand . . ."

"What?"

She focused on a spot in the distance behind me, like she
was suddenly thinking of something else. "Do you ever just
want to be believed?" she asked.

"Pardon?"

She looked at me. "Maybe it's a little bit like people not
understanding what you say. Doesn't it get old, repeating
yourself?"

"Uh . . . yeah?"

"Yeah," she said softly. "It gets old. Saying something over and over and never being heard."

I looked back down at the ravine. What was she talking about? When had she not been heard? All Liv did was talk. And she'd been heard by half the damn country.

"Seeing is believing." It was my dad's favorite phrase, trotted out when he'd secured a major shipment of those goddamn party supplies and his phone pinged with a confirmation. I think he meant it as a kind of victory phrase, but it was exactly the kind of meaningless adage guys like my dad thought nutshelled reality. It was also exactly what Liv's life had been: create the right picture and people will believe it.

And they'd believed. The hashtags didn't lie.

"I want to disappear."

"You can transform before their eyes."

"You created your reality; live with it."

I looked back at my sister. She was staring at the horizon.

"I believe you," I said.

LIV

A HOT BREEZE snaked through the hills, blowing my hair into my face.

"Liv?"

My hair extensions were clipped in too tight; I wasn't supposed to itch at them. I was standing in my cupcake dress at the window of our hotel room in San Diego. A woman and a little girl in rainbow-striped shorts were walking a small white dog on the sidewalk below.

"Lavinia," my mom said. "You have an important visitor."

I turned. My mom stood at the door with a man about my dad's age. He had thin, combed-back hair and cowboy boots with shiny metal toes.

My mom gestured for me to come closer. "You remember Mr. Day."

The man looked at my Mary Janes. "Pretty shoes," he said. The lump in his throat bobbed up and down. "For a pretty girl."

I tried not to frown. Those pale eyes . . . Yes, I remembered. But I didn't want him looking at my shoes. I didn't want him in our hotel room.

"What do you say, Livy?" my mom prompted.

"Thank you."

"Mr. Day is a talent scout," my mom said. "That means he looks for winners."

"Are you a winner, Livy?" the man asked, smiling at me. My stomach got tight. I didn't like the way he used my mom's nickname for me. He should've called me Lavinia, shouldn't he? But I nodded. Of course I was a winner.

"You saw her win Ultimate Grand Supreme at Beautylicious in Houston," Mom said to the man. "She loves that stage."

I was supposed to say something like "And the stage loves me." That's what we did for the cameras all the time. Mom would say something like "The judges are good to her" and I'd knock 'em dead with "Because I'm good to the judges!" Mom said it was good to look right at the camera when I did that. But there were no TV cameras—they weren't allowed in our hotel room—and this felt different.

The man leaned forward. His shirt was unbuttoned at the neck, and that bothered me too. "Why don't you show me your walk?"

"But I'm going to be onstage right away," I said.

"I know," said the man. "But you'll be distracted by the crowds, and I won't have a front-row seat. How about a private show?"

"Liv?"

The point on the horizon where the mountains met the sky blurred in my vision. I pulled a strand of hair from my mouth.

"I believe you."

I glanced at him and swallowed hard. "I had Dad's cell phone," I said. "Before the edge crumbled. I had it in my hand."

Jory looked at me sharply. Then he dropped to his knees and peered over the edge again. I should've helped him look, but I couldn't bring myself to get near the cliff. "Mom and Dad were here," he said. "I found Mom's necklace."

The air whooshed out of my lungs. "Let's see?"

Jory spread his hands. "I . . . I think I dropped it when I reached for you." He scanned the ravine.

"You're sure it was Busy Bee?"

"Yeah. I had it."

I should have felt better about all this. Finding our parents' things meant I'd been on the right track, that I hadn't brought us out here for nothing. But all I could feel was a dull sense of dread. We were still stranded, and even if we somehow got unstranded, we'd need our parents' things to prove they'd been here. That we hadn't made up some story . . .

"Horror show."

Jory stared into the ravine a long time. Finally, he stood and brushed dust off his shirt and jeans. "Let's get out of here."

I nodded, shivering despite the hot wind. There was a memory pricking at the back of my mind—something about cliffs, about climbing . . .

That girl I thought I'd seen.

"Come on." Jory held out a hand.

The way down was far trickier than the climb up, and my shoes weren't helping. Jory had to lower me down the last little rock wall, then he scaled a craggier part of it to land beside me, next to the highway. My water bottle stood where I'd placed it.

I picked it up and cleared my throat, trying to steady my voice. "Now what?"

He pointed in the direction of the station. "If it's still there."

I was no longer shaking, but it wasn't because I was on solid ground—I felt better because Jory was here. I felt better because he'd come after me. Even though he hated me, even though he said the most terrible things sometimes . . .

A little white block stood in the distance, wavering in the heat. The station was still there. I picked up my pace, ignoring the fact that my heel was rubbed raw and the soles of my feet were screaming.

"Pretty feet, Livy." Mom stood at the side of the room, coaching. I paused at the back of the pretend stage and turned, swaying slightly as I stepped forward again.

"No!" my mom scolded. "Don't walk like you're drunk!"

I looked over at Jory, walking with that slight hitch in his gait.

"Wow, are you that drunk?" The guy stood with a hand on Jory's shoulder, holding him at arm's length.

"He's not drunk; he just looks like that."

Hand up my shirt, tongue in my ear, vomit splashing the back of the toilet—

"Why were you there?" I asked.

"What?"

"Why were you there?"

"I heard you scream."

"No, not now." I shook my head. "Before." The memory was nagging at me, tangling my thoughts together. It was so hot, and I was so tired. "The Year Opener party."

Jory stared at me.

"You never went to parties. Why did you go to that one?"

He looked at me like I had two heads. Maybe he didn't even remember.

"I'm sorry," I said.

"Pardon?"

"I'm sorry," I repeated. "Mom said that God gives everyone a talent. And mine was the way I looked." Why was I telling him this? My apology and the memory were related, but I couldn't connect those dots right now. Jory was still staring at me, so I continued, saying the first thing that came into my head. "I used to believe it when she said it was my destiny to do pageants. She could justify it so many ways. Like, 'Oh, your feet fit all the cute shoes—they're the perfect size for pageants.' 'Your skin is alabaster, so it takes spray tan really well—it's perfect for pageants.' I thought . . ." I waited, hoping he'd say something. Even a nod would help. Nothing. "I don't know. I guess I believed her because . . ." I waved my hands in frustration. "Well, geez, Jory, even my name is a beauty pageant name!"

"It is?"

"Yeah. That's what Mom said."

Jory stopped walking so abruptly I bumped into him. He turned. "That's how you should've known she was full of shit."

"Why?"

"She named you after a serial killer."

"What? No, she didn't."

"Yes, she did. I don't think she knew."

"No, it's French."

"French."

"Well, okay, not truly French. But she wanted a name that sounded exotic, and since lavender is French, she went with Lavinia." I'd always hated the way my mom said my name, but I did like the idea of it being French.

"Lavinia Fisher: first female serial killer in the United States." Jory started walking again.

I hurried to catch up. "You're making that up."

"Can't make this stuff up."

"For real? There's a serial killer named Lavinia?"

"Famous."

I should've been feeling upset or humiliated, but somehow

this news was . . . it was so crazy it was kind of funny. I grinned. "I think the word is *in*famous," I said.

Jory stutter-stepped, and his mouth dropped open. He'd obviously expected a different reaction. And his confusion amused me more. In fact, the whole thing struck me as so ridiculous, I stopped and started to giggle. My mom thought she'd named me something fancy. My mom thought my name was a fancy pageant name because that's how much she knew about everything. And suddenly, somehow, this was the best news ever.

Jory turned to look at me, obviously at a loss, and it made me laugh harder. It was too much.

And then Jory was laughing, too. He put a fist to his mouth and leaned forward, jerking a little. And I remembered the weird little hiccupy thing he did when he laughed. He sounded a bit like a chipmunk, which became so hilarious I started laughing so hard I could hardly catch a breath. We were stranded on a deserted road in the middle of the desert with limited water and no food, and this was somehow the funniest thing I had ever experienced. I started to wheeze.

"Oh. My. Gosh." I wiped at the tears now streaming toward my chin. "I'm going to puke if I laugh any more."

Jory's chipmunk laugh faded. "Gross."

"Right?" I patted my face. "Okay." I shook my hands and shoulders and straightened up. But then I thought, *It's French,* and burst out laughing again. Jory stood with his head tilted, watching me. I swear I could hear him smiling. And then, even though I was laughing, something heavy lodged in my throat and the tears streaming down my face became angry, not happy. I was crying—not laugh-crying, really crying. My wheezing turned into long, ragged sobs.

"Hey," Jory said, "don't do that."

That feeling of nothingness was back, that sense that everything was going to crack apart and fly away and I knew I shouldn't—Jory didn't like to be touched—but I reached for him.

He stood, stiff as a board, as I put my arms around his shoulders and pressed my face into his chest. He didn't move, didn't put his arms around me, but the fact that he didn't push me away felt like something. I couldn't remember the last time I'd hugged my brother, but it didn't feel weird, and that made me cry harder.

Finally he said, "You're getting snot on my shirt."

"Oh." I pulled back, wiping at my face with my dirty hands. I cleared my throat. "I don't know what's wrong with me."

Jory shrugged. "No painkillers out here."

He wasn't being snarky; he was watching me carefully, and not in his obsessed zoning-out way. More like as if it mattered whether or not I was going to be okay. That made me want to start crying all over again. Then something over his shoulder caught my eye. I stepped around him to see the station clearly. My breath stopped. "Oh my gosh, Jory. Look."

Our car sat in the far end of the lot, right where I'd parked it last night.

POP AND LOCK
AND
POP ROCKS

JORY

"HOLY SHIT." EVEN from that distance I could see we were looking at our parents' Audi. I took a stunned step forward, two . . . and then I was running.

"Wait!" Liv yelled.

I heard her coming after me, but I had a head start and wasn't slowing. I was halfway to the car before it sharpened in my vision, becoming more than a box on shiny wheels. I could see it now; the sun wasn't glinting off the windows from this angle. I squinted, making sure my eyes weren't playing tricks.

"Wait!" Liv yelled again. The panic in her voice slowed me up. She reached me. "Do you see that?"

"What?"

"Geez, your eyes!" She grabbed my arm, pulling me to a stop. "There are two people in the car."

The hair on the back of my neck rose. Frank and a friend? Returned to off us and cover all traces? Is that what happened to our parents—is that why we were finding their things scattered about? I tried to think. Obviously, if we could see them, they could see us. Running back and hiding in those crumbling hills was our only option. Frank wasn't a big guy; I had fifty pounds on him at least. But there were two of them. And if they had guns . . .

"Are they dead?" Liv asked, her voice a squeak. "They're not moving. They're . . ."

My eyesight wasn't good enough. I could see the car; maybe I could see shapes in the front seat? Hard to say.

"Oh my god," Liv breathed. Her fingers tightened on my arm. She pointed with her free hand. "It's us."

A cold feeling knifed through me. "What?"

"We're . . . sleeping." She stared, her mouth agape. Whatever she was seeing, she was convinced of it. Her arm started to shake. She dropped it and tore her gaze from the car to meet mine. "What's going on, Jore?" she whispered.

I needed to get closer. I needed my eye drops. But they were in my backpack, which was in the car, which was fifty yards away . . . or was it? Was it really there?

That splintering feeling was back, but it felt like it was happening on the inside. It wasn't the things around me coming apart, it was . . . me. I looked at my dirty hands—foreign objects. My heart thumped hollowly, disconnected from the arteries and veins that circulated through—

Liv stepped forward.

"Wait!" I tried to grab her, but she danced out of my grasp and crossed into the parking lot. She stopped abruptly, and I caught up to her, close enough now that I could see the car plainly. There was nobody inside.

"We're gone," Liv said. "We disappeared."

"I want to disappear."

She looked at me, fear twisting her expression. And then we were both running as fast as we could toward the car. I reached it first, a rush of relief coursing through me as my hands scrabbled for the door handle and felt it solid under my fingers. I yanked the door open. It was empty, save my bag and Liv's phone, wallet, and lip balm. Everything was exactly how we'd left it.

Liv skidded to a stop, slamming her hands on the hood as if to keep the car in place. Her eyes were wild.

The splintering feeling had vanished. But now Liv looked like she was about to come apart completely. Jesus Christ, I needed to think. The sun and desert air were squeezing my lungs. It was way too hot out here. Hot enough to make Liv see things?

"Get in," I ordered. "And get the AC on."

"I don't have the keys!" Liv said, and then a weird look crossed her face. She reached into her pocket and withdrew a heart key chain with several keys on it, one with an Audi logo. "I swear they weren't there before."

"Get in."

Liv started the car and the AC and then locked us in. She sat, gripping the wheel, staring out at the gas station.

"Okay," I said, thinking aloud in an attempt to calm myself. "Okay, let's think this through." We were wasting gas, so we couldn't think it through for long. But . . . *count from ten.* Okay. Here we were, back where we'd started this morning. We had Liv's phone and charger; we had my backpack, which wasn't good for much; we had the car . . .

"I . . . that . . ." Liv's breathing was all jacked up, like she was still running. "That happened before. I saw us before. I saw . . . I think I saw . . ."

"Slow down." Her panic was making me panicky. "What are you talking about?"

"The lizard!" Liv slammed her hands on the steering wheel. "I said that because I didn't want you to think I was losing it! It was a girl, climbing up the rock last night. It was . . ." She turned to stare at me. "It was me."

My heart hammered. Those thoughts about looping sequences, that strange feeling that I'd experienced things identically more than once; I couldn't describe it as déjà vu—it was more than that.

"And then last night there was someone walking around outside the car. It was . . ." Liv's face had a feral quality, like she was on the cusp of tearing off her designer blazer and running off into the hills to live with mangled cats. "It was you."

I stared back. A thought was on the tip of my tongue, clamoring to be considered. There was no non-crazy way to say it: "Have we done all of this before?"

Her forehead creased and the spark of wildness in her eyes faded as she tried to understand.

"Maybe that's how Frank knew your name and where we were going. Maybe we've done everything already." I could see the gears grinding in her mind, could see her trying to reconcile this impossibility with everything else.

"Did we die?" she asked. "Back on that road, when I followed that SUV?"

I hadn't considered that possibility. I mean, I'd pondered this road trip being purgatory, but—

"No." I wasn't trying to reassure her—what she said felt wrong. Like that line of thinking was missing the point, even though my own theory was impossible. "It just doesn't feel like the first time we've done this."

She was quiet a moment, staring out at the station. When she spoke, her voice was flat. "If some hillbilly appears, I'm going to run him over."

I reached forward and pressed the buttons on the radio and found static, then more static. I needed someone to say the date. But all I was getting was fuzzy crackling.

The clock on the dash read 11:30 A.M. We'd been stopped at the station about three times longer than I would've guessed.

"What time does your phone say?" I asked.

"It's dead, remember?"

"So charge it!" I slammed my hands on the dash. Liv jumped, and I sat back, gripping my hands into fists. "Sorry."

"No, I will." Liv fumbled with the device, making sure the cord was still plugged into the port. "It'll take a minute—it was completely out of juice."

We sat in silence for several minutes. My pulse was slowly decelerating, but it was being replaced by a numbness.

"Your repeating things idea feels like it proves my we-died-in-a-car-crash idea," she said finally.

Prove was a strong word. Still, she had a point. "I don't want to be dead," I said.

Liv closed her eyes and breathed deep, in through her nose, out through her mouth, like she was in some New Age yoga class. Her eyes flew open. "Frank!" she said. "He's . . . he's Mom and Dad's new help."

"What?"

"At the house. He . . . he cleans the pool or something. Right?"

I stared at her. Did he?

"That's why he looked familiar to me! It's because I've seen him before!"

"When would you have seen him at the house?" It was implausible, but something about this felt right. The pool guy usually came during the day and had only been around the past month. Maybe we'd crossed paths once? Or I'd seen him from a distance, but . . . the voice. Yeah, the voice seemed totally familiar.

"That's how he knew my name!" Liv banged her hands on the steering wheel. "And he put their stuff out here to throw us off their trail!"

"And then gave us back our car? Why?"

"Um, because he's in the business of aiding and abetting people who are trying to disappear, not murdering teenagers by dehydration in the desert?"

"You think he was trying to slow us down."

"Or freak us out so bad we'd go home. And it's worked. Like, I'm *seeing* things, Jory."

Was she? Frank planting fake clues didn't account for finding this gas station three times, but maybe it was possible we'd been turned around in the dark.

"I'm going to drive," Liv said firmly. "Okay?"

"Okay."

She put the car in gear and pulled slowly out of the parking lot, checking over her shoulder as she maneuvered onto the road. That struck me as hilariously unnecessary.

Keep it together.

But there it was again: that damn sensation that things could fly apart at any moment. I gripped my hands into fists.

Focus.

Liv's explanation was at least logical. Except she'd never answered my question: When had she been at the house to see the new pool guy?

"You created your reality; live with it."

I'd said that. I remembered now. I'd said it to Liv. Recently. But when and why?

"We turned right last time," Liv said, approaching the intersection in front of the station. "I'm going straight."

"Like Frank said?"

"Yes," Liv said. "Unless you have a better idea."

My heart sped as Liv gunned it through the crossroads and approached the hills we'd been climbing around in moments ago. She guided the car carefully through them, gaze fixed on the road ahead. And then we were out and onto the straightaway. A building sat alongside the road to the left. It definitely hadn't been there before, when I was searching for Liv.

"Goddamn it," I whispered. Was I right on the verge of losing it for good? It felt like maybe I was. It felt like—

"No, look!" Liv said. "It's not the station!"

I leaned forward and peered out the window. As we approached, I could make out a tiny house with a sagging porch, and a garage beside it. It looked completely deserted, and the sight of it sent a surge of hope through me. I racked my brain for what Frank had told us. He'd talked about a ramshackle place . . .

"There's supposed to be a right turn."

Liv slowed the car. Sure enough, to our right was an intersecting road, and in both directions the highway stretched out for miles. No signs or markers. Liv looked at me. "What do you think?"

We had under half a tank of gas and no idea how far the 95 was from here. We couldn't afford to make any more mistakes. The time on the dashboard clock was 11:51 A.M. "Turn," I said. It seemed like we were headed north—the car said as much—but with the sun so high, it was hard to tell.

It occurred to me then that Frank was the only living thing

we'd seen out here. Didn't the desert have vultures or rabbits or something? Was it weird we'd seen nothing, no animal life at all, save that damn faceless cat last night?

"Jory, what I saw—"

"Heat exhaustion." I cut her off. "A mirage. Some fucking trick of the light." I couldn't go there. I wanted what she'd said about Frank to be true. My chest was sore again.

"But that girl, climbing the rock. And then finding the gas station three times. And last night after you got back into the car, I saw you—"

"We *aren't thinking straight*."

Liv must've heard the desperation in my voice because she clammed up. We drove in silence awhile. Eventually she offered me her water bottle, and I took a quick sip. Even though I must've been dehydrated, I realized I really had to pee.

"Pull over?"

Outside the AC, the heat of the desert soaked into me. I tried to hurry. Standing on the side of the vast expanse of highway didn't feel any safer than being in the car with Liv.

Silk flowers and candles in cylinders and teddy bears were piled up on the miniature church shrine. They were covered in dust—like they'd been there for some time. I scanned, looking for shade to stand in while my car sickness passed. My dad was out of the car, talking on his phone. Liv sat inside with her arms crossed, glowering straight ahead.

My mom wandered nearby. I watched her pass under the arch of the cemetery gates and head down one of the rows. An old tin shack— maybe a groundkeeper's or something—stood on this side of the gates, so I moved to its shade. My nausea started to ease.

Mom was well inside the cemetery now, standing in front of that weird little treasure mound. I watched her bend low, grasping at something. She stood, looking at her hands.

What was she doing? Praying? Over someone she didn't even know?

That was pretty funny. She didn't seem to like other people enough to do that. I watched her turn and make her way back.

"You feeling better, Jory-boy?" she asked as she passed. She swiped at her brow with a clenched fist. "Let's get this vacation started."

I got back in the car and reached over to turn the AC down from full blast—it was a bad idea to waste fuel. Fuel. If we didn't find civilization soon we were going to be in serious trouble.

Goddamn it. There was nothing for miles: not a car, not a damn sage hen in sight. And now I had another inane memory to add to my burgeoning collection.

A strange thought began to form. Maybe it was the memories that were screwing everything up, making us see things that weren't there. Maybe, when I'd found my mom's necklace, I was somehow experiencing the moment Liv had buried it in the potted cactus years ago, and it just . . . seemed like now. Maybe Liv thought Frank was wearing Dad's shoes because she was seeing something from a different moment.

"Are you okay?" Liv glanced at me.

It felt like my bones were splintering away from my muscles and tendons, my skin peeling off. I could picture myself coming apart like the enemy warriors in Cloud Dynasty when you shred them with your *jian* and they burst into pieces. In fact, this whole damn thing—the car, the desert, the heat—was starting to feel like a badly rendered RPG world. "No."

Her forehead creased. "How not-okay are you?"

"I . . ." I couldn't finish. I put my head in my hands and tried to breathe. No good. I massaged my chest with one hand, trying to rub away the burning.

"That was really impressive." Liv's voice was unnaturally

loud. I pulled my head up in confusion. "Back there." She cleared her throat. "You deadlifted me up a cliff."

I stared at her.

"Seriously. Right up the side of a cliff. Back there, in the hills. When I ran away? How did you do that?"

Oh. Conversation: she was trying to distract me. I reached for the quickest explanation. "Adrenaline."

"Still." She glanced at me again, forcing me to make eye contact. "Is that a new thing? Working out or whatever?"

"Sort of."

"Good for you," she said.

I wanted to say something sarcastic about doing it for her approval, but the sincerity in her voice stopped me. I studied her. She'd somehow pulled herself together emotionally, but she still looked like a train wreck, and the effect was so incongruent, so un-Liv, it was kind of awesome. "It's not a big deal." The tightness in my chest eased.

"You think that about everything," she said, clearly trying to keep the conversation going.

"Do I?" How would she know what I think?

"Well, you probably think getting into BU to study your rocks isn't a big deal."

"My rocks?"

"That's what you're studying, isn't it?"

"I'm taking biochem." Did she honestly think you could major in "rocks"? Whatever, I was breathing easier now.

"I thought you liked rocks."

"When I was, like, eight."

She shrugged. "Okay: biochem. That's even more of a big thing."

"It's not; it's just an actual thing." An actual thing, and

hopefully my way into a job where I didn't have to interact with idiots: a researcher for a biotech firm or something.

"Yeah, well, I probably won't even get into community."

This was news to me—such news, in fact, that I forgot all about potentially hyperventilating. I stopped gripping my T-shirt. "You want to go to college?" My sister had never expressed any interest in college whatsoever, and she'd barely passed her remedial subjects.

"I was thinking about communications?"

I tried not to gape. The thought of my sister being a professional communicator was pretty hilarious, in that three-syllable-max-vocabulary sort of way. In fact, the visual image of her at college was providing me with all kinds of ridicule fodder. Maybe she'd start a Club for People Who Want to Talk Good and Do Their Hair Good, Too.

"But . . . I don't know. I'm not smart like you."

That stopped my asshole train of thought.

"So it probably won't work out." She seemed resigned to that idea, which, for some reason, bothered me.

"How would you know?" I asked her.

"What do you mean?"

"If you're smart or not. Not like school was a priority."

"Because I wasn't smart enough for it. I've always known that. It doesn't really bug me." She shrugged like *that* was no big deal.

It was kind of infuriating. "That's bullshit."

She frowned. "What is?"

"Those damn pageants," I said. "You didn't have a chance to be smart."

"I did pageants because I wasn't going to do well in school anyway." I started to protest, but she held up a hand. "No, not just because Mom said it. I struggled. School came naturally to you." She shrugged again. "You're naturally smart; I'm not."

"You never tried."

"You don't get it. It was really hard for me."

"It's hard for everyone! I *had* to be smart," I said.

"Don't get mad again!" Liv said. "I was trying to compliment you."

"I'm not mad." And I wasn't; I was frustrated, but not at her—for her.

"Well, sometimes it's difficult to know."

"Yeah. I'm tricky like that."

This time Liv caught my irony. She smiled. Then her expression turned serious. "Did I used to know? When you were upset or happy?"

I shrugged.

"I did, didn't I?"

I stared out the windshield, glad that my chest wasn't sore anymore; Liv's powers of distraction had worked, at least for the time being. So, okay. Maybe talking wasn't the worst thing we could be doing, under the circumstances.

The heat danced off the highway that stretched out in front of us. From this perspective, it looked absolutely never-ending.

It had to end somewhere, though.

"Tell me the worst part," I said.

"The worst part of what?"

"The pageants."

Liv stared at me. "For real? You want to hear it?"

"For real."

LIV

IT SOUNDED LIKE Jory was interested, but it was so hard to tell.

But maybe it didn't matter. I was trying to keep him from losing it—the last thing I needed was Jory completely wigging out in the passenger seat—and it was working.

And I needed the distraction, too. Everything that had happened was clinging to me like a dirty second skin: our fight, me slapping him, the cliff crumbling away, seeing us in this car, remembering Frank from my parents' house—

When?

Talking wasn't the worst thing we could do.

"The truth is, that's been the hardest thing to figure out," I said, wriggling in my seat to try to reset. "Like, I look back at all the footage, and I seem so into it. And . . . I guess I was? I really thought I was doing something important."

"What changed your mind?" He still wasn't using his sarcastic tone.

"It wasn't any one thing. And maybe if other survivors hadn't reached out, online, I'd still be caught up in it."

A silence. "Because you thought you didn't have a choice?"

"I guess? Like, yes. I . . . I thought it was what I was meant to do. But my therapist says that those ideas aren't natural; they're . . ." I searched for the words she'd used. "*Suggested and reinforced* by people you trust, so you believe them. There are lots of things that were wrong, but they're hard to explain."

"Try?"

I paused. I realized that I actually wanted to tell him, but it felt like a risk because it was nothing that bad—it's not like I was abused. It *felt* wrong, which apparently is a problem when you're trying to prove something in court. So even though Sandra had heard it all and seen it all, some things hadn't been registered as part of my testimony.

"Okay, well, there's this one . . . incident. I'd been doing pageants for about a year?"

The sky was a pale, whitish blue, and the desert horizon was blurry against it. It felt like we were driving into nowhere, into nothing, and my only anchor was Jory.

"*Mr. Day is a talent scout,*" my mom said. "*That means he looks for winners.*"

"*Are you a winner, Livy?*" the man asked, smiling at me. "*Why don't you show me your walk?*"

"*But I'm going to be onstage right away.*"

"*I know,*" said Mr. Day. "*But you'll be distracted by the crowds, and I won't have a front-row seat. How about a private show?*"

"*Do your pretty feet,*" my mom said. "*Just pretend this*"—she pointed to the space between the bed and the wall—"*is the stage.*"

"*I don't feel good,*" I said to Mom.

"Livy," she reproached. "Don't go making up stories." She flashed an embarrassed smile at Mr. Day.

I walked back to the window and looked for the woman and the little girl in the rainbow shorts. They were gone.

"Maybe your mom's making you nervous," Mr. Day said. His voice was smooth, but there was a rattle in his throat. He pulled out the chair at the desk by the wall, turned it around, and sat.

My stomach churned.

My mom laughed. It sounded like she was apologizing for something. "Do you need your music?" She tapped her phone. "Here." The tinny sounds of a pop song started.

"Maybe you should wait outside?" Mr. Day said to my mom.

No. No, she couldn't leave.

"We like to see that they can perform without any coaching."

"Mom—"

"Hush, Livy." She placed her phone near the TV and reached up to undo her necklace. Busy Bee dangled from her fingers. "Just show him what you can do." She made sure I could see her set the chain beside her phone. She turned to leave.

I wanted to shout no, I wanted to run after her, but Mr. Day was staring at me, freezing me in place. The door clicked shut.

He spread his legs and leaned forward, resting his elbows on his thighs. "Go on."

After I'd done about a minute of my routine, Mr. Day left. Mom told me he clearly wasn't impressed and that it wasn't acceptable: I needed to be able to turn it on anywhere, whether I was onstage for the judges or not.

"You just ruined your chance."

When I told her I didn't like how he sat—he'd kept moving his elbows in a weird way—my mom had lost it.

"I don't care what you don't like! There are people you have to perform for whether you like them or not. There are people you'll have to work with. You don't like the other contestants, do you? But you stand onstage and smile pretty right alongside them. It's not difficult, Lavinia."

Jory was staring at me.

I drummed my fingers on the steering wheel, feeling a flush creep up my neck. "Like I said, it's hard to describe? And I know it doesn't sound that bad. It was only a minute. It's not part of my testimony because it's not like it's not common practice for talent scouts to see girls on their own, but—"

"No," Jory said. "I get it." There was something different in his tone—sadness or disappointment or something.

"You do?"

"In elementary school I had to attend special-ed classes because Mom didn't explain my syndrome to the teacher. I was put with the kids who couldn't read or do math."

I hadn't known that. "Why didn't you say anything?"

"I did."

He did. Just like I'd told my mom . . . "Well, I know my story isn't as bad as that, but—"

"No. It's fucked up, Liv."

No sarcasm. My breath caught. I drove in silence, pushing down a lump that was rising in my throat. Finally, when I could speak, I said, "I just want to hear someone say that, you know? I want to hear a judge tell them that."

Jory hadn't stopped looking at me.

"The other survivors say it helps." I cleared my throat. "It makes it real."

"You mean Asia."

I stared straight ahead. "And others."

"Liv," Jory said. "I don't care who you're into."

My stomach dropped to my ballet flats. I squinted at the road, pretending the sun was blinding me. I should've corrected him; I wanted to, but I couldn't get the words out.

It was good that Jory was so accepting, I guess? Like, if I were into Asia, at least he wouldn't be all judgy about it like Mom would've been.

In one of the *Divas* episodes, after we'd been to the wig-maker's place, Mr. Anton's, the TV camera crew had asked Mom about her religious beliefs and about what she thought of Mr. Anton, who I realized much later was gay. Sandra says they were showing how hypocritical she was: the producers knew Mom didn't think gay people were God's people, but she was only too happy to go to the "best wigmaker in Vegas" if it got me a better shot at a crown.

"I try not to think about it. The good Lord will judge Mr. Anton at the end of the day."

I'd seen the clip a dozen times.

But I didn't care what my mom believed—not anymore. Asia was someone I wanted to be around all the time, but that didn't mean that I was "into her."

Did it?

I pointed at an object in the distance. "Hey! Is that a road sign?" Not like Jory could see it better, but I needed to say something. I slowed as we reached it, and his statement left my thoughts completely. "It says a town called Mina is twenty miles away!"

"What?" Jory said. "That makes no sense."

"Why?" I checked my phone—still not powering up. How was that possible? I threw it down in disgust.

"Mina is outside Hawthorne, the town closest to Walker Lake. We were south of Tonopah when we got lost. That's a hundred miles from Walker Lake."

"Maybe it's a different Mina? Or maybe we took a shortcut."

He tilted his head at me.

"Okay, no. Never mind. Let's not even go there. Besides, this is good, right? I mean, if it's the Mina you're thinking of, we'll be back on the 95 in like a half hour! And even if it's not, there are probably phones there."

"You're going to call?" Jory sounded surprised.

"I'm totally going to call!" I said. "There's a creepy, car-stealing hillbilly after us."

"Not convinced that's what happened back there."

"Well, whatever. We're in over our heads. And I didn't mean for this to happen, Jore. I just . . . I wanted it so bad. I wanted to find them." I took a deep breath. "But maybe I *was* trying to prove something."

Jory was quiet. Then he said, "Don't go all 'God is punishing me' on me again."

I studied him. He wasn't mocking me; he was making a joke. Okay, well: "Or what?" I said. "You'll take away my designer jeans?"

"Jesus," Jory said, shaking his head, but I could tell he was amused, not annoyed. "If you get us out of here, I'll buy you some damn designer jeans."

"Okay then!" I banged the steering wheel triumphantly and accelerated. The thought of not being lost in the flipping desert was making me giddy. "Mina, here we come! Take that, hillbillies and disappearing SUVs!"

Jory shook his head. I grinned. "We are badass!" Jory hiccupped. I glanced at him. No, he'd laughed. "So badass." I did the Brush Your Shoulders dance move, switching hands on the steering wheel. "They should write a song about us."

He hiccup-laughed again.

"Or . . . a rap! Wait—" I held up a hand. "It's coming to me, here it comes . . ." I nodded my head in time to the beat I was imagining. "Gather round and listen to this riff," I rapped. "Jory saved his sister from falling off a cliff." I petered out, trying to think of more words that rhymed with *cliff*.

"That's awful."

"Awful or awesome?" I bounced in my seat. "We need tunes." I turned on the radio before remembering we were out of range. A voice blared on, making both of us jump:

"*—information about the Brewers' whereabouts are asked to contact local authorities. And now for a look at our short-range forecast, we go to meteorologist Claire Dansby. Claire?*"

The meteorologist's voice chimed in with the usual weather report: sunny, hot, dry. I forgot about finding music and turned it down. "So," I said.

"Yeah," Jory said, but something in his tone made me look over at him.

"What is it?"

"Just . . . it's weird that we keep hearing it."

"It is?"

"Well, we skip around the stations, right? They're *all* broadcasting an APB about Mom and Dad?"

I shrugged. "Maybe?"

Jory shook his head. "It's weird."

"As weird as this?" I said, doing a pop and lock with my right arm. It wasn't enough to distract him though, I could tell.

I let my arm hang from my bent elbow.

It wasn't enough to distract me either.

"Turn up the AC!" I tried to move away from Jory. We'd been in the backseat forever and the gravel road was so bumpy it was jostling us together.

"The AC's up," my mom said from the front seat. She put down her hairstyle magazine and squirted lilac hand cream onto the backs of her hands, then rubbed them together. "Lord, but the road is bad this summer." She looked at my dad. "You should contact the county."

He grunted from the driver's seat. "You should contact a Realtor." He braked, swerving to avoid a pothole. The movement forced Jory and me to bump shoulders. My purse slid off the seat and dumped onto the floor mats.

"Get on your side!" I hissed, shoving him. "Look what you did." I bent down to pick up the contents: a mirror, two different lip glosses, a brush, and some Tic Tacs.

Jory was staring at me. Like always.

"What?" I demanded, shoving my things back in my purse, not expecting him to answer. He never answered anymore. My dad said it was his way of getting attention. Like a few minutes before when he'd kicked up a fuss about feeling carsick. Dad was mad, because we'd stopped in town and Jory had refused to get out at the gas station and get fresh air. Then, as we were going past an old cemetery, he'd decided he couldn't be in the car anymore. He was so weird.

The car lurched again. "Honestly, Brenda. This place is a shit hole. It's deadweight. We should light it up and collect the insurance."

My mom turned around. "Livy, did you bring that swimsuit I bought you? The red one?"

I nodded.

"Good. We're going to take a few candids on the beach tomorrow."

My dad snorted. "That toxic shore?" He looked down at his phone. "Perfect," he said. "Still no reception up here. I'm going to have to drive back to Hawthorne tomorrow morning—a shipment's coming in."

"Mmm-hmm," Mom murmured. She was flipping through the magazine again. "Ooh, Livy—look at this one." She held up a picture of a woman with curly ponytails, dressed in a half shirt, with her tummy showing. "That'll be perfect. And I've got a little surprise for you, too. A little bling for your outfit."

My dad's head snapped toward her. "What did you buy now?"

"I didn't buy anything."

"You better not have. These pageants are sucking me dry."

"What do I do?" Jory asked.

My mom turned again. "What do you mean? When?"

"Tomorrow."

There was a silence. "Didn't you bring your books?" my mom asked. "Your rock books? There are rocks on the shore you can look for."

My dad laughed. "How's that for a good time?" He shook his head. "Go hang out with some rocks."

Jory shrugged. "I like rocks." The car jostled us again.

I wrinkled my nose. "How can you like rocks?"

"Now, Livy," my mom said. "A diamond's a rock."

"Diamonds are pretty," I said. "Jory likes the boring ones. The ones that sit there and don't sparkle or anything. What good are they?"

"They don't talk back," Jory said.

My dad laughed. I gave Jory my fiercest look. "Shut your mouth," I hissed.

Jory turned and looked out the window.

JORY

WE'D LEFT THE abandoned gas station long ago, and Liv's phone still wasn't charging. I blew on its port, wiggled the cord, and checked the USB connection on the dash. "I don't know," I said, giving up.

"There'll be phones in Mina," Liv said.

"Who are you going to call?"

"Ghostbusters."

God, she was punchy. Possibly dehydrated. "Seriously," I said.

She sighed. "I guess Sandra." She glanced at me. "I mean, first. I'll definitely call her. I guess I'll call her first." She looked like she wanted to say something more.

"What is it?"

"Okay. You know, when we were walking back to the car, I started wondering how far I'd go to find Mom and Dad. Or, you know, to see my lawsuit through. Like, it's obviously not worth falling off a cliff or dying of thirst in the desert, and I didn't mean for you to get caught up in it. Like, if I'd known . . ." She chewed her upper lip. "And . . ."

"And?"

"And then after I thought that, we somehow got unlost. It's pretty . . . coincidental, don't you think?"

"You said Frank gave us back the car because teen homicide wasn't his jam."

"Well, that's what I thought at first. But I've been rethinking it, and now I'm not so sure. It feels like something I did, or thought, changed things."

We were nearing a major road—definitely the 95. As Liv coasted to a stop, I read the sign on our side of the road. It pointed left toward Mina—half a mile—and right toward Coaldale, twenty-five miles. Coaldale was in the direction of Vegas. Liv looked at me.

"We need gas," I said. "And I'm going to eat my backpack pretty soon."

Liv turned left, north, onto the 95. I was relieved to see an oncoming car, and then another. It wasn't a busy stretch of the highway, but there were people around at least. We were back to civilization—sort of. Still, I looked closely at the oncoming cars, making sure they had actual drivers. It was crazy, maybe, but it had been a weird night.

"Something I did, or thought, changed things." Liv was clearly feeling responsible, which should have made me feel vindicated. For some reason, it didn't. I told her I blamed her for all this, but now that she was blaming herself, I couldn't bring myself to rub her face in it. Even if that idea—that a choice she had made, that we had made, had altered things—was resonating in an uncomfortable way.

I stared out the window as we drove into "town," which was

about four stores and a trailer court. Oh, and a brothel, of course. Skeletal trees dotted the town, and the dwellings were sad and run-down, with vehicle graveyards instead of front yards.

"I'm going to guess there's probably not a Starbucks here," Liv said.

"God," I muttered. "What do people even *do* here?"

"Sell gas, I hope," Liv said. "Oh, there!" She pointed to a square sign in the distance. "I think that's a station."

"Hallelujah." I slumped back into my seat.

The station was decrepit—peeling paint and weathered tin. As we approached, it occurred to me that we hadn't seen any people, and for a terrible half moment, I suspected Mina was another creepy Pussy Cats scenario. But as we pulled up to the pumps, I spotted a neon OPEN sign illuminated in the window. An AC unit whirred away, and a woman with round glasses peered out at us from above it.

"I'll pump," I offered.

Outside, the air was dense—the way it gets before it rains. The sky was cloudless, though, so I decided Mina must be in a valley of some kind. After I filled the tank, I opened the door to grab my wallet, but Liv stopped me.

"I'll pay," she said. "And I'll see if there's a phone."

"I'll come with."

"No, stay here. Remember what happened the last time we left the car?"

I studied her. Liv had never been that good at lying. "You'll phone Sandra?"

"Cross my heart."

I reached in, across the passenger side, and pulled the keys from the ignition. "Safekeeping," I said. "I want details."

Liv nodded. "I promise."

I got back in the car and watched her disappear inside the mini-mart. She approached the clerk at the counter and talked for several seconds, then turned and walked to the washroom at the back of the store. I was reminded of how dumb it was that she'd refused to pee along the deserted roadside. Was that a girl thing? Or an ex–beauty queen thing?

Hurry up.

She disappeared into the washroom. Several minutes later she reappeared but stopped at a tall, white box and fiddled with her wallet. I realized the box was an ATM, which made me feel better; any place with an ATM would have a phone. She was likely procrastinating making the call, and I couldn't totally blame her. Her lapdog lawyer was going to be pissed, but . . . well, at least this ill-fated road trip would be over. I mean, we still had to drive home, but I was going to make sure there were no accidental detours. Maybe her lawyer would even drive out and escort us back.

Liv would die of embarrassment. Her Queen Survivor crown would be revoked for sure, but again: not my problem.

Was it?

Why was I even asking myself that? This trip had been one impossibly screwed-up thing after the other, and we were lucky we hadn't perished out here after a series of questionable decisions. Besides, if there was an explanation for all the weirdness, we wouldn't find it at Walker Lake.

Liv was wandering around the store now, a little zombielike. God. I really should've gone in with her.

I waited until she was finally at the counter again and the clerk was passing her the phone before I put the keys back in the ignition and turned on the AC. The radio was still on.

"Reno PD have been called in to help with a case of arson in

Mineral County, as a recent discovery has turned it into a potential criminal investigation. Bones were uncovered in the wreckage of a burnt lakefront property, discovered by a local man during his walk. Police did not confirm whether or not the remains are human; the investigation is ongoing. In local news, LVPD are asking for the public's help in locating two people who disappeared from the Clark County area Friday—" The radio crackled and fuzzed into static. What the hell was up with radio stations out here? I waited, trying to will the announcer's voice back. *"—a gold necklace with a letter P pendant, and blond hair. Anyone with information about the Brewers' whereabouts is asked to contact local authorities. And now for a look at our short-range forecast—"*

Liv opened the door, slid back into the car, and dumped a ton of junk food into the console: potato rings, Twizzlers, Swedish Fish, two mega Oh Henry! bars, a can of soda, Pop Rocks. Seriously? The sight of it jarred my train of thought. This couldn't be typical beauty queen fare, even ex–beauty queen. Hey—there was even a package of chewable Rolaids.

I held them up, ready to make a dig at her for becoming my dealer, but then noticed her ashen, freshly scrubbed face. "What's wrong?"

"The clerk wouldn't let me use the phone without paying," she said, her voice strangely pitched. "Five bucks for a long-distance call. So I went to the ATM to get cash." She held out a white slip of paper.

I took it from her fingers and unfolded it. "What's this?"

"My bank statement."

I peered at the small type, scanning for the balance.

$667,821.09

Holy shit. I glanced up at Liv. "Is this for real?"

She swallowed. "I think so?"

"How can you have more than half a million dollars in your account?" I stared at the paper again. "It has to be a mistake."

"I called the bank," she said. "The depositor was undisclosed."

I stared at the paper. "You called the bank," I repeated. "Not Sandra?"

"I wanted to show you first!" she said.

"Why?"

"Well, I was trying to stay calm, so I started shopping"—she gestured to the pile of junk—"and then I started thinking: What if this is Mom and Dad paying me off? What if they disappeared and put that money in my account so I don't go looking for them?"

"It's not the full amount you're suing for, is it?"

"It's over half, but that's what I would've ended up with after lawyer fees and whatnot." She didn't look angry; she looked sick. I'd always known the lawsuit wasn't about the money for Liv, though I was beginning to understand her motives on a different level. Still, her reaction seemed a bit over-the-top.

"Where would they even get that kind of cash?" I asked. "I thought your earnings were held in trust. I thought that was what the lawsuit was going to unlock."

"They are. It was," Liv said.

"There's no way Mom and Dad had that lying around." The more I thought about my dad's behavior this past year, the more I was sure that he was in financial trouble.

"Maybe he borrowed it," Liv said, although she didn't sound convinced.

"I doubt he could find a lender. Unless it was a shark."

"I know." Liv hesitated, then: "Sandra said Par-T-Own was in serious debt."

Not surprising. "Too many bottles of Jack, I guess."

We were quiet a moment.

"Jory," Liv said softly. "I think part of it is your college money."

I froze. My college fund was about half that.

"It's the only thing I can think of."

No. There was no way.

"Like, I'd say it's unbelievable, except . . . is it?" Liv shook her head. Then she sat up straight. "I'm going to call Sandra. I'm going to tell her everything, and then we're driving back to Vegas, and I am giving this money back."

I stared at the dash, feeling numb. No—numb wasn't the word: *detached*. "You really think they drained my college account?"

"Well, is there any way you could check?"

I shook my head. My bank card wasn't linked to my college fund for a reason—there was no way I could touch it without my parents' consent. So it was entirely possible that they'd thought I wouldn't notice for a month or more—not like Liv and I had been on speaking terms lately.

"When was it deposited?" I asked.

"Yesterday afternoon."

"From where?"

"That's all the guy would tell me. He said they needed my account cosigner on the line to discuss anything further."

"Mom."

Liv nodded. She reached over and touched my arm.

Jesus. Was this really happening? Would they actually destroy my college plans to avoid taking responsibility for their shitty parenthood? It was like the penultimate irony. That panicky feeling from before was back, and with it, a growing anger.

"My college fund wouldn't be enough," I said. There had to be a different explanation. Where else could they get that much money?

I tried counting down from ten, but it was useless. Rage was sweeping up inside me, hot and bright, and that, combined with a persistent crackling noise, was making it difficult to think.

The radio. It was hissing. I stared at it, fighting the urge to put my fist through the dash. Like she was reading my mind, Liv reached over and turned the radio off. And I remembered looking at it moments ago, when she'd returned to the car. I'd been thinking something about that APB . . .

"Reno PD have been called in to help with a case of arson in Mineral County."

I stared at Liv, my mind racing.

"It's never-ending deadweight," my dad said into his phone, drink in his other hand. I stood in the doorway, unnoticed. "But I still want to double it to at least a half mil. Who knows? We might get lucky and lightning will strike it."

"Insurance money," I blurted out. I sat up straighter in my seat.

"What?"

"The cabin." Yeah. This felt right. The anger was still there, but it was muted by a surge of excitement that I was onto something.

Liv frowned. "Explain?"

"There's been an arson in Mineral County. A property burned down."

Liv looked at me blankly.

"*This* is Mineral County. Walker Lake is in Mineral County."

Her forehead creased. "You think they burned down the cabin and collected the insurance money?"

"Would you put that past them? It couldn't be sold."

"But how do you know this?"

"The radio. It's been playing in front of the APB about their disappearance."

Her frown deepened. "I haven't heard it."

"Well, I just did! There's been an arson at a lakefront property. It can't be a coincidence."

"But . . ." Liv chewed her lip. "Doesn't it take a long time to get money after a fire? The insurance people send out . . . what are they called—the people who decide what happened and whether you get to claim insurance? They would've had to burn it down a long time ago. It would hardly be news now."

Shit. I hadn't thought of that. "Well, maybe they did, and the media was slow to report . . ." Liv looked at me skeptically. "I don't know!" I said in exasperation. "It's a feeling I have." It shouldn't have mattered how they got the money, but it did. Even if I didn't want anything to do with my parents, I didn't want them to have sold me out. That idea felt like a little death.

Death.

"Remains," I remembered.

"What?"

"The radio talked about remains being found at the burned property. So maybe *that's* why it's on the news now—"

"Slow down," Liv pleaded, holding up a hand.

"It's on the news because the adjuster found human remains."

"Okay, first, ew? And second, it still seems pretty quick for a payout."

But my dad always had ways of getting what he wanted, skipping the line, fast-tracking his profits. And the more I thought about it, the more it seemed to make sense. I'd gotten my tattoo three months ago; I'd overheard him talking about the cabin when I'd brought him the consent form the day before. Liv's lawsuit had long been filed, and the evidence looked overwhelmingly in her favor. It was the exact kind of thing my dad would think of to protect his own interests.

My mind raced. "He could've borrowed the money, sure that he'd be able to pay himself back with the insurance claim." That was definitely something he would do. Yeah. I was totally onto something.

Liv considered this. Nodded. "Okay, but . . . if what you think is actually what happened, there's only one way to find out."

Damn straight there was only one way. "Let's go." I knew it wasn't a great idea. Heading back to Vegas with everything we knew, telling the authorities—that was a better one. But . . .

"I can call Sandra first," she offered. "Tell her where we are, at least."

"No, don't." The panic was dissipating and the energy of it was focusing into a single intent. I hated that I cared, but I couldn't help it: I needed the truth. "You can call after. When we know."

"Are you sure? It might be dangerous."

"That money is in your account for a reason," I pointed out. "They wouldn't expect us to go this far." Because they'd always underestimated us. Because they'd always sold us short.

"Are you sure? I'm only going to go if you're okay with it a hundred and ten percent."

I curbed a smartass comment about her impossible math. "I'm sure."

"But—"

"Liv!" I caught myself and softened my voice. "Let's see what's what. Then you can call."

Liv searched my face. "Okay." She started the car. Then she drew her shoulders back and sat tall. "We're doing this."

I clicked my seat belt. "We're doing this."

LIV

HAWTHORNE WAS BIGGER than Mina, and it seemed like people actually lived here. That should've made me feel better, but I was too on edge to care. The entire half-hour drive I'd been trying to talk myself down. I ate most of the junk I'd bought—except for the Pop Rocks—as a way to distract myself, but all that did was make me feel sick.

A part of me had really wanted to call Sandra from the gas station. Honestly, a part of me wanted to turn the car around and drive home. I couldn't wrap my head around what Jory had been talking about—about all this having happened already—which is why I didn't tell him about what happened at the ATM. I didn't mention that a second before I got my bank statement, I'd known what it was going to say. Not the exact number, but a big sum—kind of like I'd already seen it.

Just thinking about it made me want to panic.

I didn't want what Jory said to be true: not this happening before, and not the cabin being burned down. Because if it was like I thought, if my parents *were* at the cabin and had somehow orchestrated all this craziness to try to keep me from finding them—how amazing would it be to make them pay for that? They'd gone to such lengths to make me fail, and I still wasn't broken.

Getting to the cabin would prove it to everyone, to myself.

But I was scared, which was another thing I didn't tell Jory.

I crawled the car along, looking for something I might recognize. I was pretty sure there used to be a corner store with an oval sign along the highway somewhere and that the road to the cabin property was near it. But the only building with a separate sign we saw was when we hit the town limits—a gas station with a tall square sign and no roads going anywhere from it but into town.

"We'll have to ask someone," Jory said as I came to a four-way stop in the "downtown." A diner with a sagging porch and a metal sign that read EXTRAORDINARY TREATS sat on the corner opposite us. He pointed. "I could eat something semi-real."

I was too nauseated to eat. And drawing attention to ourselves by hanging out at a restaurant didn't seem like a good idea, but I also didn't have a better one.

I pulled over.

Inside, the diner was clean but shabby, with old space and alien movie posters tacked to the walls. A sign beside an old pedestal gumball machine said BEAM YOURSELF UP, which I guess meant "Seat yourself."

An old man nursing a coffee at the counter glanced our way. He gave Jory a hard stare, then looked me up and down. Unease gripped me, and with it, a spark of anger. I breathed deep and redirected, forcing myself to notice that the curtains had little spaceships on them.

We slid into a window booth that had UFO-shaped menus tacked under the plastic tablecloth. The man at the counter was still looking at us. I squinted at the UFO, trying to ignore him and the bit of darkness that was crowding into my mind.

"What'll it be?" Jory asked. "Saturn rings? Probes?"

"Probes? Seriously?"

"I think they're fries."

"Hi." The waitress appeared. She was wearing a black shirt with ET silkscreened on it, a name tag that said PATRICIA, and a headband with little sparkly balls on springs that bobbed when she moved her mane of red hair. "Can I get you something to drink?" And then she got a good look at Jory. I could tell because she glanced down right away, took her pad and pencil out of her apron, and started chewing her gum faster.

"Coffee."

Jory was still studying the menu.

"And what about him?"

I tilted my head. "Not sure. Hey, *him*." Jory glanced up. The waitress shifted. That black cloud was hovering close, I could feel it.

He drummed his fingers on the menu, deciding. "Number Five Is Alive," he said.

The waitress paused and looked at me. I stared back.

"Number Five Is Alive combo," Jory said again.

"Combo five?" she repeated, still looking at me.

"Yeah," Jory answered.

She scribbled on her pad like she'd actually need to write it down to remember.

"And just the coffee?" she asked me.

I glanced at the menu. "The combo comes with a soda, right?"

"Yeah. Did you want one?"

"No. I want you to ask my brother what kind of soda he'd like." The inside of my head felt fuzzy.

"Well, most people order Pepsi, so . . ." She cleared her throat and looked at Jory. "Do you want Pepsi?"

I looked at the spaceships on the curtain again. *Don't.*

"Sure," Jory said.

She left. The man at the counter had watched the entire exchange. He'd been watching with his stupid piggish eyes and—

"—eating?"

I pulled my gaze to Jory. "What?"

"You aren't eating?"

"No." I shook my head, trying to ignore the geezer but unable to keep myself from glancing over at him. He'd turned around, but I knew he was exchanging a look with the waitress. I pictured myself grabbing the back of his head and slamming his stupid face down on the counter so hard—

"Weren't you going to ask about the cabin?" Jory asked.

Right. But now I couldn't imagine asking that waitress for anything. All I could imagine was taking her stupid pencil and stabbing it through her—

Redirect.

"Are you having second thoughts?" Jory asked.

"No. Are you?" Jory shook his head in answer, but something about it looked a little unsure. *Sugar.* I looked out the window, at a woman and a child who were walking a little white dog on the opposite side of the street. They were going slowly, letting the dog stop and sniff everything. Something about staring at them through a streaked pane of glass felt familiar. Like I'd seen it before, but not here. I'd never choose to be in this sad excuse for a—

"I'll be right back."

I banged out the diner door, inhaling the dry air. Okay, that was a fail in there. Part of my recovery meant rejecting my old coping methods and choosing new ones; I shouldn't have to physically remove myself from a situation.

But I was off my game. This ATM business and carjacking-hillbilly scene was messing me up. I tried to smooth my hair back from my face.

"Hold your hair outta the way," my mom instructed, fiddling with the little gold chain. It glinted in the sun. Out on the pier, my dad was standing with a glass in his hand.

I pulled my curly ponytails to the side and looked down at my strawberry-red two-piece as she put my new necklace on. My suit had a band of ruffles along the top, which Mom called "very Bridget Bar-doe," whoever that was. When she was doing my hair, she'd called me Daisy Duke. And now . . .

"Ow!" The pendant was hot against my skin. It must've been sitting in the sun.

My mom ignored me, clasping it at the back. "There," she said. "Princess Liv."

"Where'd you get it?"

"Oh, just somewhere. I spotted it and thought it would be absolutely perfect." She picked up her camera. "Okay, let's see. We need the lake in the background."

I looked behind me. Jory was standing near the water. "Jory!" I yelled. "Get out of the picture!"

I caught up to the woman and little girl halfway down the sidewalk. "Excuse me!"

The woman turned. She was older than she'd seemed through the window—maybe forty. Her hair had an inch of gray roots, and she was wearing a nylon tracksuit. The little girl holding the white terrier's leash was wearing rainbow-striped shorts.

Those rainbow shorts were so familiar.

"Hi," I said, then stumbled for something else to say.

"Hello." The woman was holding a cigarette with about a mile of ash on the end. The little girl let the dog sniff the curb and peered at me from under her eyelashes. "Say hi," she instructed the girl. "Don't you look at the person who's talking to you?"

My stomach twisted. Maybe I was hungrier than I thought. "Uh. I'm not from here, and I'm looking for this place. A cabin property? It might have . . . burned down?"

"You're looking for a place that burnt?"

"Maybe? I don't know."

"You don't know." The woman raised an eyebrow.

"Well, I think it might have burned down. Do you . . . know of any fires around here recently?"

The woman looked me up and down, and I was suddenly aware of how awful I looked: dirt-stained blouse and blazer, dusty jeans, stringy hair, and no makeup. I tried to stand up straight. "Like, in the last week?"

The little girl spoke up. "I heard a siren."

"Really?"

The woman rolled her eyes. "She hears all kinds of things." The ash fell from her cigarette onto the sidewalk between us. "I don't know about any fire."

"It was a loud siren," the little girl said.

"That's enough," the woman said. "Don't go making up stories."

Suddenly I could see it: my hand ripping the cigarette from the woman's mouth and stomping on it. *Dang.* I couldn't have "problematic thoughts" right now. I pressed on. "Are there any lake properties around here? Ones you can get to from a road off the main highway?"

The woman took a drag of her cigarette. She looked completely disinterested in me, as if she had something important to do in the middle of this stupid town and I was holding her up.

"Sticks," the little girl said. "Road."

"Sticks Road?" I asked.

The woman shrugged. "Maybe. It's north out of town. I think it used to lead to some cabins." She flicked ash. "'Course, all them properties haven't been used since the lake up and died."

My heart sped. "Can you tell me where it is?"

"Not even sure that road is passable anymore. Not like the county's maintained it."

"Okay, but—"

"There's a haunted house," the little girl said.

"Shush," the woman said.

"A haunted house?"

"She means an abandoned building—maybe it was a store at one time, I don't know. Sticks Road is behind it."

Just like I remembered. "And the road goes to the lake?"

The little girl nodded enthusiastically; the woman took another drag of her cigarette.

"Is the road obvious? Like . . . we'll be able to see it?"

"I suppose," she said. "Depends on how bad you want to, probably." She had a strange way of answering. "Just don't miss the turn at the ramshackle place five miles up this road." The girl went to speak, but the woman put her hand up, cutting her off. She threw the girl a warning look.

I suddenly didn't want to talk anymore. I was the reason the little girl was getting into trouble. "Okay. Thanks." I turned away to return to the diner. Halfway across the street, I looked back.

The two were walking away, but the little girl was looking over her shoulder, too.

A few clouds were gathering in the west behind them—light, fluffy, and white. Like that dog. That dog. Those rainbow shorts . . .

I'd seen them before. They'd been outside the hotel room that time Mr. Day came to "look at me"; I'd seen them from the window.

Except it couldn't be them. That was almost ten years ago, and I was probably remembering it wrong. Or maybe I was remembering it right and the memory was, like, affecting me and what I thought I was looking at?

"Don't go making up stories."

The little girl turned around and continued down the sidewalk. That bit of darkness was edging back into my mind. *Redirect.* I needed to focus on getting to the cabin. We were so close.

My coffee was waiting for me, and as I slid into my seat the waitress brought Jory's order. I stared at the steam from my cup to give him some privacy while he ate, and breathed deep, trying to think about the positive. I was right about the way to the cabin, and I was starting to remember being there, too. That was good, wasn't it?

I glanced up at Jory, who was halfway finished with his meal. He was losing some of the fries out of the corner of his mouth as he ate and using a napkin to try to catch the bits.

"Refill?" The waitress was suddenly beside our table with the coffeepot. She was asking me but staring openly at Jory. The coffeepot hung from her hand like an afterthought. She chewed her gum furiously.

"Were you asking me?" I asked.

"Yeah." But her gaze was still on Jory. "Did you want more?"

"More what?"

"Huh?"

"I said, more what?" That forced her to look at me.

"Coffee." She gestured with the pot like it was obvious.

"Oh, *coffee*. I couldn't really tell what you were asking because you weren't looking at me. You know, you should really look at the person you're talking to. Basic customer service. Like, the most basic."

She frowned. "I just wanted to know if you want more coffee."

"Well, I don't. What I *do* want, *Patricia*, is for you to leave us the flip alone until we're ready for the bill."

"What?" Her mouth hung open. I could see her stupid gum in her back teeth.

"Actually, here." I opened my wallet and grabbed a twenty. "Keep the change." I waved it at her. "Begone."

She snapped her mouth shut and took the bill, tucking it into her apron and giving me a look she probably thought was withering, then headed back into the kitchen. I almost laughed; she didn't know withering looks. Get her backstage with eleven other beauty queens vying for Ultimate Grand Supreme and she'd know.

Oh. Now Jory was staring at me. "'Begone'?" he asked.

"Her headband was annoying me." I shrugged, but my anger was back, working its way through everything, down my throat, into my stomach. The techniques I'd learned to manage it weren't working. We needed to get out of here. I pushed my cup away. "This coffee is freaking terrible. Are you almost done?"

He picked up the burger on his plate. "I'll take it to go."

I tossed my hair behind my shoulder, trying to look calm. "Then let's blow this dumpster fire."

We stood and headed for the door.

"Beauty queen!"

I spun around. The waitress was standing at the entrance to the kitchen. One hand held the swinging door open; the other hand held a smartphone. "You're Princess Liv," she said triumphantly, waving the phone. The man at the counter turned around, his little piggy eyes roaming all over me. I froze, unsure if I should deny it or leave or—

"I wondered if it was you, but the bitch fit clinched it." She crossed her arms, leaning against the door. "You know, you look like shit in person."

The man snorted, amused. I flushed bright red. I did look like shit. All of a sudden, I wanted to disappear—sink through the floor or, better yet, turn and run—but I couldn't. I was stuck there, in their gaze. And they were right about me.

"Guess airbrushing really can fix anything."

The man's amused face and the woman's satisfied smirk grew bigger and bigger, and a jumble of voices started in my head—a soft buzzing that grew in volume.

EatYourCakePrettyFeetDoesn'tMatterIfYouDon'tLikeIt.

"Don't they teach manners in beauty school?" The waitress's voice was dulled, far away. The voices became a loud hum, drowning out the sounds of the diner.

Don'tGoMakingUpStoriesPrincessLiv.

The waitress was speaking again, but it sounded like she was underwater. The darkness hanging at the edge of my mind pushed forward, competing with the voices for space.

KillYourselfYouHorrorShow.

Jory stepped in front of me. A muffled "Fuck you." And then he had my arm and was turning me, guiding me toward the door. The waitress's voice was shrill behind us, like someone speaking on an unadjusted microphone, but one word cut through the tangle of sound in my head: "freak."

The voices stopped.

Jory continued, pushing open the diner door, but I turned on my heel.

"What did you say?"

She unfolded her arms, looking less sure, but her voice was cutting. "I said, I see you've moved from pageants to freak shows."

The dark cloud rushed back, boiling up under my skin. My hand reached out for something—anything—and landed on a glass ashtray on the nearest table. I picked it up. The weight of it was solid, reassuring.

"You want a show?" I whispered.

The dark was pushing at me from the inside, tearing at me. I had to let it out or it would swallow me whole.

"Liv—" Jory said.

I pulled my arm back and whipped the ashtray at the counter, aiming for the man. It smashed spectacularly against the skirt of the counter beside his leg, and he jumped, nearly falling off his stool. Shards flew everywhere—small crystals, like breakaway glass.

"Liv!" Jory's hand was on my arm now.

"You want a show?" I screamed, pulling out of Jory's grasp. I spotted the gumball machine and lunged for it, grabbing its

square glass body with both hands and pulling it with all my might. It tipped, teetered on its round base, then fell with an ear-splitting crash to the diner floor. A rainbow of gumballs broke free in a wave, spilling across the entry of the diner and toward the tables and chairs.

The waitress's face went a ridiculous beet color. "You spoiled bitch!"

The man at the counter pushed himself to standing. "You kids'll have to pay for that—"

But Jory was stiff-arming me out the door—Geez Murphy, he was strong—and I set my sights on our car across the street, letting him pull me into a run.

SPATTERING HER
ALABASTER
SKIN

JORY

I DOVE FOR the passenger seat like some perp in a B-movie crime scene, flinging the half-eaten burger onto the sidewalk behind me. Liv slammed her door and started the car. Then she sat there, her face pale and her eyes glassy.

"Drive," I urged her, "before they take down our license plate."

There was a slim chance of either the waitress or the old dude navigating that sea of million-year-old gumballs to chase after us in time, but I needed to snap my sister out of whatever this was. Goddamn. That rage. I hadn't seen Liv like that in years.

She threw the car into gear and pulled onto the street with a jerk, squawking the tires and inadvertently continuing the B-movie scene I had rolling through my head.

"Jesus." I knew Liv had been annoyed with the idiot waitress, but I hadn't anticipated that kind of dramatic exit. Honestly, I was sort of in awe. Was it cathartic, unleashing like that? It looked more satisfying than a Sixty-Day Shred, that's for damn sure.

We were barely through the four-way stop when a furry shape darted across the street. Liv swerved violently, but there was a muffled thump.

A cat. Had we hit it?

I could tell by the look on Liv's face we had, but she didn't slow. We ripped along the main street, past a dollar store, another gas station, and a sad-looking grocery store. To the west, dark clouds were crowding in over the few low buildings. Liv was gripping the steering wheel like a younger, blonder Cruella de Vil.

There was a moment in the diner I'd almost reneged on all this. Food in my stomach had given me some clarity of thought, and heading to the cabin to make sure it was burned to the ground seemed like a less than stellar plan. But after Liv's display, it would've been a super-dick move to pull the rug out from under her feet. She was sure our parents were there. Better to just . . . make sure she didn't get hurt. "Um, do you know where we're going?"

"Oh, I know all right," Liv muttered, accelerating as we reached the town limits. We tore past a row of trailers. "I remember."

The exact route to the cabin? Impossible. "What do you remember?"

Liv faltered, easing up on the gas. She frowned, like she was confused, and we slowed to just under Guaranteed Fiery Crash velocity. "I remember that pageant."

"What?"

She chewed her lip, eyes fixed on the road. "The cemetery," she said.

"Uh—" Shit. She wasn't making sense. But then I noticed we were approaching something on the right. I stared hard out the window. Rows of stone markers were coming into view, standing in a crooked formation. We passed a wrought-iron arch that fronted the site, which was fenced with barbed wire.

My mom turned and made her way back through the cemetery.

"You feeling better, Jory-boy?" she asked as she huffed her way past me. She swiped at her brow with a clenched fist. "Let's get this vacation started." She let out a high-pitched laugh, like she was nervous.

I stared at the shrine. Above the mound of items, little yellow flags were attached to the roof, unmoving. I glanced back. It looked like my dad was still on his phone, because he was pacing with his head down. My mom was halfway to the car.

I turned and passed under the arch, making my way to the miniature church. When I got within a few feet, I could see a picture of a little girl among the mounds of stuff. She was maybe four, with dark curly hair, a pink dress, and a gold necklace. On the bottom of the wooden frame the name CICI was written in silver pen. Plastic rosaries were hung on its corner. There were a few things tucked in and around the mound of teddies: a jewelry box with a faded rose on the top, a leather purse, a little china dog. Cici's things, I guessed.

Was this what my mom had been looking at?

Weird.

I looked closer at the picture. Maybe the girl was a beauty pageant kid, like Liv. Maybe that was why Mom had acted so weird.

Tucked between a teddy bear and vase of silk flowers was a printed card with the same picture of her on it, only smaller—from her service or something. I leaned forward, squinting. NUESTRO ANGEL: PATRICIA DIEZ.

I turned and headed back to the car.

I thought I could see that little church-shrine thing from

here. It looked bare now, except for the flags. Nobody in the Diez family had died recently—

Patricia. That was the name of the waitress at the diner, wasn't it?

Weird, but hardly important. The important thing was that it seemed like we were on the right track, even if Liv still looked a bit unstable.

"What are we looking for?" I asked her. "Is there a landmark, or—"

"A haunted house."

"A haunted house."

"That's what the little girl said, and I believe her."

Maybe questions weren't a good idea right now. I craned my neck to see out the driver's side window. The clouds in the west were closer than they'd appeared from town, spreading over the low hills toward us. It looked like we were in for a bastard of a storm.

Something to rival Hurricane Liv, maybe.

I could feel my heart rate slow down the farther we got from town. The initial shock and bolt of adrenaline were wearing off. In its place, a weird euphoria was washing in.

My sister stared straight ahead, determined. Wow. What would it be like to be all or nothing like that? She'd frozen solid when that waitress commented on her looks—she couldn't brush it off and chalk it up to the waitress being a douchebag. If I froze every time people did that to me, I'd never move. And then she'd completely lost control. It was something to behold, but . . . well, it made me feel bad for her, too.

Control the narrative.

That's was Liv's sole MO. But what happens when the narrative controls you?

"She was an idiot," I offered. "Her headband was annoying me, too."

Liv took her gaze off the road for a split second to glance at me. She cleared her throat. "I shouldn't have done that."

"The gumballs were probably forty years old. Choking hazard. You saved a customer's life."

Her forehead creased. "You think?"

"Sure. Plus, they needed to redecorate."

That drew a smile from her. She pulled her shoulders back and sat up taller. "Well, they're welcome."

"Yeah, they are."

She laughed. The color was returning to her cheeks. "Okay," she said, shaking her head a bit. "So, we're looking for an abandoned building. There's a road near it that leads to the cabin."

I guess that was all she needed for a debrief. Fine with me. And it reassured me that she actually did have a plan beyond fleeing that one-horse town. Still, it seemed like a good idea to keep her grounded—manage her expectations. "Maybe the cabin," I said, "or maybe what's left of it."

"Right." Liv was quiet for a minute. "Hey, if the cabin *is* burned to the ground, could we prove they did it?"

"Maybe."

"Hopefully," she said. She darted a glance at me. "But . . ."

"But what?"

"But if I'm right—if Mom and Dad are hiding out up there—will you . . ." She took a deep breath. "Will you accept my offer? Of paying for your surgery?"

I looked at her in surprise.

"I'm . . . I didn't mean what I said about you not deserving it." A few drops of rain hit the windshield and streaked along the pane like tiny tearstains. The dark clouds were above us now, obscuring the sun. "You do. You deserve something you want."

"How would you know what I want?" I'd said that to her. When? When we argued after our car had disappeared?

"Why?"

"I just want to."

"Tired of being embarrassed of me?" That was from before, too, but not from the Pussy Cats station. *Before* before. So what would happen if I said it again? "Tired of being embarrassed of me?"

"No!" Her cheeks flushed, the way they did when she got angry. Then she sighed. "Okay, yes, I guess I'm trying to make myself feel better."

Huh. That felt like something she'd refused to admit in our previous argument—arguments?

"Like, I feel bad . . ." She hesitated.

"That Mom and Dad spent that money on your pageants instead?" No. We definitely hadn't had *this* conversation before.

"Well, not like I asked them to, or had any control over it, but yeah, I guess?" She chewed her lip. "No. Actually, no. That's not the whole truth."

"Okay."

"I just . . . I want to make it up to you, and I know that's probably impossible and I'm insulting you by saying it. But I think I understand why you hate me, and that's not Mom and Dad's fault. It's mine."

I cringed a little at the "hate me" but kept quiet. I had said it, after all. And whatever was on her mind, two things were true: she was certain of it, and while it didn't seem like she wanted to tell me this, she needed to.

"It was that Halloween pageant."

Not what I was expecting. "What?"

"That one I was asking you about before? You know, where I was that mad scientist and—"

"I remember." I just couldn't wrap my head around how she was connecting these dots. One pageant? *That's* what she felt bad about? "Explain."

"Getting you involved in my Theme event was wrong. I've . . . I've always felt bad about that." Rain was now pattering on the roof of the car, the windshield. Liv switched on the wipers.

"Why?"

"Because I shouldn't have asked you. It was probably only the sixth pageant I did, and I was still nervous . . . pretty scared onstage, still. I think I thought if you were there, it'd be okay."

"You wanted me there because you were scared?" *Don't.* But there it was: that little shred of hope. I tried to tell myself it didn't mean anything. But hearing her say this was knocking something loose inside me, something I'd kept closed so tightly for so long that it scared me to feel it coming apart.

"Yeah. And then we didn't even win the stupid event," she said bitterly.

It wasn't important, but I didn't know what else to say, so I corrected her. "Yes, you did."

"No."

"Yes. It was revoked. For attacking that girl."

"Oh." She paused. "I guess I'd forgotten that. I . . . blacked out, or whatever."

"Blacked out." For some reason, this didn't strike the same false note it usually did.

"Yeah."

The wipers sped up as it began to rain more heavily. I

positioned myself so I had a good look at Liv's face. "You really don't remember the attack?"

"No." She seemed sincere and also unconcerned, like her memory of it didn't matter at all.

"After the crowning, backstage, you lost it. You grabbed the girl's crown, pulled some of her hair out. Then you hit her in the face with her broomstick. It tore her retina."

"Yeah, I . . . saw the report. They tried to charge me with assault."

"But no witnesses."

"Yeah."

"And no footage," I added.

"No, it was before the cameras. Honestly, it's probably why I got the TV deal. Those guys are so slimy."

Hang on. "It was before *Divas*?"

"Yeah."

"You sure?"

"Sandra says it's okay—it doesn't damage our ability to prove that my tantrums and the TV show were related." Liv turned the windshield wipers even faster. "She says she framed it like the stress of the pageants was already getting to me and the TV show pushed me over the edge."

"But you hadn't been doing pageants that long, had you?"

"Shows you how toxic they were."

I didn't remember it this way. I thought Liv was already on *Divas*. I thought she was pissed she hadn't won the big crown and she'd figured the next best thing was airtime, that she knew that freaking out would give the TV producers what they wanted. I mean, she'd figured everything else out so fast—how to turn it on for the judges, how to be exactly who Mom wanted—was it such a stretch?

But she was saying *Divas* wasn't even a thing yet when that had happened. And clearly, she'd know. She would've been over the sequence of events dozens of times with her lawyer. It was probably in her testimony—which I'd never bothered to read.

"That's why I was asking if I used to be able to read you better. Like, I think I must've? But asking you to be there wasn't fair to you. And it was my fault. What happened to you that day."

"What happened?"

"That girl—mocking you?"

"What girl?"

"The witch. The girl I attacked."

I searched Liv's face. "That's why you attacked her?"

"Well, yeah. She was mocking you, offstage, while we were doing our routine. And then after the crowning she told me she couldn't believe I'd done Theme with a . . ." She hesitated. "A freak."

I stared at my sister. That image of her in the diner, screaming, smashing the gumball machine . . . *"I see you've moved from pageants to freak shows."*

And I suddenly saw her First Blackout Rage Performance, really saw it, for the first time.

"You shouldn't have been there." Her voice quavered.

It hadn't been a performance. It hadn't been to impress the producers. It had been about *me*, over some stupid comment I hadn't even heard. "Liv, I didn't know the girl was—"

"That's not the point! I knew how awful they were. Some of those girls and their moms were so nasty. Like, I was . . ." She faltered. "I was 'pageant material,' and I got tons of mean comments. But I wanted you there because you were my older brother. So even though I knew it was a bad idea, I put you in that position because *I* was scared. And that's pathetic."

"You were seven."

"I should've known better." She shook her head. "I should've never made you participate."

A part of me wanted to laugh. I mean, she was right—her pageants did screw me over. But a snarky comment by some inappropriately dressed child-witch was hardly part of that picture. The real picture: she'd left me with an addict who drank until he couldn't see my face so she could be surrounded by people who'd die before associating with someone who looked like me. And just because she stopped playing dress-up with Mom didn't mean she could insert herself back in my life, playing savior.

I wanted to set her straight, tell her that. It was there, itching my skin, my teeth.

But that look in her eyes. She was apologizing, truly apologizing, for something she felt responsible for: putting me in harm's way. Her reaction to it at the time had been violent and inappropriate.

But maybe instinctual, too.

"I should never have made you," she said again. She was telling me her truth. What would happen if, for once, I did the same?

How would that change things?

"You didn't," I said. "I wanted to be there."

LIV

JORY WAS TRYING to make me feel better, obviously—which was unlike him—but at least this was going better than before. I almost hadn't brought up the Halloween pageant, but I'd suddenly wanted Jory to understand my offer, even if it meant admitting something kind of awful about myself. "Yeah, right."

"No, for real." Jory stared at the dashboard. "I only really hated the pageants later. When you were gone all the time."

I frowned. "What do you mean?"

"I hated being alone. With him," Jory said. "Dad was hard to be around. So sarcastic and harsh . . ." He pressed on like he knew what I was thinking: that Jory was pretty much the exact same. "And drunk."

Okay, I guess I'd known Jory didn't like it when Dad drank—I didn't like it either—but I always sort of thought that being hard to get along with was something they had in common, maybe even something that made them good companions.

And after the pageants, he'd spent so much time being a jerk to me . . .

He looked out the window and cleared his throat. "I missed having someone who understood me without asking eight times."

Shoot. "I knew it," I said. "I knew I used to know you better."

He kept talking like he hadn't heard me. "And I didn't get why you left—why you didn't want to be around me anymore."

I sat in the foyer, waiting for Mom to put a few last things in her purse. The car was already packed with all my costumes and bags, but I'd never get in until she was ready to go. I noticed a quarter on the tile floor but didn't try to pick it up. My nails were fresh, and Mom would kill me if I chipped them.

My dad was in his office down the hall, talking loudly on the phone.

"Can I come?" Jory was sitting on the last stair to the second floor.

"Jory," Mom reproached, stuffing a bottle of water into her purse. "You know you don't like these things. You'd be bored. We'll be so busy with Livy's hair and makeup, and we still need to go over her routines. Livy, carefully get your jean jacket—the one with the rhinestones." She checked her watch. "Dang it, we're late already."

"You said the show is tomorrow," I said, opening the closet and gingerly taking my jacket from a hook that was my height.

"Not for the pageant—for Divas. *The crew is going to meet us at the hotel to get some preshow footage." She paused in front of the hall mirror. "Oh shoot!" Her hand flew to her neck. "I'm not wearing Busy Bee. Livy, you're supposed to remind me!" She sat her purse down and hurried up the stairs, brushing past Jory.*

Jory looked at me. "Can I come?" he asked again.

"Why?"

A curse word rang out from Dad's office. Jory glanced down the hall and back at me. "I don't want to stay here."

"You'd be bored," I said, repeating what Mom had said.

"I could bring my books," he offered.

I looked down. Jory couldn't come to the pageants—Mom had said so, and besides, we'd tried that once. It was better if he stayed home; then we didn't need to worry about anything. And neither did he.

Mom bustled back down the stairs and grabbed her purse from the stand near the mirror. "Let's go."

"Liv?" Jory was standing now, on the bottom step. He sounded . . . nervous or something. I looked down at my nails—why was he asking me, anyway? It wasn't like I made the decisions.

"Come on, Livy." Mom was standing with the door open. "Judas Priest, we don't have all day."

The door closed behind me.

I stared at Jory. Standing on that cliff after he'd pulled me to safety . . .

"You left me."

Oh my gosh. I pulled the car to the side of the empty highway and threw it in park. I turned to face him. "It wasn't you," I said. "You know that, right?"

"I know it was nothing I did," he said. "But it *was* me. I didn't fit there, right?"

"But that's not a bad thing! That's what I've been saying! Seriously—those places are stupid and toxic, and I should've never made you go there. You're way smarter than all of those people put together—"

"That's why I was left at home?"

I chewed my upper lip. I wanted so badly to say yes. But was that for his sake or mine? And was I really "warrioring through the pageant stuff" if I was still saying what I thought people wanted to hear?

"I think . . ." I swallowed. "I think after that Halloween pageant I was way more aware of how people saw you. And I hate myself for it, but . . . yeah, I was embarrassed." Jory flinched. Like, visibly freaking *flinched*, and my heart tore wide open. My throat got tight. I forced myself to continue. "And then I got so far into that world, I think maybe . . . I think I forgot. About you. Us." I swallowed. "And then after I was so busy trying to fit in at school, I didn't even see you."

The rain was coming down hard now, pelting the windshield and drumming against the roof in sharp taps. My heart was hammering the same way. I searched his face—his eyes were glassy.

"And that's horrible, because you obviously used to know me better than I knew myself."

He made a self-deprecating sound and shook his head.

"You did! You still do!" I could see I needed to prove it to him. "You know that comment you made about me being into Asia? Well, maybe I am into her. In fact, maybe I'm *way* into her. Actually, the fact that she has a boyfriend really, really freaking annoys me because sometimes I'm sure she's into me, too. So there. You're not just book smart; you read people. And that's something I'll never be able to do. I'm too worried about what they think of me." I said it in a rush, half expecting a sarcastic reply. He didn't speak. I couldn't tell if that was good or bad. Like, he wasn't responding, but he also wasn't dismissing me with snark. I decided if I ever had a shot at this, it was right here and now.

"You think you can buy me?"

"I try to be strong and fierce," I said. "I like to pretend that

I am. But it isn't true. And I can't blame that all on my messed-up childhood. I've been a horrible person, but I'm trying to get better. I know I can't buy you. I know no amount of money or whatever could make you want to be my brother, just like no amount of money would make what Mom and Dad did to me okay, and that's not the point. The point is, even if you can't forgive me, you deserve something you want."

I pressed my lips together. Jory was still, so still, in the passenger seat, staring straight ahead. The wind gusted.

"Jory?" I said.

More silence.

"Say something," I said. "Please?"

He looked over at me. "I pushed Dad that day," he said. "I pushed him off the pier."

JORY

LIV'S FACE WAS so completely confused, in normal circumstances it would've been hilarious.

"That memory you had at the house, the reason we're out here."

"I'm not following—"

"I *pushed him in*," I said. "He hit his head, and I ran. You don't remember that part." The memory was clear in my mind, finally. How I'd felt everything coming apart, how I'd acted on pure instinct, putting my hands on his back and shoving him hard. That telltale clunk as his head hit the pier . . .

Liv's mouth dropped open. "Oh my gosh, Jory."

"I didn't remember. Until now." The sun glinting off the surface of the water, the clink of the glass against my dad's teeth. He was in a suit jacket, of all things. He'd just returned from town, where there was cell service.

"Right now?"

"Well, a few hours ago. In the desert."

Liv looked at a loss for words. "What were you . . ." She stopped and rephrased: "Why did you do it?"

Good question. Impossible to answer, even though the answer was obvious. "I don't know. I sort of always hated him, or knew that he hated me. And he called me out there, said I was a monster, that we all were, and I . . ." I trailed off.

"Lost it," Liv finished for me.

I was quiet.

I came to my senses in the shallows, doubled over; somehow I'd lost the moments it took to run from the end of the pier. *Click.*

And then my mom noticed him. She was so busy trying to fish him out, it didn't occur to her I might've had something to do with it. And Dad couldn't remember anything.

Liv cleared her throat. "I keep flashing to this image of you as a young kid, maybe eleven or twelve? I think it's from that day." She was looking at me strangely.

Suddenly I wanted to distance myself from that kid she was remembering. "It freaked me out. My anger, I mean. I didn't want to be like Dad. So . . . I made sure I shoved it all down, after that." Recently, though, it had started to surface. It had reappeared around the time Liv had filed her lawsuit.

"Well, that's not very healthy." She put the car in gear and started driving again. "If you bottle it all up, it might come out in a really bad way."

I stared at her. Like trashing a diner?

Her eyes darted toward me like she knew what I was thinking. She shrugged. "I used to get so angry I'd black out completely. But I've been working on that. I can feel it coming now. And . . ." She drew herself up. "Now, after years of therapy, I can remember when I rage." Her lips quirked. She was making a joke.

And, actually, it was pretty funny.

"So anyway," she said. "Do you . . . think that memory is important?"

"Um . . ." Was she serious? "I mean, I was . . ." Finding common ground? Trying to say I didn't totally blame her?

"I know *why* you told me." She waved her hand. "But I'm wondering if it's important that this trip made you remember it."

She wasn't joking anymore, but her chill was almost comical. "I just told you I nearly killed him."

"I know."

"Okaayy . . ."

"Honestly, Jory? He probably deserved it."

I stared at her.

She pushed a chunk of hair behind her ear. "What?"

It wasn't that I disagreed. But I'd always thought that even though she was making a big dramatic show of suing our parents, when it came down to it, she was still a daddy's girl.

But why would I think that?

That story Liv told me about the hotel room was haunting me in several ways. That incident was like a microcosm of that whole damn world: tear down your instincts, teach you that your pretty smile is what matters most. I guess I thought Liv wouldn't be capable of realizing that only a piece of shit would let his daughter dress up to impress men his own age.

And there it was.

Liv had been raised to tune out her gut feelings about things, to stay quiet when she was uncomfortable . . .

To follow Frank to the water.

Damn.

Maybe her choices weren't all her fault, which was the basis for her entire lawsuit. Liv raised her eyebrows like she was waiting for me to explain my reaction.

"Nothing," I said. "Yeah—you're probably right." I suddenly realized that we hadn't seen a car in a very long time. Again. "Hey, how far is this haunted house supposed to be?"

"I think five miles? Feels like we've been driving forever." She peered ahead. "Oh—what's that?"

An abandoned husk of a building came into view. Out front sat a rusted oval sign that probably used to rotate, its facade long ago defaced. As Liv slowed, the wind picked up and the rain increased. A piece of cardboard gusted across the street in front of us and the few skeletal trees on the side of the road bent from the force. We crept by the old store, slowed further, and then Liv turned onto a gravel road that met the highway. There was an old sign, green with white lettering: STICKS RD.

"This is definitely it," Liv said.

The road was lined with bare trees on either side, and it followed the contours of the lake, curving back and forth, dipping down into gullies, and rising slowly up low hills. The way it meandered, I remembered, you never saw the cabin until you were almost right on top of it.

Liv accelerated. The road was bad, marred with potholes. I hoped she noticed.

"Okay," she said. "So this trip, that memory. Why now?"

I shrugged. "I'm remembering lots of things."

"Me too," she said. "But . . . why? Are we remembering certain things because of the decisions we're making? I feel like we're missing something."

Okay, so my sister wasn't always as simple as she seemed. What she said felt right somehow; we *were* missing something.

But I'd been thinking about it the opposite way: that, somehow, the memories were affecting our decisions.

Liv created her reality. The thought was back, nagging and persistent. Maybe I'd done the same thing. Maybe repressing the memory of trying to off my own dad was part of that. And maybe that was more significant than anything else, right now.

So, what else had I constructed?

Liv's eyes widened.

"What?"

They darted toward me and away.

"Liv," I said. *"What?"*

"Nothing." She shook her head. "Just . . . this road is really bad."

"Bullshit," I said. Yes, the potholes were terrible, and the mud the car was churning through was getting thick and dangerous—we were fishtailing here and again—but the look on her face wasn't *that*.

"I . . . I saw something—in my mind, I mean. Not a vision. I think it's a memory."

"Okay."

"Just . . . well, was I at the house Thursday night?"

"You mean the night before the verdict?"

"I feel like I was there. With you."

A weird feeling came over me. Something about that was familiar. "Why would you have been there?"

Liv shook her head and chewed her lip. "I don't know . . . but I remember Asia dropping me off. I remember walking up the steps."

Thursday night. Thursday night. I closed my eyes and tried

to picture what I'd been doing that evening but couldn't. *Impossible. Think.* What did we have for dinner? I'd worked out . . . twice that day. So I would've been hungry. A microwave meal—that was familiar. My mom must've talked about the next day, about the court date.

"That's when I met Frank the first time."

My eyes snapped open. "What?"

Liv nodded vehemently. "That's how I know he's their pool guy. He was leaving when I was arriving. And he said something, too—but I can't remember what . . ."

"Are you sure? What would you have been doing at the house? Maybe you're . . ." I swallowed. "Remembering it wrong?" Except her text: *Can I come over?*

And now I could see myself coming down the stairs to the foyer, where Liv was standing. Our parents weren't home, or one of them would've answered the door. It couldn't have been Thursday. Except . . .

They'd told me not to wait up, I remembered that now.

"I was at the house," Liv said adamantly. "And I saw Frank. He said he was checking the water pump." She looked at me. "And he said something about Mom and Dad not being home, that they went away to deal with an investment."

An investment: the cabin. I sucked in a breath. Maybe that's why we were out here. Liv thought her memory of Dad nearly drowning made her think of the cabin, but maybe it was the other way around: maybe the mention of the investment—the cabin—was what made Liv remember Dad nearly drowning.

Suggested by Frank. Reinforced by . . .

My chest was getting tight. None of this made sense. Why couldn't I remember?

Liv squinted out the windshield and braked hard. The rain poured down around us.

"What . . . what else do you remember?"

"We were arguing," Liv whispered.

I stared at her.

She looked over at me. "We were arguing about the money."

LIV

"*THE* MONEY?" JORY asked. "Like, the six hundred K in your bank account?"

"*It's not about the money, Jory.*"

"*You think you can buy me?*"

"Maybe?" My heart pounded.

"*You're so pathetic.*"

"*I'm telling the truth!*"

"*Tired of being embarrassed of me?*"

"So what happened then?"

"I honestly don't know. It's like . . . a blank. But maybe . . . maybe when we get to the cabin, we'll remember."

"Why would you say that?"

"I don't know." I chewed my lip. "It feels like we're going for a reason. And it's connected."

Jory was silent. I leaned closer to the windshield and tried not to think about how nervous I was. The wipers couldn't go any faster, and it was getting really hard to see. Huge streams ran down the middle of the road, and the car bumped into potholes that were hidden by the water.

The car jostled us together again.

I wrinkled my nose. "How can you like rocks?"

"Now, Livy," my mom said. "A diamond's a rock."

"Diamonds are pretty," I said. "Jory likes the boring ones. The ones that sit there and don't sparkle or anything. What good are they?"

"They don't talk back," Jory said.

My dad laughed. I gave Jory my fiercest look. "Shut your mouth," I hissed.

Jory turned and looked out the window.

"Did you get me a diamond?" I asked my mom. "Is that the bling you got me?"

She laughed. "Not that blingy."

I crossed my arms and stuck out my lower lip in a pout the way Mom said was cute. "But I want a diamond."

"Someday, Livy," my mom said. "When you win enough crowns."

The rain pounded harder against the windshield.

"She never did get me a diamond," I muttered. Seriously. How many crowns was I supposed to win?

"What?"

"The last time we were up here. She said she'd get me a diamond."

Jory looked at me for several moments. "Diamonds aren't actually that rare. A red beryl would be better. More appropriate."

"I don't even know what that is."

"It's got a different beauty. Not ordinary. And it's strong."

Geez Murphy. I cleared my throat over the lump that was rising in it. "Yeah, well. I got a gold necklace, I guess."

"I guess," he said. "So that incident on the pier—that was the same day."

"Yeah." We crested a hill and started down. I could now see only a few feet in front of the car. "We'd stopped at that grave-yard we passed a while back. You were carsick?"

"Wait. That was all the same trip?"

"Well, I don't remember taking pictures on the shore twice. I'm pretty sure that was the last time we were here." Jory was quiet. He was thinking about something. "What is it?"

"Nothing," he said. "I figured something out, is all."

"What?"

"That stop at the cemetery. Your photo shoot."

"Yeah?"

"Well, I know where Mom got that little prize for you."

"What prize?"

He shook his head. "What a piece of work."

"What prize?"

"The necklace she gave you." He shook his head. "She stole it from a grave."

Cold crept into my hairline. "What?"

"Yeah. I saw her. I didn't figure that out until just now."

The necklace I'd worn with that red swimsuit had been stolen from a grave? What kind of person did that? My stomach churned. I remember grasping at the pendant, running my fingers over it, feeling so pleased . . .

My thoughts stopped. "That necklace," I said.

"Yeah?"

"It had a *P* pendant on it. Mom said it was for Princess Liv."

Jory shrugged. "Makes sense," he said. "The girl was named Patricia—Cici for short. Don't know why I remember that—"

"No. The radio announcement." My voice was tight. "It keeps saying Mom is wearing a necklace with a *P* pendant on it."

Jory tilted his head. "You're right."

"Why would she be wearing that necklace?" I asked. "I don't even know when I had it last."

"She wasn't wearing it. The cop heard me wrong."

My heart beat fast. "But . . . it's a really weird coincidence, don't you think?"

"I guess."

"But what if it's not?"

"What do you mean? How could—"

A huge splash of water pelted the windshield, and I slammed on the brakes, lurching to a halt in an enormous puddle. It stretched out before us and disappeared into the curtain of rain.

"Back up," Jory instructed, "before we get stuck."

I threw the car in reverse and backed up the hill as quickly as I dared, then put the car in park once I was sure we were at the top.

"Should I go for it?"

"Wait. Let me look." Jory opened his door and disappeared into the rain. I hurried to unbuckle my seat belt and follow. The road was slick; my flat shoes slipped and squelched down the hill to where Jory stood at the edge of the puddle. We were already soaked. Water streamed down my face and neck into the collar of my blouse.

"It's washed out!" he called over the roar of the rain, gesturing at the ditches on either side, which were filling with water too. The only place that wasn't covered in water was inside the trees, where the car obviously couldn't go. The puddle stretched down the road at least twenty feet, raindrops peppering the surface so hard it looked like it was boiling. "Could be really deep in the middle!"

A crack of thunder split the air.

Jory gestured for us to get back in the car. We slipped and slid our way back up the hill, the narrow road getting soggier every minute. There was no way I could turn the car around safely—I'd slide into the ditch for sure.

We slammed our doors, sealing out the torrent, and sat, dripping on the Audi's leather seats. The rain pounded on the roof; a grumble of thunder followed a flash of lightning. It seemed really close, and we were sitting on top of a freaking hill . . .

"I can't back up all the way to the highway," I said.

"No," he agreed.

I rested my head on the steering wheel. We were going to have to wait for the rain to stop and the roads to dry to continue, and who knew how long that would take? I banged my forehead softly once. That, or walk back to the road and ask for help.

That was the safe thing to do. The way the rain was coming down, it might be dangerous to stay in the car with the water rising. We should probably get off this road and back to town. And then . . . and then phone Sandra.

And give up.

His voice broke into my thoughts. "What did you mean, about the necklace not being a coincidence?" He sounded strange. A little desperate.

I shook my head, forehead still on the wheel. I didn't know what I was thinking. "It doesn't matter." That was a lie. All of this mattered. It mattered so much that the thought of failing now made me want to scream and burst into tears. *Redirect.* I wasn't going to let myself cry in front of Jory—not again.

I heard him sigh. "You ready to hike?"

I raised my head and looked at him. Nodded. "Maybe we can hitchhike once we reach the highway." Right. Catch a ride with all the cars we saw?

"Not to the highway. *In.*"

I stared at him.

"You said you'd hike in," he said.

"But . . ."

"Where are we going to go—back to that diner?"

"But what if the cabin's not there?"

"What if it is?"

I searched his face. "You don't have to do this for me."

He shrugged. "It can't be much farther. And then we'll know."

My throat got tight. "Okay," I said. "Yeah. Yes. I'm ready."

JORY

THE RAIN WAS coming in sheets. Liv grasped my arm as we put our heads down and stumbled on the sodden road. Every part of me was soaked; putting my hoodie on had been useless. The wind had picked up, and the trees on the sides of the road swayed violently in the torrent.

I was starting to shiver.

Was this the stupidest plan I'd ever had? It was going to be if we arrived and there was no cabin left. But it might be there, and for whatever reason, I couldn't bear the thought of Liv giving up now. Whatever we'd find, at least she'd see this through like she wanted.

"It shouldn't be too much farther!" I called over the wail of the wind. I didn't know that at all, but didn't distances always seem farther when you were a kid? For sure if it had been a clear day, we would've been able to see the lake from where we were walking. Now we could barely see ten feet in front of us.

I glanced at Liv. She was moving stoically forward, like some kind of discarded wind-up doll. Her hair was a mat of hair-spray clumps, sticking to the sides of her neck and her forehead, and her eyes were narrowed tight against the wind. She was a goddamn mess, but she was a determined mess, and there was something oddly beautiful about it. In fact, in the storm, Liv was practically glowing. What had she called her skin? Alabaster. The wind gusted the rain in muddy sprays, spattering her alabaster skin.

I'd always assumed the pageant world had hollowed her out, but maybe surviving it had actually strengthened her—in ways she didn't even know.

And her reaction to the news that I'd tried to off Dad—I hadn't expected her to reframe it, think about it as a memory that was telling us something. And I couldn't figure out what it could mean, especially given her claim about Frank. I mean, it was possible we were out here because of him, but I couldn't imagine a scenario in which Liv would've showed up at the house the night before her court date.

"Why can't you believe me?"

"I'm not your grief puppet, Liv."

That argument—from when?—was on the outskirts of my memory, out of reach. I turned my head against a sudden gust of wind, trying to think. We'd heard that radio announcement several times. So why had Liv claimed she'd never heard the part about the arson? That was impossible; I *knew* I'd heard it before we stopped in Mina . . .

"Reno PD have been called in to help with a case of arson in Mineral County, as a recent discovery has turned it into a potential criminal investigation."

Criminal investigation. Human remains.

In the cabin.

Ice shot through my veins. Where had that thought come from?

Liv said something to me, but her voice was ripped away by the wind. She ducked her head closer and spoke loudly over the storm. "I don't know what to hope for! I don't know what to hope we'll find."

I glanced at her in surprise. Didn't she want to be right? Didn't she want to find our parents? I stepped carelessly and slipped in the mud, nearly taking Liv down with me.

She clung to my arm, righting herself, and pulled me to a stop. "But I want you to know: whatever it is, I'll fix it."

Fix it. My chest was starting to constrict again. Why had I left that new package of Rolaids in the car? Thunder rumbled in the distance.

"I'll fix it," she said again, adamantly.

"Liv," I said as clearly as I could. "It's not your fault."

Her eyes widened, and her face changed from determined to something so vulnerable, so sincerely grateful, it felt like my heart was cracking wide open, splitting in two. And suddenly, I didn't care if my parents *had* bankrupted me to try to get out of jail free. I hoped they were at the cabin—I was going to drag them back to Vegas myself. I'd do it in a goddamn hurricane, and I would be smiling so hard on the inside, they'd be able to see it from fucking space.

Like it was echoing my thought, a blast of wind came, causing Liv to stumble into me. The trees lining the road heaved violently, and there was a loud crack overhead.

And then a sharp pain coursed through my shoulder, buckling my knees.

LIV

I HEARD THE tree branch crack but had no time to react. It hit Jory, its long branches scratching my face and catching my hair, and dropped him like a rock at my feet.

"Jory!" The tree branch lay across his back, pinning him to the muddy road. I pushed at it, but it was so heavy, my shoving only made Jory cry out. "Hang on!" I leapt across his body and tugged at the branch from the far side. It moved slowly, and Jory swore loudly, but I didn't have another option—I wasn't strong enough to lift it off him.

When I got him free, I touched his shoulder where the branch had come down. He swore again and tried to sit up, pushing himself to kneeling with his left arm, like he didn't want to use the right. When he eased himself up to sitting I saw that the shoulder of his gray hoodie was starting to discolor with a dark stain.

"Oh geez," I said. That was blood. For sure it was blood.

He winced.

"Is it . . ." I swallowed. "Is it broken?"

He reached up to touch his shoulder, then his skin went a kind of gray and he toppled over into the mud. The rain pelted down on his slack face.

"Jory!" I didn't want to shake him. Had he fainted or was he—

No. No. Do not panic.

Except I was panicking. He was hurt, and I couldn't call anyone and I couldn't leave him here to go find someone and—

Oh god.

Why had I thought we should hike in? Why . . . why had I done any of this? The rain screamed down around us. I pulled my blazer off and tried to hold it over Jory's white face. He looked so small suddenly—like a child.

Jory looked at me. "Can I come?" he asked again.

"Why?"

A curse word rang out from Dad's office. Jory glanced down the hall and back at me. "I don't want to stay here."

"You'd be bored," I said, repeating what Mom had said.

"I could bring my books," he offered.

Mom bustled back down the stairs and grabbed her purse from the stand near the mirror. "Let's go."

The door closed behind me.

A sob rose in my throat. What should I do? How could I fix this?

"You created your reality; live with it." Jory said that to me. At the house, Thursday night. I couldn't remember what had happened the day before our argument, or what happened directly after, but I remembered that. We were arguing about . . . about the surgery and the money. And I was so angry with him, probably because I knew it was true. A small part of me knew that the court case was me continuing to play a role I thought people

wanted me to. I'd never asked myself what I truly wanted; how *I* thought I could heal.

Well, I didn't want this. And I wasn't going to accept it. My parents could keep their money, they could disappear and never be brought to justice, they could burn down whatever they needed in order to get ahead. But they didn't get to take Jory away from me now. And I didn't care if I ever found them.

"You win," I whispered. "I'm done." I tilted my head back and raised my voice over the roar of the storm. "Just let us get to shelter!" Tears spilled down my cheeks, mixing with the rain-drops. I held my blazer over my brother. "Please."

The rain let up; I actually felt it slow against the fabric.

Had that worked?

I dropped the jacket and saw the curtain of rain part. A glimmer of light flickered through, and as the rain slowed to a soft patter I saw it: the cabin. I choked back my tears, staring hard. It stood, solid as anything, dark brown clapboards and shake-shingled roof. The porch light was on. We were in the cabin's drive—not even twelve feet from the house. We were here. And it looked like someone else was, too.

I shouldn't have been scared. Hadn't I been sure of this all along? Besides, I didn't have much choice now; I had to get Jory inside.

I covered him with my jacket again. It was soaked, but that seemed better than letting the rain fall on his face. I stumbled toward the front door, slipping in the mud. A crack of thunder rumbled overhead. The porch was covered, and being out of the rain was like surfacing from a deep swim. I steadied my nerve and pounded on the door. "Mom? Dad?" I called. I fumbled with the doorknob. Locked.

I thought hard. My dad always left a key . . .

I scrambled back down the steps and dropped to my knees, searching under the second step for the little hook that held the door key. A thrill went through me when my fingers touched metal. I hurried back and fumbled with the lock until it clicked.

Jory pushed at the door. It swung open with a creak. A musty smell wafted out.

"Mom? Dad?" I called into the dark space.

No answer.

"Come on," Jory said. "They'll show up." He stepped inside.

I paused at the doorway. That hadn't felt like a memory. Was I imagining what would've happened if Jory hadn't been hurt on the road right now?

I stepped inside. The living room was nothing more than shadows. Lightning flashed over the lake, illuminating the room and with it, a series of dark, shapeless masses—the living room was full of people or—

No. As my eyes adjusted to the dim light, I realized that all the furniture was covered with bedsheets. The entire room was filled with shapes. Some had human forms, but I knew they were only furniture.

I kicked off my ruined ballet flats—they were slowing me down—and grabbed a sheet off the small table near the door. I left the door open a crack and sprinted back down the drive. My feet were so numb from the cold that I barely registered the bite of pebbles on my soles.

On the ground, Jory was squirming, coming to.

"Take it easy!" Relief washed over me as I helped him to sit again. "Here, we should tie your arm to your side. It's hurt." I wrapped the bedsheet around his shoulder. Dazed, he raised his left arm so I could tie it around his other side. "It's going to be okay," I said. "We're here." I gestured at the cabin. "We need to get inside."

He whimpered as I helped him to his feet with his good arm. "Hurts," he said.

"I know," I said, pulling his good arm around my shoulder. "But you're going to be okay. Let's get inside."

BEFORE

BEFORE

JORY

THE INSIDE OF the cabin was dark, fuzzy. My vision swam as waves of pain rolled through my neck and shoulder, and I halted on the threshold, trying to see what we were walking into.

Ghosts. The living room was full of them.

"It's the furniture—it's covered." Liv crossed into the space and fumbled for the pull chain on a lamp a few feet away. The lamp clicked but didn't turn on. It took a few seconds for the light to even out in my vision. She was right: all shapes of bedsheets stood at perfect attention. Some were obvious, like the couch and armchairs positioned toward the fireplace. Some were a mystery. But nothing moved.

And nothing looked recently disturbed.

"Mom and Dad?"

She shook her head. "Doesn't seem like anyone is here." She moved to an adjacent wall and flicked on the light switch. Nothing happened. "No power," she said.

"Then how is the porch light on?" I reflexively gestured with my bound arm, inciting a swoop of pain so intense my stomach lurched. I whimpered.

Liv looked alarmed. "Sit down," she instructed, pointing to the sofa. I moved gingerly forward and let her help me awkwardly lower myself onto the dusty bedsheet covering it. She returned to the open door and stuck her head outside. "It looks like it runs from a little box—like maybe a solar thingy?" She closed the door, sealing out the storm. "So." She crossed the room to stand beside me. "The cabin's still here."

"Yeah."

"It wasn't the one in the APB."

"I . . . guess."

Liv bit her lip. "It's okay," she said. "We'll fix your account." She was talking about my college money. But I didn't care about that now; unease was creeping around inside me, drowning out the terrible reality of my parents' bribery attempt. Something about all this felt . . . wrong. I mean, it was the right cabin—everything was as I remembered it, pretty well—but . . . "It was unlocked?"

Liv held up a key. "I remembered where Dad kept it." She set it down on the covered side table beside the couch and placed her blazer on the couch arm.

"You're sure no one is here?"

"Doesn't look like it."

The muffled wind gusted against the cabin, finding its way through unseen cracks with a thin wail. There were no sounds inside the cabin, though that didn't mean much. There weren't many places to hide, but there were some.

"I'll go look for some aspirin," she said.

"I'm fine," I said.

"You're definitely not fine."

"I don't know if you should go alone."

"The cabin's basically three rooms," she protested.

"Wait a second. Please?"

She shrugged and sat down on the hearth in front of the empty fireplace, stretching her soggy pant legs toward the couch and pulling her arms around her. In the gloom her face was pale and almost glowed—like a marble statue from some gallery in Europe. The real thing, not some Vegas imitation.

"What . . . happened?"

"A tree branch broke off in the wind and hit you," Liv said. "You passed out for a minute."

I shifted uncomfortably. "Thank you. For getting me here."

Liv was quiet.

"Doesn't look like anyone's been here," I said. "Seems like no one's been here for a really long time."

She nodded.

"If there's no power, there's no phone. We'll have to wait out the storm." Again, a nod. Her silence was making me nervous. "Are you okay?"

She cleared her throat and drew her knees up, looking at me carefully. Finally she spoke. "I made a pledge," she said softly. "When you got hurt on the road. That if I could get you to safety, I'd drop the lawsuit."

"A pledge. To who?"

"God? The universe? Myself? I don't know." She looked around the room. "But we got here." The storm was lashing the cabin, railing at the weathered siding with violent gusts of wind and rain. Liv, by contrast, was still and calm; either the eye of the storm, or a hurricane candle, burning bright despite the tempest. "And it was like . . ." She tilted her head. "I got lighter, when I said it. Like I got free, somehow."

I realized what she was doing. "Liv, nothing got me to this cabin but you."

"I don't know if that's true," she said. "But maybe it doesn't matter. I've always felt this . . . dark thing, inside. Anger. But what I want, deep down, is to be happy. And I want you to be happy."

"The lawsuit is part of that—"

"Coming to terms with what Mom and Dad did is part of that. But I don't need a moment in court for that."

"Well, maybe I do."

She squinted at me. "Why would you need it?"

I looked away. Why was she talking like this? After what we'd been through to get here, why would she suddenly decide it didn't matter?

"We can still do your surgery," Liv said. "I have savings."

"It's not the surgery!" Anger sparked in me. "What about what you deserve?"

"But what *is* that now? Because I think I deserved a normal childhood, but that's not going to happen. What's done is done. I'm the person I am because of what happened, and nothing can change that."

"So you're giving up?"

"I'm not giving up."

"Yes, you are!"

"No. I'm . . . creating a new reality. To live with."

I stared at her. My words. Yes, those were definitely my words.

She tucked her hair behind her ear and looked at the ground. "I want it to be different from now on."

Did she mean different between us? I didn't want to let myself consider that, in case I was wrong. I focused instead on why I was so upset about this. It was this goddamn road trip. I remembered that Liv had been someone to cling to in the storm of our childhoods. And I knew now that it wasn't her fault, getting swept up in the gale. She was finally back on dry land. Why shouldn't she be rewarded for that?

Why shouldn't our parents pay?

"You were right," Liv said. "A large part of the lawsuit was about how it looked. I knew the other survivors wanted me to go through with it, and I thought it would make me seem more . . . *self-actualized* for Asia, whatever that means."

"I was talking shit before."

She smiled at me. "You never talk shit. It's one of the best things about you."

"But you can't—"

"Jory," she cut me off. "I'm not afraid. I'm not afraid anymore."

Something in me was bottoming out, creating a big hollow space where there had been anger. Liv was saying what I'd been saying all along, but hearing it from her reflected the emptiness of my argument back to me. It pulled back the curtain on the fact that my own misery had been part of my rejection of hers. And I didn't want her to believe that she wasn't worth restitution, but I could tell by looking at her face that she was moving beyond caring about it. It didn't matter whether making that pledge had gotten us here.

"We'll talk about it later."

She shrugged, then looked at the empty fireplace. "I'm freezing," she said. "I should start this thing."

"You know how to start a fire?"

"How hard could it be?"

"Very?" I was still rattled. "You could try. You'd need paper.

There are probably matches in there—" I tried to gesture at the box beside the mantel, but my shoulder sparked pain again. I sucked in a sharp breath.

Liv jumped to her feet. "I'm looking for aspirin."

"Just—"

"We need to dry off, too. Maybe there are towels. And I'll look for paper."

She disappeared, moving out of my sight behind the couch and heading for the front door. I craned my neck to see her put on her shoes, then she crossed the room toward the kitchen. I heard a loud whine. Then silence. "Water doesn't work!" she called.

No surprise there. I listened to her thumping around in the kitchen, opening drawers and cupboards. Our conversation had been a bunch of bullshit—I hoped I could make Liv see that—but something else felt wrong, too.

"You think you can buy me?" Liv's eyes were shiny with rage.

But so were my dad's.

Wait. *I'd* said that to Liv. So why would I picture her saying it to my dad? I lay still, trying to flesh out the memory, and realized that under the vaguely familiar smell of mildew and wood, there was another odor—acrid, slightly chemical. I shifted in my wet clothes, trying to place it. Was it the smell of something . . . burning?

"Did you check the bedroom?" I called. There was only one; Liv and I had camped out on the living room floor in our sleeping bags when we were kids. There was no answer. A gust of wind came again, shaking the panes of glass in the living room window that faced the lake. I listened for sounds of her rummaging. Nothing. "Liv?" My voice rose a notch.

"What?"

"Jesus!" She'd appeared back in the living room without a sound.

She crossed toward the couch with her hands full. She was carrying a flattened cereal box, a couple of towels, and a bottle of aspirin. "Can you swallow these without water?" She dumped her finds next to me.

"It won't be pretty." I pulled myself to sitting and let her put two small white pills in my hand.

"Well, don't choke." She grabbed the cereal box and knelt by the fireplace. "I have no idea how to do the Heinrich."

"Or the Heimlich." She was too busy ripping the box into smaller pieces and arranging them in the hearth to notice my joke. I cleared my throat. "Do you smell something weird?"

She ripped a piece with more energy than I would've guessed she had after our little ordeal.

"Liv?"

"It's called 'ancient cabin.'"

"No, for real."

Liv stood and looked at me.

"Something burnt, maybe?"

She swiveled without answering, opened the tin on the mantel, and took out a box of matches. She'd already somehow gotten soot all over her hands.

"Um, you'll need wood," I pointed out.

"Where would that be?"

"I think there was a woodshed outside."

Liv walked over to the picture window and drew back a portion of the gauzy curtains to peer out.

"Liv?"

"Storm's letting up," she said, her voice weirdly distant.

"That's good." I worked up saliva and took the pills one at a time, watching her carefully.

She stood stock-still at the window.

"Can you see the lake?"

"No."

"Then what are you looking at?"

She turned. "What do you think would've happened if Dad *had* drowned that day?"

"What?"

"If Dad had drowned, would we have had the money for pageants?"

"I don't know. I mean, he must've had life insurance?"

"That would've lasted only so long. Mom has never had a job; she's always depended on Dad, right? If he'd drowned that day, we would've had to quit the circuit. I would've been at home, with you—before I forgot . . . everything. Before I forgot about us. I shouldn't have pointed Dad out to Mom. She didn't see. *I* noticed. If I hadn't . . ." She shook her head. "Hindsight. Right?"

I couldn't be sure from this distance, but it seemed like she was trembling. "It could've gone a million ways."

"But it didn't. And if I had known? If I could've seen the next six years, I think I might've kept my mouth shut."

My unease was back in full force. Maybe she was going into shock? "You should dry off," I said. "Get warm. There must be a blanket." When she didn't move, I hauled myself up off the couch, wincing as fire shot through my shoulder. I stepped toward the bedroom.

"Jory, don't—"

"Don't what?"

"I'll look. You rest."

"I'm not dying. I can walk." I moved around the couch.

She took a hurried step toward me.

"I'm *fine*."

She stopped like she'd been caught. She was being so weird. "What's wrong?" I asked. Her eyes flicked toward the adjoining room. "What's in there?"

"It's not good. Jory . . ."

I turned and crossed to the bedroom, and she scrambled after me. Inside the doorway, I stopped abruptly. There was a heap of something dark on the floor at the foot of the bed. "What is that?" I asked, bending close. It looked like someone had dumped a wheelbarrow of soil onto the floor. There were whitish lumps in the dirt. I moved closer.

"Jory," Liv whispered.

I bent down and brushed away a clump of dirt with my free hand. An oblong shape protruded. As I pushed, the object emerged from the soil, a long, pale . . . bone. The air left my lungs. The white was bone. And this was a . . . femur? I recoiled, stepping away from the mound, and stared at Liv.

"Remains."

"What?" I scanned the room, looking for anything that would explain what this was—why it was here. But that smell of burning I'd detected earlier . . . this was it. I knew that without a doubt.

"Those are human remains." Liv's face was pale.

"We don't know that," I said, but something told me she was right. I noticed the ash on her hands. "Did you touch it?"

"I needed to see . . ." Her voice was faint. She looked at me, her face unreadable. "These are the remains the radio talked about. Right?"

I scanned the room a bit more desperately. This couldn't be

that. The report had said arson—a property burned down. This was not a property burned down.

That splintering feeling was starting again. I hadn't had it since being lost in the desert, but here it was, washing over me, like the cabin was about to fragment into a million pieces as we stood there looking at—

What? Whose remains were these? And why was I feeling responsible?

I reached out a hand, found Liv's wrist, and gripped it tight. It was solid. Real. Liv was real.

Stop it. Don't panic.

Liv's hands were smeared with black streaks of ash and her nails were caked—as though she'd dug into the pile. Why would she do that? It was all over her. The remains were all over her . . .

Goddamn.

Had Frank mentioned the "investment" deliberately to Liv, in order to get us to come here? Was it to find . . . this? My brain clicked into survival mode, like we were back in the desert with only a few inches of water and no rescue in sight.

"You should . . . We should go," I said.

"Why?"

"We shouldn't be here."

"But why?"

"Think about it! We leave Vegas without telling anyone and come to a remote cabin and just happen to find human remains?"

"But . . ." Liv stared at me. "You think it looks like we did this?"

"I think it looks bad. Can *you* explain why we're here?"

"F-F-Frank."

Exactly. "Long gone by now."

"But we were on Mom and Dad's trail. The traces of them in the desert—"

"Buried under a rockslide we'll never find again." The SUV we saw, getting lost, Frank finding us—was it all part of some elaborate setup to slow us down?

A look of horror crossed Liv's face. "Oh my god, Jory. Would the police really think we did this?"

"I don't know." I wasn't even sure I was thinking about this the right way. Being set up like this would be almost impossible. I mean, it wasn't like my parents could've programmed the radio in their car to . . .

Play the same music and APB over and over?

Fuck.

"We need to go." I grabbed her hand and pulled her through the doorway to the living room, but before we could reach the door, a sound froze us in our tracks.

Footsteps.

Someone was on the front porch.

LIV

I **SWEAR MY** heart stopped.

The front door didn't have a window, so I couldn't be sure, but it sounded like whoever that was had stopped directly outside it. The doorknob began to turn.

Frick.

I hadn't locked the door behind me. It was one of those weird locks where you needed to use the key from the inside. The key sat where I'd placed it on the side table near the couch. And we were right in plain view, frozen in the middle of the room like scared rabbits.

I watched uselessly as the door began to open. Jory snapped into action, pulling us around the side of a deep bookcase that stood against the living room wall. I heard the door swing open with a long creak and I pressed into the dusty sheet. I felt my heart speeding.

Cold air rushed past us. The floorboards creaked once, like the person was shifting their weight on the threshold.

Who would be out in this storm? A nosy neighbor who'd seen us arrive? Would they really walk around in this? We hadn't heard a car.

Wait. Maybe this was a good thing. If they'd seen us show up, they could verify our story that we'd found the cabin like this. A witness. And there'd be more than one. The waitress in Hawthorne. There was no way she'd forget our visit. For sure the police could determine when the remains were burned? Maybe we should show ourselves—maybe whoever was there could help. Unless . . .

Unless whoever was at the door was the person responsible for what we'd found in the bedroom.

My skin prickled. Something about that felt absolutely true.

Jory was standing stock-still, his head tilted like he was listening.

Another breeze blew into the cabin, gently tugging at the sheets on the rumpled couch. We'd tracked in mud, and Jory's soaked hoodie was lying beside my blazer on the arm of the couch. It was obvious we were here. Plus, our car was parked halfway down the lane. I nudged Jory. We needed to run, didn't we?

He put a hand on my forearm and squeezed, keeping me in place.

The unseen visitor stepped into the cabin and stopped. But now . . . more footsteps coming up the porch steps. There was a second person.

And there was a smell—fake lilacs or something. My heart raced. Mom and Dad?

That wasn't possible. I put one hand to my pocket, feeling the lump of ash-caked metal inside, hope and disbelief and fear mixing together in a ball in my stomach. The door creaked again, then closed, sealing out the fresh air. The smell of rain lingered.

I waited for the sound of footsteps moving across the living room toward us. Jory's hand tightened on my arm.

Silence.

A weird, heavy silence. My breathing was too loud. I tried to take little sips of air. The wind shrieked quietly through the unseen gaps in the old cabin. More silence from the front door. Then Jory shifted noisily, and I gripped his arm in fear.

Nothing came in reply. No movement. No sound.

Jory peered around the edge of the bookcase. I heard him exhale. He moved, shaking off my arm and darting toward the side table near the couch. He grabbed the key, and I peered around to see him hurrying to the front door, which was closed.

No one was standing inside the cabin.

The small window near the door showed a portion of the gravel drive winding off through bare trees. I couldn't see much from where I stood, but there was no vehicle on the road.

Jory was fitting the key in the lock, awkwardly using his left hand. He turned it, then checked the handle to make sure it was locked. He made his way quietly back to me, grabbing our clothes off the couch on the way and tucking them under his sling. He took my hand and pulled me farther away from the front door and into the kitchen, heading straight for the door that led out the side of the cabin into the woods. He checked that it was locked too, then put his head to the doorjamb.

I tucked in beside him, out of sight of the one window that sat over the sink, and looked out at the woods. The storm was letting up, but the inside of the cabin was growing darker; the kitchen was washed in a kind of gray-purple hue. There was no sound from outside but the staccato of rain dripping from the eaves. He passed me my blazer wordlessly and, not knowing what else to do with it, I put it on. I watched as he shrugged out of the sling and let it drop to the floor. He rolled his bad shoulder easily, like it didn't hurt anymore. Like he'd never been injured.

Impossible.

I thought again of the heap of ash in the bedroom and pressed my back to the door, doubling over, suddenly feeling like I was going to be sick. As I hung my head and tried to breathe, I noticed a bright-red plastic can—the kind you store gasoline in—tucked under the curtain-lined kitchen counter. Beside it was a thin blue cylinder with a curved metal tube protruding from the top. A blowtorch? Was this what was used to—

"I thought they were setting us up," Jory murmured.

I looked at him.

"But there's no way they'd show up here, if they were." He pulled his hoodie over his head.

"Who?"

"Mom and Dad." His voice was muffled until his head emerged. "That was them, at the door."

My stomach lurched again. "No, Jory, it wasn't."

"Yes, it was. I could feel it."

But he didn't know. "No . . ." I hesitated, twisting my ashy hands.

He kept his voice low. "I was trying to figure out how they did it. I thought maybe that radio APB was a fake and Frank was a plant, but they wouldn't do all of that and then show up here—"

"It wasn't them."

Jory peered at me. "Why do you keep saying that?"

I hesitated.

"*Liv.*"

"Because . . ." I dug a hand into my pocket and pulled out the little chain. I brushed it off and held it up so Jory could see that it was a necklace. A dirty gold chain, with a letter *P* pendant.

"*—a gold necklace with a letter* P *pendant, and blond hair. Anyone with information about the Brewers' whereabouts is asked to contact local authorities.*"

I could practically see the radio announcement register with him.

"Where did you get that?" His voice was a whisper.

"It was . . ." I swallowed hard. "It was in the pile of ash."

The floor in the cabin creaked loudly. We froze. It creaked again. Someone was moving around in the bedroom.

Jory's face paled. He fumbled the key into the lock of the kitchen door, unlocked it with a twist, and pulled the door open quietly. We slipped outside, onto the rain-soaked porch in the quickly falling dusk. Jory pulled the door shut gently, then locked it behind us.

"Come on," he whispered, taking my hand. I stumbled down the little step that led from the kitchen door onto a path that wound through the trees. It looked like we were alone out here; those two were now locked inside the cabin. That was good, wasn't it? I didn't know. I couldn't think straight. My head was swimming, my stomach tight with fear.

I put my head down and followed Jory into the woods.

JORY

SKIRTING THE SHORE was the only way to get back to the road without being seen from a window. Liv stumbled along behind me, gripping my hand as she slipped along the muddy path. The pain in my shoulder had inexplicably disappeared. The soggy forest was silent. Not even a damn bird chirping.

I went as fast as I could. My head was spinning, but we had to leave—had to get away from . . . them. Liv's fingers dug into my hand.

I understood, now, why she'd been so weird and cagey, even if what she was thinking was impossible. I knew who'd been at the door.

But why would our parents turn up at the cabin?

To torch it.

So who was in the bedroom? A chill touched my neck. That feeling of foreboding that had been growing since we'd arrived was coming over me full force.

The path led us away from the cabin and through the trees toward the pier. The leafless saplings didn't provide much cover, but dark was falling fast. By the time we reached the dingy shore, we could barely see the weathered cabin through the trees. The sun was going down, its rays coating the surface of the lake with an orange haze. The water's edge was rimmed with a yellow scum, and the rotting pier sat crookedly in the water.

I peered down. The ripples I'd made had dissipated and the surface calmed. I stared harder, searching for what my dad was pointing at.

"Can't you see it?" His breath was acidic and sweet. He leaned close, and I turned my head away. "No," he said, pushing my chin and pointing at the water again. He put his other hand on my shoulder and gripped it so hard I bit back a whimper. "There."

My chest was tight. I halted on the shore, staring out at the lake.

"We're all monsters inside."

"Jory?"

I glanced at Liv. She was clutching that necklace in a tight fist, her eyes glazed with fear or shock; it looked like she was on the verge of a full-blown freak-out.

"That"—I pointed at her clenched hand—"is not what you think."

She stared at me.

"The ashes. It's not Mom and Dad."

"Yes, it is," she whispered.

"No. That was them at the door, Liv."

She blinked. "No."

"Yes. It was." Why were we arguing about this? We needed to get to the car, and we didn't have much time before the light was gone. Stumbling around the woods in the pitch-black near that cabin was one of our worst options. But there was something stalling me out. Something niggling at me about the necklace in her hand. About those remains . . .

"The radio announcement," Liv said fiercely.

I tried to push the niggle away and think about this logically. The only way Liv could be right was if I was wrong about the necklace and someone else had told the cops what Mom had been wearing. But who would that have been? The person actually responsible for their disappearance? That didn't make sense.

Besides, I couldn't put my finger on how, but I knew it had been them at the door.

"What are you doing here?"

My dad stood at the threshold, looking out of place in his suit jacket. My mom appeared beside him, eyes widening with alarm. Her hands flew to her neck, a nervous gesture.

"You're wrong," I reiterated, trying to catch hold of that image. It had to be a memory, but I couldn't place it. It almost felt like a . . . a premonition.

"Then who was it?" she asked. "Who was wearing the necklace identical to the one in the radio announcement?"

That fucking radio announcement. I wanted to ignore it. It was obviously wrong—possibly bogus—but it was why we were here. And something about it had always bothered me. I thought hard, trying to remember.

Police did not confirm whether or not the remains are human; the investigation is ongoing. In local news, LVPD are asking the public's help in locating two people who disappeared from the Clark County area Friday . . .

Holy shit.

"The arson," I said. "The human remains."

Liv wiped at her face, leaving a smudge of ash.

"You said you hadn't heard the radio talk about it."

"I hadn't."

"But *I* had. I knew that I had. I'd heard it before. That's why it was so familiar and weird: I'd heard it before any of this. Before we parked, I heard it in the car—"

"Slow down," Liv pleaded. "I'm not catching everything—"

"The *courthouse parking lot*," I enunciated. "*Before* before. I heard it then."

"I don't understand—"

"It was the same APB we've been hearing all along: the one about Mom and Dad's disappearance."

"Wait." Liv narrowed her eyes. "You heard about Mom and Dad's disappearance before they disappeared? That doesn't make any sense."

"I know." But I was remembering now, them leaving the house—Thursday night. Telling me not to wait up, as if that was something I would ever do.

"We'll be late," my mom had said.

That's when she'd said it, not at the courthouse.

"It was the same. It already happened. Before any of this."

"What do you mean?"

"They were already missing. That"—I pointed at the cabin, thinking about those remains—"already happened. We were always coming up here because—"

"Stop!" Liv threw up her hands. "Just stop! I don't understand!" Her eyes were wild. "I don't know what to do! Do we go back to the car? Do we try to hike back to Hawthorne and call the police? I don't know what's going on! Please tell me what we should—" She broke off, cocking her head to the side. "Do you hear that?"

The soft sound of a familiar tune reached my ears. A pop song, something about *calling me maybe* . . .

Liv's hand went to her back pocket. She pulled out her phone—her dead phone—and the ringtone became distinct. She squinted at the screen, then looked up at me in shock. "It's Sandra."

Liv held it, frozen with indecision . . . too long. It silenced. Her eyes flew to mine. "I didn't know what to say."

No shit. My thoughts were tangling together, making it hard to focus on what was happening, what had happened, what our options were now.

"Hey." Liv's face changed into a confused frown. She unlocked her phone and started pressing buttons and scrolling. She stood, mouth half-open, swiping at the phone like a person possessed. Reading, scrolling, swiping. "Oh my god," she said. "Oh my god." Her head snapped up. Back down. She scrolled up with one finger, then held her phone out with an unsteady hand. "Look at this."

I grabbed it and held it close to read the small font. She'd opened a message thread from Asia and scrolled back to a text that was time-stamped 9:05 P.M.:

How's it going with Talky Tom?

Let me know if you need backup. Ha, ha.

Talky Tom. Me? Wow, clever. I read on.

Ping me and I'll pick you up.

9:41 P.M.

Maybe you should've waited until after.

?

Aren't your parents home by now? You should get out of there.

10:05 P.M.

Hello?

What's going on?

Then there were two missed calls fifteen minutes apart. I frowned. "Home by now"? Asia must've had some serious doubts about my parents' intelligence if she thought they'd go home after—

10:35 P.M.
Answer your phone!

Talked to Sandra. She said your parents are out of town? Right before the court date? I take it you're staying with Jory tonight? Super weird.

What did he say about the $?

Tonight? The money? I glanced at my sister—her face had lost its pallor.

"The texts are from Thursday night."

What was she talking about? I glanced back down:

Soo . . . See you at the courthouse tomorrow morning I guess?

"I knew the money would be there," she whispered. "At that ATM. I had a feeling." Her face was stricken, bordering on helplessness. And I'd seen it before.

"It's not about the money, Jory."

"Then why do you think you can buy me?"

"Why can't you believe me?"

I stared at Liv, remembering our argument. It had gotten heated. Really heated.

"Keep reading."

8:01 A.M. Missed call.

8:17 A.M.
Is your phone dead?
Do you want me to bring this shirt you picked out?

9:37 A.M.
We're in the hall outside the courtroom. Sandra's here. Where r u?

Worried.

Then fourteen missed calls.

I dropped my hand and stared at my sister in disbelief. "Liv—"

"There's more." She snatched the phone from my hand and stabbed at it, then shoved it in front of my face again. This thread was initiated by her lawyer:

8:15 A.M.

Good morning, Lavinia. Hope your talk with Jory went well. See you soon, my warrior. Victory is near!

9:41 A.M. Missed call.

9:42 A.M. Message converted to text.

"Hi, Lavinia, it's Sandra. We are standing outside the courtroom and I'm . . . well, actually I'm pretty concerned because I thought you'd be here by now. I thought you were coming with Asia, but Asia said you stayed with Jory last night and didn't call for . . . <cannot be converted to text> *. . . haven't seen your parents . . .* <cannot be converted to text> *. . . and we'll wait, of course, for you outside the courtroom, but please call me when you get this."*

11:05 A.M. Message converted to text.

"Lavinia, I don't know what's going on with you, but I wanted you to know that it's normal to get cold feet. So if that's what this is, just please—talk to me. <cannot be converted to text> *and we missed our hearing, obviously, but we'll be assigned a new date. And we can talk about that, if you're confused or unsure or whatever. Just call me."*

Six missed calls.

The air left my lungs. I looked up at her. "You weren't at the courthouse yesterday."

Her face was white. "Neither were you."

LIV

"HOW IS THAT possible?" Jory stared at me, fingers clenched white against my pink phone.

My mind was drifting, racing, pulling out bits of memory and knitting together a picture. "I came to tell you what Mom and Dad had done. Thursday night. Asia dropped me off at the house."

Jory stared at me. "But—"

"It's why I already knew what I'd see on my statement before taking money out in Mina. They'd tried to bribe me to drop the charges."

"When?"

"I . . . I don't know for sure. Earlier in the week?"

"You think you can buy me?"

Jory hadn't said that; *I* had.

His sense that we'd done things before. My head swam with images: the girl I saw climbing the rock in the desert, Jory appearing outside the car last night, the cat I hit on the way out of Hawthorne . . . everything had already happened, and it was glimmering through to now, but all out of order. The story was wrong—

I sucked in a breath. Another. And another. I suddenly couldn't get enough air; I opened my mouth, but my throat felt blocked.

Jory clamped a hand on my shoulder and gripped it tight. "Breathe out. Slow."

I leaned into him, trying to do as he said, but it was like blowing into a too-big balloon. At least his touch was keeping me from flying apart completely.

"Help me remember," he said. "What happened when you showed up?"

Help him. I found my voice. "I . . . I only remember little bits. I saw Frank leaving. He was talking about the pool—something about the water pump." Like when we'd met him in the desert. "Then he said Mom and Dad had gone out of town to deal with an investment. Then you showed up. And we talked."

"Okay."

I hesitated. "But it didn't go well."

"What do you mean, didn't go well?"

"We were standing outside, by the pool. It wasn't totally dark yet—the pool lights weren't on. And we were arguing." And I was suddenly wishing I'd asked Asia to come in. I'd promised I'd text if things went wrong . . .

"You're so pathetic."

"I'm telling the truth."

"About the money? Why would we do that?"

"Yes and no." I cleared my throat. "We were arguing about the surgery."

"Tired of being embarrassed of me?"

"Why can't you just accept my help?"

"Because you're a joke? A horror show."

"I . . . I told you what I planned to do with it, but I didn't explain it very well. You got angry. I got defensive."

"I'm not your guilt puppet, Liv. It doesn't work like that."

"I am trying to make things better!"

He scoffed. "You created your reality; live with it."

Talking it out was helping me remember. "It was kind of like when we were stuck at that deserted gas station. I was making some pretty big assumptions about what you wanted," I said. "That was stupid of me."

"Did it end the same?"

"I . . . don't know."

We looked at each other.

He dropped his hand from my shoulder and took a step back. "Fuck."

"What's wrong?"

He held my gaze. "How did it end?"

JORY

LIV INHALED SHARPLY. She knew I was thinking about those remains.

My heart thumped loudly, pulsing in my throat.

That little seed of thought—*you created your reality*—had been growing in my brain since she reminded me about that argument.

"What are you doing here?"

"You think you can buy me?"

Our fight. Liv's abandonment of me, my disdain for her, her slapping me in the face with her assumption that I needed to be fixed, that I'd be grateful for her help . . . I'd become so angry I could hardly see straight. I could remember that, although I couldn't feel that part of me anymore—that deep pit of rage. It had disappeared in these last hours. But Thursday night, I'd known exactly how to draw on it. A sick feeling was making its way through me.

"Jory," Liv said.

"What if it ended really badly? What if I'm creating all of this to—"

She grabbed my hand. "That's not what's happening. It's not what happened."

"How can you be sure?"

"Because you wouldn't. You *didn't*. Even if you should've."

"Why would you say that?"

"Because the argument wasn't your fault! When I found that amount in my account, I . . . I was pretty sure where they'd gotten it, and I didn't want you to blame me." She hesitated. "I decided offering you the surgery with my lawsuit winnings would get you on my side. I guess I didn't . . . know how angry you were about . . . everything. I mean, I should've. But I was too full of myself. I hadn't thought about what you'd been through because of me."

I shook my head. "Because of *them*," I said. "Liv, I *am* on your side."

Her eyes widened, then welled with tears. She ducked her head, wiping her wrist across her forehead and smudging it with ash. She could hear the truth in my words, couldn't she? I needed her to, because I'd finally realized what was missing when I thought about my new life. I'd found that missing piece.

She blew out a ragged breath. "We got in the car. Right? We got in the Audi and drove away from the house. I was angry, and you weren't talking anymore."

"But if we were still mad at each other, where would we have been going?"

"There's only one place they could've gotten the money!"

"How do I know you're not lying?"

Liv's cheeks were scarlet. "It's. The. Truth."

"Prove it."

"We were going to the bank." I answered my own question

as the memory pinged. "I told you to show me a bank statement. I wanted an actual piece of paper."

And that was me being vindictive. It wasn't that I didn't believe Mom and Dad would bribe her with my college money. It was that I was pissed about her showing up at the house, waving around her magic lawsuit wand. I wanted her to feel like she had to prove something to me. I wanted her to feel powerless.

Liv nodded. "Yeah. Yes." She chewed her lip. "But we figured out what Mom and Dad were up to while we were driving there. I told you what Sandra said about Dad's business being broke. You remembered him talking on the phone about insuring the cabin when you were getting his consent for your tattoo. And we changed our route."

Except those voice messages from Sandra made it sound like no one had noticed we were missing until the hearing. If we'd left Thursday night someone would've noticed . . .

No. Because my parents hadn't come home, and Liv never called Asia to come pick her up.

"So Thursday night they came . . ."

"Here," Liv finished.

And we'd come after them.

Footsteps.

Someone was on the front porch.

Liv drew close to me in the center of the living room as we watched the handle turn and the door swing open.

My dad stood at the threshold, looking out of place in his suit jacket. My mom appeared beside him, eyes widening with alarm. Her hands flew to her neck, a nervous gesture.

Where had they come from? We hadn't heard a car.

"What are you doing here?" His voice was a knife on granite.

Liv was thrown momentarily, and she stepped back. But her face hardened. She held up her phone and pressed record. "You think you can buy me?"

My dad stepped into the cabin. There was a sharp, sweet odor in the air: he'd been drinking. "I don't know what you're talking about, but you'd better—"

"Six hundred K to drop the lawsuit?"

My dad stopped. "Turn that thing off."

"After you tell me how you freed up that much money."

My mom fiddled with her necklace. "Now, Livy, don't go making up stories."

Liv drew a breath; it sounded like a hiss.

"Give me that." My dad pointed at Liv's phone.

"Or what?"

My dad's eyes were shiny with rage. He hefted the jerrican.

I jumped in front of Liv.

It felt like a memory, but also somehow . . . not.

That caustic smell of burning was back, faint in my nostrils but gaining strength.

"You should call Sandra and tell her where we are." Liv didn't move. "We can call her," I tried again, "then get to the car and get out of here and let the cops . . ." I trailed off. Liv had put her phone back in her pocket and was staring at the pier.

"Liv?"

"We don't have to do anything," she said softly. "We've done it all already."

The tone of her voice made me go still.

"We heard what we wanted—needed—to hear. Just like we saw what we needed to see. To remember." She turned to face me. "We remembered what it used to be like before. *Before* before."

Somewhere in the back of my mind, alarm spiked, but it was drowned out by an overwhelming feeling: *hope*, trilling inside, unable to be shoved down and drowned in a bottomless well of rage. My breath was caught, stuck in my throat like some winged creature that would take my heart with it if it were set free.

"I'm sorry," she said. "I'm sorry it took this long." And she looked so sad . . .

Say it. "Liv, whatever happened—whatever *happens*—we can restart."

The phone pinged again. That smoky odor was increasing, drifting around us and out onto the cooling lake.

Liv regained her composure. She straightened up, put her phone on speaker, and pressed a button. She held it up, her face unreadable.

"Lavinia, it's Sandra. We are . . . we're filing a missing persons report."

Liv looked at the phone in her hand. "You're right: it's not Mom and Dad in there. It was never about them." Her eyes found mine. "This was always about us."

The radio announcement, the road trip, that pile of ash and bone on the floor . . .

She raised a hand and pointed to the woods at my back.

I knew before I turned to look that the cabin was ablaze.

Great plumes of smoke were drifting through the spindly trees down onto our little patch of shore. High above the tops of the trees, tongues of flame reached up from the cabin and lapped at the night sky. They licked along the top of the roof and down the sides.

Crackling, tearing. A great whoosh came as something inside caught and went up. And then, underneath and faint: a muffled sound. Cries. Fists pounding.

And even from here, I knew the sound was coming from that windowless bedroom.

LIV

IT WAS ALWAYS about us.

"I don't want to be dead." Oh, Jory.

The cries were getting faint. But somehow, now they were as familiar to me as perfect posture.

"We've done this before."

Yes. Many times. How many times?

My mom fiddled with her necklace. "Now, Livy, don't go making up stories."

I drew a breath, letting that darkness funnel in, fill me up.

"Give me that." My dad gestured for my phone.

"Or what?"

My dad's jaw worked. And I saw it on his face: desperation.

He hefted the bright-red gas can. As he swung, Jory jumped in front of me, knocking me backward and catching the can on the side of his head.

A roar came as the fire sucked at the air and consumed the

cabin, like it was made of gasoline. I moved closer to Jory, need-ing his silence, wanting his strength.

Jory was on the floor. He was bleeding from his nose, and his shirt was discoloring with a dark stain. My mom stared at him, gripping her necklace. She didn't move toward him, didn't speak.

My dad turned unfocused eyes on me. I backed toward the fire-place. My hands, trembling with rage, fumbled behind me. I found the fire poker.

And let the black rush in.

The flames were rising high now, a neon glow above the trees.

"Stop!" My mom's voice. Was she shouting at me or my dad?

I couldn't see, couldn't feel anything . . .

My throat was tight, a sob building in my chest.

Smoke billowed from the walls as the curtains caught and erupted in flames.

The smoke was thick in the air now, coating the shore.

A searing heat. Stinging eyes, raw throat. My rage was burned out; in its place was sheer panic. Where was everyone?

I dove to the floor, searching for fresh air. Everything was so dark, it was impossible to see which way was out—

"Liv!" Jory. He was there. He was beside me, reaching out his hand.

I gripped his fingers. "Don't leave me," I said.

JORY

LIV REACHED OUT and gripped my hand. "Don't leave me." Her voice was small, like when we were kids. The smoke unfurled onto the shore, the water, toward the last rays of sun.

Through the spindly forest, the fire raged; columns of orange shot high and erupted in sparks above the trees. The cries, the pounding, had gone silent. Because . . .

No.

Liv's fingers tightened. This couldn't be what she thought.

"Give me that." My dad pointed at Liv's phone.

"Or what?"

My dad's eyes were shiny with rage. He hefted the jerrican.

I jumped in front of Liv.

I pulled the key from my pocket with my free hand and ran a finger along its teeth, staring at the inferno engulfing the cabin.

Searing pain, blackness. Images were blurring, layering on top of one another.

Someone was screaming.

I rolled onto my back and found Liv, standing over me with the fire poker, eyes wild, mouth open in an earsplitting screech. She stepped over me and swung.

There was a dull thud.

"Stop!" My mom's voice.

Liv's hand in mine felt so tiny.

I turned my head to the side and found my dad's dirty shoes. That telltale round buckle was dusty—like he'd been walking a long time. Maybe they'd parked the car where it wouldn't be seen and hiked in . . .

I gripped the key tightly. *Focus.*

I pushed to my knees. My dad was crumpled on the floor. He moaned and shifted, coming around. I pulled my gaze up and found Liv standing, staring down at him with a vacant expression. Her hair fell in front of her face.

Click.

The sound of a camera shutter startled us both.

I glanced to the doorway to find the source.

"You just ruined your chance," my mom said, holding her phone in front of her face. She took another picture and dropped her hand, looking terrified and vindicated at once. "It's over."

I looked to Liv. And saw a darkness overtake her.

Aggravated assault, attempted murder, whatever the allegation, it would've been the end of Liv's lawsuit.

The smoke was thick through the trees now, concealing the cabin. I tried to reach back into my thoughts, to flesh out what had happened next.

Instead, the memory of my parents leaving our house Thursday night came to me. My mom, standing in the foyer, telling me not to wait up, fiddling with the gold chain around her neck. That pendant between her fingers: it wasn't Busy Bee. She hadn't worn that since Liv moved out.

"We'll be late."

I could see it plain: the *P* pendant at my mom's throat. The Princess Liv necklace. My *mom* had been wearing it. I'd been wrong all along, but it didn't matter . . .

Because *we'd* never filed a missing persons report.

Wait. Was the memory real? Or was I conflating two moments in time, or a dozen moments in time, and creating something that felt like a memory?

I sucked in a breath.

Conflating moments in time. That was the explanation: moments, glimmering in and out of my consciousness. How else could it be? Piecing this together in a linear way was impossible—things didn't make sense. Like how the burned cabin and remains were reported before anyone was missing. Like the necklace, in those ashes.

Time was blurring; it was folding and looping back on itself. I'd felt that all along, like we were experiencing everything all out of order and somehow, all at once. Which meant . . .

"We haven't done this," I said. "This is the first time."

"No," Liv said. "You don't understand."

But I did.

Liv swiveled, opening the tin on the mantel and taking out a box of matches.

Moments—past, present, future—were bleeding through at the same time, coalescing, making it seem like we'd done things before, or that we knew what was going to happen. And if that was true, then what had happened, and what could happen . . . there was no difference. *Create your reality.*

Her hand—no, my hand?—on a match. Striking. Dropping.

A great whoosh of flame.

My hand. Before today, this moment, there was no way I

would've set the fire, locked them in. I would never have torched the evidence to protect my sister.

"I'm sorry it took this long."

But I'd do it now.

Everything was hot. My T-shirt was sticky with blood. I found Liv on the ground, below the smoke, and fumbled for her hand.

"Don't leave me," she said.

And I wouldn't.

It didn't have to be us in there. If I'd protected my sister, just now, for the first time, then we could still be missing. All I had to do was . . .

I took Liv's free hand and opened her fist so that the necklace was lying on her palm. I brushed away the bit of dirt that clung to the pendant and picked up the chain. "Put it on." Her hand trembled. "We're going to be okay."

She searched my face.

"Trust me."

She took the necklace, unclasped it, and fastened it around her neck, pulling the pendant to sit against the hollow of her throat. It left a smudge of black ash on her collarbone.

I hoped Liv could feel my smile. That splintering feeling, that sense of temporality, was gone. It was Liv and me, standing on the shore, the sun setting on the horizon. Solid. Real.

Liv raised her eyebrows in surprise and smiled back—a smile I hadn't seen in forever. No red swimsuit, no tiara, no audience: Liv. And I believed her.

My fingers drifted to the *ouroboros* on the inside of my right arm. Everything—everyone—could start again.

That was the thing about infinity.

LIV

WE FOLLOWED THE path out of the woods and skirted the burning cabin, listening to the fire crackle and the air scream.

When we got to the front, we paused in the driveway, watching black smoke pouring out of the places the fire had eaten through. Jory's face was lit with the faint orange glow of the fire. It looked like victory.

A great whoosh rose up as the fire caught hold of something and exploded higher; flames roared and the beams groaned as they split. And then the roof gave, careening down into the center of the small square building. Burying dead ends.

And revealing what we truly deserved.

Because everything happened exactly the way it should have. Jory and I had taken something unchangeable and created something new. Something I'd wanted all along.

"What do we do now?" I asked.

"What do you want to do?"

The fire was losing strength, petering out without so many things to burn. Great blackened chunks of wall were exposed through the crumbled roof.

The violence was over; the damage was done. I could picture the road stretching out in front of us.

"I want to go back to the car," I said. "And keep driving."

"We can do that."

I could feel ash and dirt and tears drying on my face, and it felt beautiful and fierce. Jory's face was a blank slate, and he was brave and vulnerable and complicated. There was so much I wanted to know, so much I wanted to tell him.

And I could see him now—really see him.

I held up the car keys. "Let's go."

Radio News FM:

"Reno PD have been called in to help with a case
of arson in Mineral County, as a recent discovery has
turned it into a potential criminal investigation.
Bones were uncovered in the wreckage of a burnt lakefront property, discovered by a local man during his
walk. Police did not confirm whether or not the
remains are human; the investigation is ongoing.

"In local news, LVPD are asking for the public's
help in locating two people who disappeared from the
Clark County area Friday. Sixteen-year-old Lavinia
Brewer and her brother, eighteen-year-old Jory
Brewer, disappeared before the verdict in a high-
profile lawsuit in which Lavinia was suing her par-
ents for legal emancipation. Parents Brenda and
Stephen Brewer have not been reached for comment.

"Jory is described as six feet tall with an
athletic build, brown eyes, sandy blond hair,
and a partial paralysis on the right side of his
face. Lavinia, who also goes by Liv, is five
foot seven with blue eyes and blond hair. She is
wearing a gold necklace with a P pendant.

"Police are asking for anyone with information about the Brewers' whereabouts to contact
local authorities."

ACKNOWLEDGMENTS

I am surrounded by wonderful people who helped bring my strange and slippery book into existence.

Heartfelt thanks to . . .

My editor, Christian Trimmer, for loving Liv and Jory, for making their story infinitely better with brilliant, non-soul-destroying (!) critique, and for being so welcoming and lovely.

My agent, Michael Bourret, for helping me narrow the lens on this one, for setting up the perfect match, and for always being so generous with your time and knowledge.

Assistant editor Mark Podesta, designer Rich Deas, publicist Morgan Rath, and everyone at Holt for your kind attention to all of the many production details.

Matthieu Bourel, for the most perfect cover art imaginable.

Roger Kreil, for sharing your experience of Moebius Syndrome and responding to my long-winded queries so good-naturedly. (Small-town connections FTW!)

Jennifer Ruttan, for sharing your legal expertise and time. (Family reunions FTW!)

My writer friends—Dana Alison Levy (treasured cheerleader

and partner-in-mulling), Rachael Allen (in-line commentary queen), the magical Alina Klein, Nikki "Be Gone" Vogel, and the equally furious and fabulous Natasha Deen and Hope Cook—for reading drafts, for offering feedback, for commiserating and celebrating with me.

My friends and family, for all of the love and encouragement. (I'm who I am because of you. Take that as you will?)

My husband, Marcel, and my kids, Matias and Dylan, who are my *before* before, my now, and my ever after . . . for everything.